SHIFT HAPPENS

SHIFT HAPPENS

T. M. BAUMGARTNER

SPECULATIVE TURTLE PRESS

A ngela should have brought her gloves.

She hadn't really planned on crouching on the roof of a building, talking down a freaked-out porcupine, and yet it hadn't been completely out of the question either. But no, the black leather gloves, newly washed after the encounter with a very apologetic hamster, were still sitting on the stand by her apartment door. Right where she'd put them so she wouldn't forget to take them to work.

"Darren?" Angela edged a bit closer, roof gravel crunching under her shoes, and tried to look non-threatening, which wasn't all that hard for a short pudgy fifty-six year old white woman. She aimed for the aura of benevolent aunt, but was aware that she sometimes achieved crazy cat lady instead. "Darren, can we talk about this?"

"Just leave me alone!" The voice should have sounded odd coming from a little woodland creature, but Angela had been doing her job too long to even notice any more. "Why won't anybody ever leave me alone?"

Angela's left calf started to cramp up as she held her crouch. "Look, I'll be happy to leave you by yourself for a while, but first we have to get you back to your human form. What do you think about that?"

The porcupine took a step back from her, quills rattling. "I'm not going to live in a cage in some secret military facility!"

With a sigh Angela knelt on her right knee and stretched out her left leg, massaging her calf. The young guys always brought that one up, as if they couldn't imagine a world where everyone didn't realize how important they were. Still, it looked like they might skip the whole "Why me?" conversation, which was a relief because Angela didn't have a good answer for that one. Everyone had the potential to shift into another form, but most people were lucky enough to never do so. "Darren, what the heck would the military want with a porcupine that doesn't want to leave his room? Let's get you back to human and then we can get you in a class so you can control your shifting and get you on a probation schedule." He seemed like a nice kid. If she could just get him through this crisis, he could go back to writing the web comic his mother didn't understand, and playing the final scenes of *The Last Salamander* with his online guild.

"You're trying to trick me. I've seen *Shift Enforcers*."

Shit Enforcers, Angela thought but didn't say it out loud. "Darren, do I look like some guy on steroids who's going to knock you out? I knit. I do yoga. I have a book club that meets every other week to talk about the latest romance novels. I don't knock people out and put them in magical handcuffs while I chant Latin at them." She took a breath and continued in a quieter voice. "Now why don't you move away from there and we can talk about what to do next."

After a long career of talking accidental shifters off ledges usually more metaphorical than this, Angela could tell he was starting to listen. Maybe she wouldn't need those gloves after all.

Silence. His nose twitched. "No cage?"

"Absolutely not. We'll get you changed back, then I'll put a spell on you so you won't accidentally shift. It'll wear off in a week or so, but that will give you a chance to get some training." She scooted back a foot. At least she didn't need to worry about the building being destroyed by the amount of magic released even if he did happen to dive into the concrete below. "Let's move away from the edge, though. I don't want you to end up falling when we get you back to normal size."

He waddled forward on little feet, maintaining the same separation. "What now?"

Angela relaxed. "Now I just need you to think about letting me help you." She probably could have shifted him without his cooperation — his magic didn't feel all that strong, an M7 or maybe M6 at best — but this way would be easier on them both.

"That's it?"

"Yep. It's a little anticlimactic, isn't it?"

"No Latin?" He sounded disappointed.

"I mean, if it makes you feel better I can throw some in." Angela looked at the energies flickering in his core, the threads of both forms spiraling together, and bumped them with a spark of power to get some separation.

"Wait!" The porcupine sidled off to the left. "I'm not going to end up naked, am I?"

Angela smiled. "Were you wearing clothes when you shifted?" At his nod she opened a hand. "Then you'll have them when you shift back." She raised her eyebrows. "Ready?"

"Okay."

She readied the spell to bind him to one form. "Quod erat demonstrandum. Quid pro quo." The net settled over him and she shoved a little more power into it, lighting up the strands. "Veni vidi vi—"

Then disaster struck. With a bang the door to the roof flew open and two cops rushed through guns drawn. "Freeze!"

The porcupine eeped, all spines suddenly erect, and jumped backward. Not, Angela thought later, in an attempt to jump off the roof, but in the startled reflex of a small prey animal. Either way, he sailed toward the edge of a three-story drop and she did the only thing she could do.

She really should have brought her gloves.

PORCUPINE QUILLS WERE a pain to get out. As the emergency department resident dug out forty-seven quills, Angela had plenty of time to think about the significance of the third magical lightweight shifting within two weeks. She tried to decide if the background hum of magic in the hospital felt abnormal or if she was just thinking about it too hard. She'd spent the weekend driving around asking herself the same question without finding any source.

While he worked, the resident quoted his favorite bits from *Shift Enforcers*. Tug. "'Looks like we *steered* that one on a path back to humanity!'" The resident snorted and pulled another quill out. From the compactness of his magical core, he'd never shifted, but from the buzz of his fingers against her flesh, even through the latex gloves, she suspected he was one of the few that could be trained to work magic. Maybe that explained why he was so obsessed with the show. "The 'Salamander's Bones' episode was one of the best. It was the one where they trained him for that mission in Spain where he ran with the bulls and they gored that spy."

Angela wondered if the doctor was aware that steers were castrated. Probably not. She worked on her breathing and tried to tune him out. The local anesthetic was starting to wear off, but there were only a few quills left.

At least she'd managed to shift Darren back and settle the binding on him before the cops had handcuffed her. Darren hadn't even complained about the bald spots he'd been left with, although it was possible he hadn't noticed them yet. In any case, she'd done her job and Darren was safe for the next week or two.

Tug. "'Go *cluck* yourself!'"

True fact: the script writers for *Shift Enforcers* were only allowed to write characters that shifted into animals already tested on camera and approved by the star, Guy Barron. At 5'8" Guy was sensitive about looking too short, and after the first season there were more and more mini-horses, small dogs, and chickens. He'd even passed on the opportunity to film with a dragon shifter who'd been passing through. The world may have lost some spectacular cinematography but the sets were easier to clean up afterward.

Angela's phone rang before the resident could think up another quip. With her free hand cuffed to the rail of the nearby bed, she couldn't raise it to her ear. "You're on speaker, Captain." Maybe that would convince him to be a little more professional. "I really think we need to get a team in to survey downtown to see if there's—"

Her attempt to direct the conversation failed. "What the

hell, Jones? How the fuck do you go out on a simple bitch-n-switch and end up assaulting a cop?"

The resident's eyes lit up at the lingo. They hadn't used that term until after the *Shift Enforcers* writers had come up with it. Until then they'd just called it "talking to a new shifter."

The silence lengthened and she realized the question hadn't been rhetorical. "It was...an accident?"

"You kneed the guy in the balls so hard he's still packing ice around his nuts and it was an *accident*?" Captain Rosenthal's voice got louder until by the end of the question he was yelling, and she could picture his face getting redder and the vein on his temple pulsing. She'd certainly seen it happen enough times to know what it looked like. "Moore and Young never have *accidents*" — he drew out the word — "like that. I don't get calls from the chief of police about their conduct on a regular basis."

To be fair, this would only be the third time he'd been called about her in the five years since he'd transferred in, so "regular basis" was a bit of a stretch, but she didn't think pointing that out would help her any. "I'd just talked this guy off the ledge, I mean literally, and those guys ran onto the scene and almost ruined everything. He's lucky I just kneed him instead of throwing him off the building. I'm in the emergency room now." She paused for a moment then brought out the big guns. "This could cause...long term disability."

The resident looked up in confusion at that and opened his mouth, but her look was enough to make him stay silent. He angled his groin further away from her knee and went back to pulling out quills.

While she'd expected to derail the captain's argument a bit by bringing up permanent disability, Angela hadn't expected to silence him completely. She glanced at the phone to make sure he hadn't hung up, but the line was still open. "Captain Rosenthal? Are you still there?" Finger on the disconnect button she paused. She couldn't hear him talking, but if she used her imagination that background noise was labored breathing. "Captain? Can you hear me?" Nothing. After another five seconds, Angela hit disconnect and scrolled through her contact list. The phone on the daytime dispatcher's desk rang. Twelve-oh-five. Candace would be at lunch, the emergency calls automatically rolling over to the main police dispatch center. Angela didn't have the number of the building guard station. Gritting her teeth she dialed again.

Matt Moore's voice had a patronizing edge when he finally answered. "Angie! Hey when we said you didn't have any balls, we meant you should grow a pair not take someone—"

She interrupted. "Are you in the office?"

"What's it to you?"

"If you're in the office can you go check on the captain?"

"Yeah, right, like I'm going to fall for that. He just got off the phone with the police chief. I'm still working on this stupid survey about new incidents that we all have to do because of you."

"Matt, seriously, he was on the phone with me and I think there's something wrong."

"Not happening, Angie. Hey, if you're still over by the stadium can you swing by one of my—"

She hung up and dialed the only other person who might be in the office.

Caleb Young answered right before it would have transferred to voicemail. "What. I'm busy."

Busy doing online training for yet another useless

certificate if the past was any predictor of the present, but she tried to keep her voice level. "Can you go check on the captain? We were on the phone and I'm worried he might have had a medical emergency."

"No way. He's so pissed off right now I'm staying out of sight for the afternoon." The bright ding from a question correctly answered came over the line. If Caleb spent as much time helping his clients as he did following the checklist to get the next promotion, he probably wouldn't spend as much time complaining about his workload.

Angela leaned toward the phone and dropped her voice. "Young. If you don't go check on him right now I swear I will call your wife and tell her exactly" — she split the word up into three distinct syllables — "what you were up to after the last holiday party." Not that Angela knew anything, but she'd heard him trying to fill gaps the next day.

The resident's eyebrows went up but he went back to pulling the last three quills from her wrist. One breath. Two. By the third she knew she'd overplayed her hand and she'd just have to call an ambulance and cross her fingers that she didn't get fired if the captain was just having phone trouble.

"Fine. Whatever. I'll go look."

His chair squeaked, then Angela heard him knock on the captain's door. "Cap? You okay in there... Oh my god!" His voice went up an octave and he was suddenly close to the phone again. "He's lying on the floor and I think he's *dead*!"

"Start CPR," she ordered. "I'll call for an ambulance."

"Wait! What do I do?"

Every year. They re-certified in CPR every damn year. She knew this because she was the one stuck with keeping track of it. Caleb had been with the department for five years, so he'd been through the training at least five times.

The resident put down his forceps and took the phone from her. "I'm going to guide you through this, okay?" He pulled his own cell phone out of the pocket in his lab coat and gave it to Angela. "Call 911 and get them rolling." He bandaged up her hand while talking Caleb, and then Matt a few minutes later, through chest compressions.

By the time they heard the EMTs enter the room ten minutes later and hung up both phones they were sitting next to each other on the bed. The resident sighed. "Sorry about your boss."

He looked so disappointed she patted him on the shoulder, lightly. "Maybe he'll pull through. There was nothing else you could have done."

He looked startled. "I knew that." He stood up and checked her bandage over.

"You just looked so disappointed..." Angela thought back to the point when his shoulders had drooped. "Oh. You thought they would be more like the officers on *Shift Enforcers*. Sorry."

"No, no, it was stupid of me. It's just a television show. If anyone should know how much they make stuff up, I should." He gestured at the building around him. "It's just... when I was in high school I thought that was what I wanted to do when I grew up."

"Why didn't you?" Angela flipped to her other sight. After a lifetime of practice, it was automatic, the physical world fading while the currents and eddies of magic came into focus, letting her see the resident's magical potential. He probably wasn't a powerhouse, but he certainly had enough innate magic to do her job, and he'd had enough empathy to explain what he was planning to do, instead of just treating her like she was an injured hand with a body attached to it. "I think you would have been good at it."

"Thanks." For the first time he gave her a real smile. "I guess I was just too intimidated. I'd never be able to face down a cobra with just a trash can lid and my wits."

2

"Those writers should be shot," Angela fumed later as she power-walked around the boundary of the parking lot. Deputy District Attorney Vicky Jackson strode along next to her, dressed in a silk charcoal suit and bright pink running shoes. Physically, the two were opposite in just about every way possible, one dark-skinned, tall and elegant, the other short, pale and frumpy, but their work challenges were similar and Vicky had progressed from a client to a friend years ago. "What kind of idiot would face a cobra with just a trash can lid?"

"The idiots you work with?"

Angela stopped mid-rant and snorted. "Probably. Well, no, Matt would claim he would have dealt with it but he wasn't given the right address, then somehow pass it off to me."

"And Caleb would just keep shooting his Taser at it until it ran away and lived as a snake for the rest of its life," Vicky suggested.

Angela laughed again, slightly out of breath from the pace they were keeping.

"When's Rosenthal's funeral?"

"Tomorrow morning. The whole thing is pretty awful." At Vicky's raised eyebrow, Angela elaborated. "I mean, it's awful that he died, of course, but I feel kind of bad that he dropped dead while he was yelling at me."

"We should all be lucky enough to die doing the thing we love the most," Vicky replied solemnly and increased her pace. "Come on. Don't slack off now. What was he yelling at you for this time?"

In between gasps for air, Angela told her about the porcupine on the roof and the cops who had almost sent them both off the edge. "And then while I was standing there with a hand full of quills, trying to concentrate on switching this poor guy back and not on my hand starting to swell up like a balloon, one of them was over there making fun of both of us. Misogynistic, ageist, and just...mean. And his partner just stood there and laughed. So when he did that thing guys do where they pretend they don't see you trying to get by while they block the door, I kneed him in the groin." Angela gulped another breath and tried to ignore the burning in her calves. "Possibly not the smartest thing I've ever done." She glanced up at Vicky. "Have they forwarded the case to your office yet?"

The timer alarm on Vicky's phone went off and they slowed to a more comfortable pace and turned to head back into the building. "I haven't seen anything yet. Let me ask around. I won't be assigned to it, but I might be able to find out what's going on."

"Thanks." They walked a few more steps before Angela remembered her other purpose for going on a break with Vicky. "It's been a couple of weeks. Mind if I look so I can put a check mark next to your number and make it look like I did something useful today?"

Vicky stopped and faced her. "Knock yourself out."

Angela switched to her other sight even as she worked to regain her breath. As she'd expected, Vicky's core was a stable sphere of purples and green chasing each other in a swirl that was beautiful to watch. She was in no danger of inadvertently shifting. If her snow leopard form came out, it would be because she wanted it to. Angela switched back to regular sight and smiled. "All good. Thanks for letting me look."

"You know you don't have to ask, right?"

Angela took a full breath, lungs aching, and let it out slowly. Vicky was more comfortable blurring the line between work and friendship than she was. "My mother always taught me to be polite."

Vicky shook her head slightly and they started walking back toward the glass doors. "I'll let you know as soon as I hear anything about charging you for that polite kick to the testicles."

Angela stopped halfway through pulling on her sweat-shirt and dragged it back off, using one sleeve to fan her face.

Vicky pulled open the door and waited for her. "Did the doctor give you anything for the hot flashes?"

Angela shook her head as she walked into the building. "She said I should eat less sugar and drink less caffeine."

Vicky's laughter rang through the atrium. "Call me when you need help burying her body. And try not to get arrested at the funeral."

TWO YEARS of weekly yoga hadn't done much for Angela's flexibility, but it had really improved her ability to access her

other sight while in a variety of poses. Kneeling on the mat
with her knees apart, she lowered her torso down to the
ground, the spare tire around her middle the first thing to
make contact. She really needed to stop eating so many
snacks before bedtime.

"Very nice, everyone." The instructor's voice carried
easily to the back corner. "Now hold this pose and repeat
after me: 'My body is worthy of my love.'"

Easy for the instructor to say, Angela thought. *Her*
stomach curved inward and there weren't rolls when she
contorted herself into a pretzel. Still, the instructor probably
couldn't catch a porcupine in mid-flight. Angela deserved
the chai latte she'd promised herself after class.

Following instructions, she rolled to her bare feet and
sank into the chair pose, arms up in the air. "My body is
fierce and fabulous," she mumbled along with everyone
else. Possibly more flabby than fierce, technically, but the
pepper spray she carried at work made up for that. She
blinked and took a look at the other members of the class,
since checking their stability was the reason all of them
were there. Diana flickered a little, but no more than usual.
Grace's inner light was in turmoil, which probably meant
she and the boyfriend were off again, but she seemed to be
handling it well. Just in case, Angela would offer to bolster
her a bit when class ended. It would just be a matter of
helping her balance her magic out, not spelling her magic
into a different configuration altogether.

Other MPD employees might employ more forceful
solutions, but that was why her coworkers had to keep a
cache of power stores to recharge their magic. Angela
always felt nauseated and itchy when she had to use one, so
she avoided them. Besides, anything that gave up its stored
magic more readily than obsidian was also obscenely

expensive. She preferred to enjoy her weekends instead of clocking up overtime to pay for magical objects.

Surely if there was something destabilizing the city enough to create new shifters she'd see it reflected in this room, but nothing caught her attention. Not everyone in the yoga class was a shifter, of course. It wasn't advertised as such, and anyone who wanted to come was welcome, but enough of Angela's clients had chosen to make this a part of their routine that there was a pleasant hum of magic in the air for those who were sensitive to it.

She crouched down and turned into a floating chair twist. "My body is strong and stable." Next to her, Travis put out a hand to keep from tipping over. After a rough start he was doing much better this month, and she'd only needed to help him calm his magic once.

And Lily, fierce tiny Lily whose imagination was boundless and whose form was some sort of strange reptile Angela couldn't define... Angela blinked and looked again. Unless she was mistaken, Lily was pregnant.

Lily was fifteen.

Well, *that* was going to add an interesting twist to the evening.

Back into a kneeling lunge, one leg forward, arms stretched up and behind her. "My body is full of wisdom." Angela hoped her body started sharing some of that wisdom with her mind, because she was going to need it soon. One or both of Lily's parents picked her up after class every week, and from the few conversations she'd had with Lily without her parents present, Angela understood that they guarded their daughter carefully.

The drama they'd started when Lily had first shifted three years ago had been bad enough. By the time Angela had arrived at their beautifully maintained ranch house,

Lily's mother had been crying and yelling at Lily's father, and her father had been drinking scotch and blaming his wife because they'd never had any shifters on *his* side of the family. Angela had slipped off her shoes and added them to the pile by the door, walked through the living room with its grand piano, passing two younger siblings sitting at the table pretending to do their homework, and back the hall to Lily's room where she opened the door to find something that looked like *T. rex* imagined by a girl who liked everything blue and sparkly. Lily's lizard form had been sitting quietly on her bed, splinters of a wrecked string instrument on the floor. "I don't *like* to play violin," she'd said when Angela had introduced herself.

Once her parents had realized that Lily going to one of the group classes meant no magical probation officer would ever come by their house again, they had agreed to let her go. Lily had started with knitting, tried a few weeks with the hiking group, and finally settled on yoga. As far as Angela knew, shifting into a magical lizard was the one act of rebellion Lily had ever performed.

And now they were standing, lifting one leg into a tree pose. "My body is balanced and beautiful." Excrement might be about to hit the proverbial fan, but that mantra could have been chosen specifically for Lily and her magic. She'd always been steady and in control, but now she was positively glowing with good health. The baby's magic was more than a little wobbly, though, spinning as if it were a lopsided lump in her womb. Angela had seen a few other shifters early in pregnancy, but she'd never seen a fetus so intense or off-balance.

By the end of the hour Angela's legs were burning, her pink "my other car is a broomstick" t-shirt clung to her back, and she was still no closer to figuring out what she was going to say to Lily. The only thing she knew for certain was that they needed to first talk without her parents, or the entire conversation would be derailed. But of course Lily's mother was waiting on the other side of the door.

Angela held up a finger to Grace to ask her to wait a moment, and crossed over to the front of the room where Lily was rolling up her mat. "Lily! How are you doing?"

The girl looked up in surprise, her straight black hair swinging in a perfect layer. "Oh, hi Ms. Jones. I'm fine, how are you?" Then she frowned. "At least... I think I'm doing fine." She dropped her voice even though the non-shifters had already left. "I haven't had any problems. Is something wrong?"

Angela paused. Did the girl not know she was pregnant? If that was true this certainly wasn't the time or place to tell her. But the fetus needed to be stabilized. "It's probably nothing. Do you mind if I give you a little bump of protection?" *A bump for the bump*, she thought.

Lily held her hands out. "Sure."

Angela quickly wove a net and cast it around the tiny glow in Lily's abdomen. "There. How's that feel?"

Lily gave her an uncertain smile, looking her age. "I didn't feel anything. Is there something wrong?"

One of the first things Angela had learned in her job was that confidence helped shifters maintain control over their magic more than any other thing, and conversely, self-doubt could ruin that control quickly. She smiled and waved a hand as if nothing were important. "I think you're just growing out of some of the old techniques. No big deal. Is there a time when we can spend half an hour going over some things? Maybe we could meet for coffee or tea after school?"

Lily frowned. "I have *activities* —" she said the word as if it were profanity " — after school every day this week. But I have third period free tomorrow."

They set up a time to meet at the McDonald's next to Lily's school in the morning, and Angela drove home wondering how the baby of a sparkling magical dinosaur would look.

3

The funeral was low-key, just a few people from work plus the captain's sister who had flown in to settle his affairs. The captain had been a mid-level magic user, and from the second row Angela could just barely feel the buzz of power from the bones in the casket when she concentrated. In another week even that would be gone. At least they wouldn't need to worry about someone digging up his grave to power some artifact.

The chief gave the eulogy, nobody even pretended to shed a tear, and Angela found the whole thing thoroughly depressing. Caleb and Matt had worn nearly identical dark grey suits with purple ties. When their frowns as they saw each other showed it hadn't been planned, Angela did a quick search on her phone and found the answer — *Shift Enforcers*, season two, episode eleven, when Guy Barron had attended the wake for his first partner who'd been bitten by a cobra.

As the chief shuffled through his notes after ten minutes spent describing the captain's unexceptional rise through the ranks, Angela texted Vicky. *When I die I want a wake. With a live band.*

Her phone buzzed with Vicky's reply halfway through a story about the captain when he had been the technical advisor on *Shift Enforcers. By the time something kills you half the city will be on fire. We'll call it a Viking funeral and be done.*

Ducking her head to hide her smile Angela replied. *Fair enough. But make sure there is alcohol.*

Noted. Got to go. My triple latte is almost ready.

Are you ever going to ask her out?

Hitting on people at their job is tacky. And possibly harassment.

Coward.

I know you are but what am I?

When the service concluded, Angela introduced herself to the captain's sister and offered her condolences, hoping the woman hadn't heard about Angela's contribution to the captain's massive coronary, then headed for the door, noting Matt making a beeline for the chief. That didn't surprise her — he'd be sure to drop a casual reference to something the chief said into his conversations for the next week. Angela supposed it would be a good idea to remind the chief who she was, but the thought of trying to make small talk with the man at a funeral was too painful to contemplate. Also, he might have heard about her assault on a police officer.

She saw Caleb in the parking lot and lengthened her stride to catch up with him before he got to his car. "Caleb, wait up a second." Caleb dropped his keys on the asphalt, giving Angela time to reach him. "You have a lot of clients downtown, don't you? Have you felt anything off lately?"

"Off?" Caleb straightened up with his keys in his hand. "Don't you think I would have said something if I had?"

"Of course." She held up a hand, palm outward to soothe

him. "But have you had any problems with clients being more unstable than they usually are?"

Caleb smoothed down his tie but didn't meet her eyes. "*I* haven't had any clients shift lately. Maybe it's just you." He gestured to the car door she was blocking. "Do you mind? I have work to do."

Angela moved out of the way and watched him drive off. Caleb was always touchy, but apparently funerals cranked up the dial.

She'd been hopeful when Caleb had first started at the department. He had a reputation for brute-forcing his way through magical complications instead of taking the time to untangle the problem, but he'd been near the top of his academy class and his magic level was respectable. Unfortunately, any time something went wrong, instead of learning from his mistakes, he spent his energy taking someone down with him. So he never ended up at the bottom of the pile, but as a side effect, nobody trusted him. For all the extra training he did, and all the reports he carefully massaged to make his performance look better, he remained stuck in place, with none of the promotions and awards he thought he deserved. Angela wasn't looking forward to Caleb blaming her for everything when a new boss arrived.

Still, he'd have no reason to ignore a stray magic source in the city. His clients would be just as affected as hers. Maybe she'd be able to convince their new boss to run a sweep downtown.

$\sim$

BY THE TIME she'd reached the front of the line inside McDonald's, Angela's plan to just order a cup of coffee had changed into a sugary iced coffee, hash browns, and an apple pie. When Lily slid into the booth a few moments later, Angela pushed the tray towards her. "Do you want some of this?" A quick glance with her other sight showed the baby twirling about, stable and content.

The girl broke off a corner from the fried potatoes and regarded her. "What's going on? Why are you all dressed up?"

Angela glanced down at her clothes. "My boss's funeral was this morning. I haven't had a chance to change yet."

Lily's face fell. "That's sad. Does that mean you're going to get his job?" A hint of anxiety crossed her features. "Am I going to get a new probation officer?"

"What? No, nothing like that," Angela said, although it suddenly hit her why Matt had gone to talk to the chief this morning. She shoved that image down to worry over later. Matt was bad enough as a co-worker. He'd be disastrous as her boss. "I wanted to make sure everything was going okay with you."

Now Lily just looked confused. "Why wouldn't it be?"

Angela regarded the girl for a moment and then decided she'd just have to be blunt. "You're pregnant."

Lily's mouth opened, displaying impressively straight teeth. "What? No I'm not."

Angela raised her eyebrows, doing her best to appear both motherly and nonjudgmental. "Lily, I can see the fetus. I put a stabilizer on her or him last night."

"But..." Lily's eyes were wide. "I've never even..." Her voice dropped down to a whisper. "...had sex." Her cheeks reddened.

Angela took a breath. Teenagers were masters of denial, but they could also be victims of misinformation. There was no way around it. The conversation was going to get uncomfortable. With the state of sexual education in the schools, she needed to figure out where to start. "You know how pregnancy happens, right?"

Lily's blush deepened. "I *know* that. It's from sex," she said, reproach heavy in her voice.

Angela dredged up memories of her own high school days and the lies that had floated around then. "And you know that it can happen the very first time, right? Uh, even if you're standing up?"

Lily kept her eyes on the table. "I've never done *anything* with a boy. So I can't be pregnant."

Angela sat back. In all the time she'd been looking after Lily, she'd never known her to lie, which meant either Lily was blocking out what had happened... Or she wasn't really pregnant. Angela took another long look at Lily with her other sight. It certainly looked like a fetus to her, but only a couple of her clients had been pregnant while she'd been overseeing them. Maybe this was something else — a parasite or even some form of cancer. "I think we need to get your parents to take you to a doctor."

"But I'm not—" Lily looked like she was going to cry.

Angela smiled at her again. "I believe you. But there's something going on inside you, and if it's not a baby we need to find out what it is." She glanced at her phone to see what time it was. Lily would need to get back to class soon. "If you want, I can call your parents or come by this evening and talk to them in person."

"Can you take me?" Lily blurted it out, then dashed away a tear with one hand. "If it's something bad, they'll be impossible to talk to and they'll start blaming each other. And besides, maybe this is something wrong with my magic and you're the expert in that."

Angela wondered how old Lily had been when she'd had to take responsibility for everything. "Your parents will have to set up the appointment," she warned the girl. "You're still a minor and I'm not your guardian. But I'll certainly go with you if they'll let me." Perhaps if she started with the magical aspect, Lily's parents would ask her to accompany their daughter. Angela had never seen parents so determined to ignore one part of their child.

Lily dredged up a weak smile, thanked her, and ran off to her next class, leaving Angela staring at a mound of food and dreading the upcoming conversation.

DRIVING BACK to the office Angela left a vague voicemail for Lily's mother, not surprised when the woman didn't answer the call. Either she just didn't answer calls from anyone, or Angela was being screened out deliberately. She suspected the latter. In any case, there wasn't anything she could do about it now, so she parked in the back corner of the parking lot and picked up the bag with her laptop and a more comfortable set of clothes and went into the building. After changing in the locker room she made her way to her desk, surprised to see the door to the captain's office open. Even more surprising was finding Matt sitting behind the desk, looking for all the world as if he had moved in there permanently. He'd even transferred his books, with Smith's *Power Creatures Through the Ages* proudly displayed next to Ettinger's *The Source of Magic: Essays on Power Creatures and Other Shifter Anomalies,* as if he needed them near to hand in case a salamander suddenly appeared for the first time in hundreds of years.

Candace, the daytime dispatcher, an improbably blond woman wearing the black dress she'd had on at the funeral, caught her eye, and then got up and headed toward the restroom. Angela put down her things and followed her.

"We haven't even had a chance to get the carpets cleaned," Candace growled the second the door swung closed behind them. "He just went in there and started piling all of Ron's things in a box and told me to get him coffee."

The only thing that really surprised Angela was the speed at which Matt had moved. "Does the chief know?"

Candace nodded. "He came by after the funeral and said that Matt was the acting captain until the position is filled." She flipped the water on, then off. "I asked why you weren't in charge since you had more seniority."

Angela looked at the woman with a newfound respect. "Really? You called the chief out in public?"

Candace shrugged. "He's not going to fire me. I used to work in his group. I know where too many of the bodies are buried. And it's not like it's a big surprise that you do ninety percent of the work down here."

It was a big surprise to Angela that anyone else had noticed. "So what did he say?"

"Matt has more 'leadership presence'," she said, sketching quotes in the air. "Which I think just means he has a penis and you don't. So now Matt's in there reorganizing the case load." Her headset lit up and she turned toward the door. "You've got to apply for that position. I don't think I can work here with Matt in charge." She hit a button on the headset and her voice changed pitch. "Magical dispatch, what is the nature of your emergency?"

Angela started to head back to her desk, then halfway there changed her mind and took the elevator to the fourth floor and walked down the hall to see if Vicky was around.

The deputy district attorney was in her office, but packing her briefcase to leave.

"I have to be at an arraignment in twenty," Vicky said, pausing to look around her desk then snatching a pen and putting it in her bag. "But while you're here, I have news about your testicular assault case."

Angela winced. "How bad is it?"

"Not bad at all. They're dropping the whole thing. It never happened."

At least one thing was going well. "Any idea why? Is it just because the captain dropped dead? Because Matt's in charge for the moment and if having them file charges against me will make it more likely he'll keep that spot permanently, I'm screwed."

Vicky closed her briefcase and ushered Angela out of the office, heading back to the elevator. "Don't worry. The officer in question has at least one complaint pending against him for acting like a complete asshole and making sexist remarks during an arrest. His body camera wasn't on during that arrest, so it's a he-said she-said thing. But." She hit the elevator call button and turned to face Angela. "They reviewed the footage from yesterday. Some of the stuff he said was word for word what the other woman claimed in her complaint. They gave him the choice of resigning or being fired. So your case just got tossed. No charges. Never happened."

The door chimed and they got on the elevator together. "Never happened except that now all the cops are going to blame me for getting someone fired," Angela pointed out.

Vicky tilted her head, conceding the point. "They'll forget about it in a few months when they have a chance to remember what an ass he was."

Angela sighed. With any luck she wouldn't need backup

any time soon. She shook her head to force that thought away. "Good luck in court." She ducked out of the elevator on her floor.

Walking into the office, she found Matt and Caleb at the armory cabinet pulling out the big equipment cases, the ones with stunners and magically charged restraints, the ones that only got taken out when everything was going to hell. When Matt saw her he nodded. "Oh good, Angie, you're here. One of the partners at a law firm downtown snapped and turned into a dragon, knocked down half the floor, charred the rest of it, and ate at least one person."

A dragon large enough to eat a person.

Downtown. She'd *known* there was something going on there.

A fire-breathing dragon.

That was the kind of thing that showed up once in a career. Angela grabbed her keys, adrenaline making her arms tingle. The dragon must have been what had been disturbing all the magical energy in the city.

Matt closed the cabinet and locked it. "I need you to take anything else that comes up while Young and I deal with the dragon. I was going to have you start the HQ notification for the dragon, but I think Candace has a case on hold already. We might be gone a while."

Angela opened her mouth, then stopped and tried again. "Wouldn't it be better if I went along on the dragon? I've got more experience—" Her rankings were also higher, but he knew that too.

Matt held up a hand. "I get it. Everyone wants in on this one, but this is a *dragon*. This guy isn't going to just need a few wind chimes and breathing exercises." He turned to Caleb. "Ready? Let's change this!" With the catch phrase from *Shift Enforcers* ringing through the air, they barged out of the room.

Angela waited until she heard the stairwell door slam closed and called after them. "I hope that thing burns the hair off your asses." She gave in to temptation and kicked her desk, which responded with a satisfying metal clang.

"Angela?"

Candace's voice behind her made her sigh. Angela turned. "I used my 'Get out of jail free' card on the wrong thing this week. What's up?"

"There's a woman that shifted to a mouse at the Biltmore Hotel. Seventh floor conference room." The dispatcher handed Angela a sticky note with the address.

Angela sighed again and picked up her bag. "Right. I guess I'll go deal with a mouse." She headed for the door.

4

The drive to the Biltmore gave her a chance to feel sorry for herself for a good fifteen minutes, and then she decided it was time to get over it. Sure, a fire-breathing dragon the size of a small house was cool, but a shape-shifted mouse was... Nope, she still needed a few more minutes to get over it.

At least the presence of the dragon solved one of her questions. Dragons were immensely strong, second only to salamanders in the order of power creatures. The lawyer's magic must have been over the Bernhoefer threshold, the level at which second-order effects became important in how stray magic was drawn in. He would have been attracting magical energy from all over. Latent shifters in the area would have also been absorbing it. Granted, it was a little odd for someone to exceed the threshold needed to warp the magical flux before shifting the first time, but dragons were only exceeded in power and rarity by sala-manders. Maybe that was normal for them. And now she'd never know, because while there was a dragon downtown, she was heading in the opposite direction to take care of a mouse.

Her mood wasn't helped when she got to the hotel and found out they'd turned the electricity off.

"Shutting down the electricity is in the protocol," the hotel's head of security told her, holding up the spiral-bound notebook.

Angela grabbed it from him, scanned the section, and pointed to the footnote. "Only for unknown creatures. A mouse is not going to tap into the electrical grid and start throwing lightning bolts." She pushed the notebook into his chest. "Never mind. Just point me at the stairwell." She took the flashlight from his desk, headed into the stairwell, and started climbing stairs.

Six flights of stairs in the dark with no fresh air circulating wasn't anything to write home about, but she felt a little better about the McDonald's slip that morning. Surely she'd burned off the apple pie at least. She opened the door onto the seventh floor, and took a moment to catch her breath while trying to figure out where the conference room was.

The beam of light finally hit a map for the floor, and she followed it to a small room with a round table crowded with laptops and paper coffee cups. She pushed the door open slowly. "Hello! I'm Officer Angela Jones with the Magical Probation Department. Is anyone here?"

For a moment she thought the room was deserted — and wouldn't *that* be a thing, trying to find a tiny mouse in a ten story building while the guys with less seniority, fewer qualifications, and just generally less sense were out dealing with a fire-breathing dragon the size of a house — but finally a quiet voice answered.

"I'm here." The voice sounded female. Young. Hesitant. Someone used to being overlooked.

Angela took a moment to push her irritation with the day away. There was nothing she could do about the dragon, fire-breathing and all, but right now there was a scared human who had just shifted into a mouse and needed her help. "Do you mind if I come in?" She took the silence for assent and moved forward slowly, flipping the lock on the door as it closed behind her and using the flashlight to make sure she didn't step on anything. Rolling one of the abandoned chairs closer to the table she sat down. "Are you okay if I relax here for a bit? I had to come up the stairs and my knees aren't what they used to be. What's your name?"

"Clara."

"Nice to meet you, Clara. You can call me Angela. Having a bit of a rough day today, aren't you?"

"I'm so sorry, I didn't mean for this to happen!"

Angela smiled reassurance in what she hoped was the right direction. "Trust me, I've been doing this for thirty-five years and nobody means for this to happen, at least the first time. Quite a lot of people grow to like it later, but I think the first time is a shock for everyone."

Movement on the desk drew Angela's eye and she saw a sleek brown and white mouse sitting on her haunches, nose twitching.

"My dad is going to lose it. Not about the shifting, you know, just the mouse part."

A quick glimpse with her other sight verified that this was the right creature, and also that she had a huge bundle of magic. This case wasn't going to get added to Angela's list of anomalies. Clara would have shifted sooner or later even without the city's magic going haywire. "Is he scared of rodents?"

A weak laugh greeted her words. "My dad? He's not afraid of anything. Nobody's allowed to be afraid of anything around him."

Angela nodded. Shape was nearly always determined by identity, need, and power. Darren, who had just wanted everyone to leave him alone, had become a porcupine for a reason. Angela suspected she wouldn't have to look too hard to figure out why Clara identified with the shape of a mouse. "Old school, your dad?"

Clara nodded, her whiskers shining in the glow of the flashlight. "I've always been a huge disappointment. Maybe he's psychic."

Or maybe he was just an asshole and a bully, but Angela didn't say that aloud. "He doesn't shift, though, does he? You've got magic that he doesn't. That puts you quite a few steps ahead in my book."

"But a mouse? He'd throw a party if I'd turned into a bear or a tiger. A mouse is something he'll have to hide from the neighbors. And I'll probably get fired. He'll have to hide that too."

Angela sniffed. "Most of the large predators I know wish they had turned into mice. Do you know how many of them hurt or killed someone the first time they shifted? At least you don't have to live with that for the rest of your life." She paused to let that sink in, then continued. "As far as the job goes... If you have half the magic I think you do, you'll have so many opportunities you'll have to hire someone to read through them all."

Ah, that had gotten Clara's attention. "Why?"

A sudden wave of heat made Angela start sweating and she flapped her shirt to create some air movement. Damned hormones. "Do you know how hard it is to keep a mouse out of someplace? You can go places, find out information, fix problems, and do all sorts of things just because you're so small. Trust me, if you don't have at least ten great job offers by this time next week, I'll buy you gourmet cheese for a year."

A squeaky laugh greeted her words.

"So what do you think? Want to start working on getting back to your human form, or would you rather hang out this way for a while? I have to say, they might not turn the electricity back on until we leave, and it's starting to get a little muggy in here."

Clara shuffled forward a few steps. "So, um, that's sort of what I was working on before you got here. And I'm not having a lot of luck."

A mouse with big magic *and* the self-awareness to start trying to change right after her first shift — they would be throwing money at her before she got done with the first day of training. "Not a problem. You probably just need a little help figuring out what to do." With someone like Darren the porcupine, she could overpower his magic completely and push him along the right path. With the bulk of magic Clara possessed, Angela would need to lead the way and Clara would have to figure out how to follow. In some ways they would need to cover the first two days of training just in order to get her to the class. "It might take a bit of patience, though. You ready to try some things?"

The mouse nodded. "What do I need to do?"

"First thing to do is get comfortable." Angela rubbed her arms, suddenly chilled as the hot flash passed. "Now close your eyes and just pay attention to yourself. I'm going to tug on your magic. If you can feel that, it will help you focus on what you need to do, okay? Here we go."

Angela switched to her other sight and looked at Clara. To her it looked like two different colors of light swirling around, purple and green, like two pieces of glowing thread traveling an impossibly complicated path around each other. Other people visualized it differently. One of her classmates had seen smoke and water, another some sort of Escherian tree with two canopies that blended into each other depending on how he looked. Angela didn't know how her classmates made changes, but she just visualized tugging gently on one of the threads.

"Do you feel that?"

Silence, then a slow shaking of the tiny mouse head. "I don't think so."

"Not to worry." Another wave of heat went over Angela and she leaned forward so her back wasn't touching the chair. "Yell if you start to feel something." She tugged harder, pulling on a different strand. For shifters with less magical power, she could just pull the strands apart and make the human strand dominant, essentially unraveling and reconstituting them as human. It wasn't a pleasant feeling, but that was what Caleb and Matt usually did when they had enough of a power differential to pull it off. That solved the immediate problem, and if the shifters took longer to get over the trauma and learn to shift themselves, well, that was what the training weeks were for. Angela preferred a more gentle approach, generally starting the process and allowing the shifter to finish it once it was under way. It took longer, but they didn't go into training too scared to shift.

When Clara didn't respond to the stronger pull, Angela used her magic to form a wedge between the two strands, levering them apart while pulling them in opposite directions. Sweat formed on her brow, from effort this time. Right about the time the mouse squeaked, the strands flung Angela's magic back, the rebound making her whole body vibrate. She shook her head to clear it. Clara had some of the strongest magic she'd felt in years.

"I felt something that time," the mouse said, holding her tail in her paws and looking at it as if she didn't know what it was.

Angela took a breath and let it out slowly. "Can you feel the difference between what it's like now and when I was tugging on it?" She pasted a reassuring smile on her face again. "It's okay if you don't yet. It's normal for it to take a few tries." Someone who identified with the form of a mouse was likely predisposed to be hesitant. Add that to the strength of her magic and Angela suspected this might be one of the more challenging transformations of her career. Building up Clara's confidence was going to be key.

Making a wedge with her magic again Angela forced the two strands apart a bit then stopped. "Can you feel that?"

"It tickles." The mouse lifted one back foot to scratch her belly and Angela found herself thrown back again.

The lights flickered on, followed a few minutes later by the rattle of air conditioning, for which Angela was grateful. Her shirt was already plastered to her back and her skin was burning.

"Okay, let's try again."

They kept going, Angela trying to conserve her power in the face of the tight bundle that was Clara's magic. An hour later, she pushed her hair back and sighed. Clara could vaguely feel her own magic, but her attempts to manipulate it had so far been unsuccessful. "Let's take a break for a few minutes, okay? I need to check my messages."

Angela pulled out her phone. It had been buzzing with new texts intermittently the entire time, so she wasn't too surprised to find thirty messages waiting for her. Most of them were public service announcements that Candace had sent out, advising people to avoid the area where the dragon had shifted. Apparently, Matt and Caleb weren't having the easy time of it they'd planned. Now the mayor was getting involved. The early deaths and ongoing property damage were bad, but Angela found it hard to feel sympathy toward her coworkers.

"Good news?" Clara was checking out everything on the table, reaching up to touch the flower arrangement, and getting used to her new form.

"Just the opposite," Angela replied. "I'm afraid I'm not being very nice." She gave Clara a quick summary of what was going on across town. "I really shouldn't be gloating, but I have to admit it makes me feel good that they're having problems." She texted a quick update to Candace, letting her know she'd be unavailable for a while longer.

"If I turned into a dragon, I think I'd just stay that way."

Angela cocked her head and looked at the mouse as she explored the items on the table. "It's tempting, isn't it? Still, it would be inconvenient. Can you imagine breathing fire and then getting the hiccups?" She waited until the mouse looked up at her. "Let's try something different while I'm resting. Can you tell me what you were feeling when you first shifted?"

Clara hunched down and remained silent. Angela waited.

"We were having a team meeting. My director was in town, which was why we had the meeting here. He says it wastes too much time to commute to the office."

So instead of having one person travel to the office, he made fifteen people travel to the hotel. Angela resisted the urge to sigh.

"We were going around the room giving status updates on our projects." Clara paused. "My project has had a bunch of delays because of things I couldn't really control. The lead developer's mother died, and then the requirements changed, and..." She trailed to a stop. "We're behind and I've brought this up with my boss before now, but she wasn't at the meeting, so I had to be the one to tell the director and he just kept asking questions and getting madder and madder." Clara scratched at her side. "I just wanted everyone to stop staring at me."

Looking with her other sight Angela could see Clara's core of magic tightening as she talked, until it looked like a solid purple bundle and she had a hard time seeing any strands of green at all. To the average magical eye, Clara looked like every other mouse. Intelligence agencies would be all over her when she finished training.

Angela switched back to her regular sight. "Okay, so that's how you got this way. Now let's talk about the good things in your life. Where's the last place you went on vacation where you had a good time?"

The mouse was silent for a long moment. "I spent a weekend at my family's cabin by the lake, all by myself."

"Think about being there. What did you like about it?"

"It was so peaceful. Nobody expected anything of me and I just went on walks and skipped stones across the water."

Angela continued drawing her out, having her talk about a perfect day in the cabin by the lake while she watched with her other sight. The strands were relaxing, more and more green streaks coming to the foreground. She tugged a few of them and the ball of magic moved sluggishly. If she threw all her power behind it, she might be able to force Clara to shift now, but if she failed, she'd be useless for the next day and Clara would still be a mouse. If Clara spent any more than forty-eight hours as a mouse, the likelihood increased that this shape would become permanent and she would never be able to shift back.

"Clara, can you feel the difference between your magic now and just a few minutes ago?" Someone was moving around in the hallway on the other side of the locked door. There was a hesitant knock. Angela got up and went over warily, remembering the overreaction of the police earlier. "Can I help you?" she asked through the closed door.

"Hotel security. I was just wondering how much longer you would be and when we can start allowing people back in the building."

Angela glanced at her phone to see what time it was. If she didn't leave for the fur and fiber circle soon she'd be late. She unlocked the door and eased it open, keeping her booted foot in place so nobody could force it open further. The same man who had been defending the elevator shutdown earlier was in the hallway. "You can let people back in the building." From the look on his face she realized he probably wasn't allowed to open the building again until the shifter was gone. "She's a mouse, you know. The dragon is on the other side of town." Angela thought about her schedule. "Hang on a minute." She closed the door and locked it, then went back to the table.

"Clara, how do you feel about going somewhere else for a while? I have a meeting with a bunch of shifters soon, and frankly I need to take a break for a bit. You'll get a chance to meet a bunch of great people."

"Like this?" The mouse waved one paw down at her body.

Angela raised her eyebrows. "You have no idea what kind of impact you're going to make on them. You may look small to everyone else, but some of the shifters will be able to see your magic. It'll be fun."

Clara looked around. "I guess. Uh, do you mind bringing my purse?"

Angela texted an update to Candace, checking her texts first. The lawyer was still a dragon and there were no other new cases pending. Then Clara climbed into her purse, and Angela carried it downstairs and out to her car. A crowd of people waited outside the building, most of them irritated because they weren't allowed to enter. The sight of a MPD uniform caused a ripple of questions, but none of them realized Angela had the shifter with her and she made it to her car without incident.

5

The combination of the normal evening commute and a series of detours due to the dragon situation made traffic a disaster, but they eventually made it to the community center only five minutes late, and Angela recognized three other people hurrying into the building. With Clara in her purse in one hand and her own knitting bag in the other, they crossed the parking lot and went inside. The sliding panels had been closed, sectioning off the back of the large meeting room. The larger area was occupied by a beginning ballroom dance class, a Debussy waltz playing while a woman counted to three over and over. Angela went past the dancers to the smaller room where folding metal chairs were set up around a table. Eight of the regulars were already there, three men and five women, their fiber projects spread out on the table in front of them.

"Sorry I'm late," she said as she took one of the empty seats. Angela put Clara's purse down on the table carefully before dropping her knitting down beside it. "Clara, do you want to come out and meet everyone or would you be more comfortable in there for a while?"

Clara poked her head out, looked around, then climbed out, one paw holding onto the purse strap.

"Everyone, this is Clara. She shifted for the first time today so be nice."

"When are we ever not nice?" Denise asked, looking up from her crocheting.

"Aside from when we look at your knitting," Ken added and the whole table laughed.

Angela picked up the latest in the series of potholders she was making. She was not a great knitter, even when she concentrated. When she was trying to knit and talk or monitor other things at the same time, she dropped stitches left and right. She found it easier just to stick with a simple knit stitch over and over, forming an unchanging rectangle until it was big enough to cast off and then she started another one. The deepest drawer in her kitchen was stuffed full of them. When the group got too boisterous, she would threaten to bring all the squares in and bind them together to create the world's ugliest blanket.

Switching to her other sight, Angela checked everyone as they continued working on knitting, crocheting, and lace projects. Nobody needed her help this evening, for which she was grateful. Trying to get Clara shifted back had tired her, and she still had a long evening ahead.

The fiber crowd skewed older, and for the most part that made them more stable, years of dealing with their condition allowing them to spot and avoid the triggers that would make them unintentionally shift. Not everyone shifted in early adulthood, but Angela could count on one hand the number of people over fifty who suddenly developed their talent. The hum of magic in the room felt more mature than it had at yoga, mellow from control instead of sharp angles and movement. The mouse was the exception, Clara's energy a harsh counterpoint to the comforting warmth of the older magic.

Next door the music switched from Debussy to Strauss, but the count to three went on unchanged. "So Clara..." Ken said, placing his scissors down on the table and looking up over the top of the glasses perched on his hook nose, "do you knit?"

Angela held her breath. She hadn't thought to warn Clara before they came in. Indifference to the fiber arts might be overlooked as poor taste, but pretending to have a passion that didn't exist would earn her nothing but scorn. There was no way to fake it in this crowd.

The mouse took hold of her tail again. "I'm more into embroidery." At the sharp interest from a few members she rocked back. "Mostly on clothing. I have a denim jacket that I've been working on for a while. It's a picture of the Washington Monument with Ruth Bader Ginsburg free climbing up the side."

Angela let her spine relax. Clara would fit in just fine with this group. In fact, if she could just get Clara back into her own shape and the mouse didn't accept a job that had her moving somewhere else, she would try to get Clara to come to this meeting every week. The mature energies would be a good mix with the powerhouse that was Clara's magic. And maybe Angela could switch to embroidery and stop creating endless potholders of doom.

Ken looked down at the dog jacket he was working on. He was adding a steek to form the buttonhole for the belly strap, which involved crocheting on either side and then cutting the ladder down the middle. "It does seem that it might be convenient to do the finer needlework in that form, but isn't it rather difficult to find a needle small enough?" He picked up the scissors and made another snip. "You can trust Officer Jones, you know."

Clara twisted her body to look back at Angela. "I do."

Angela paused in hooking thread around the needle. "Ken, don't push Clara. She's been cooperating. I'm just having an off day." The last part was a total lie, but the more she could avoid worrying Clara, the better.

Penelope looked up from her crochet, raising a grey eyebrow, her gnarled hands continuing their motions without stopping. Then she looked at the mouse and her eyes widened, her mouth forming a surprised "oh." Angela caught her eye and shook her head a little. Pen was one of the few in the group that could see magical energies in others. Angela didn't need her to tell the others about Clara's strength before she could get the mouse shifted back.

"If you want," Pen said, glancing back at her crochet hook again, "we could make it a bit of a group effort. I think I can work with Angela well enough to help her get you back. And I've learned a thing or two over the years that I might be able to teach you that will let you help yourself."

Clara looked back at Angela again.

"It's up to you," Angela said with a careful shrug. "It certainly won't hurt."

Clara nodded assent, the gesture looking odd on a mouse.

Pen explained some meditation techniques she'd found helpful in the past, allowing Angela to concentrate on pulling on the green threads of light, trying to invert the whole construct. She could feel Pen doing the same thing at a different spot, a little more tentatively.

For fifteen minutes the room was quiet, with just the sounds of the music and counting coming from the other room, and the quiet clicking of needles. Angela stopped trying to knit and merely sat with her eyes closed, concentrating on the magic in front of her.

A few times they came close, the whole thing on the edge of inverting, then it bounced back.

"Almost had it that time," Pen said, her voice sounding thin. "Let's try one more time."

Angela looked over at her. "You sure you're up to it? I don't want your son calling me tomorrow..." The group around the table laughed. Penelope's son watched over her carefully, and everyone had had at least one run in with him. Angela quite liked him, but she counted on at least one call every few months complaining that she was making his mother's life too difficult.

"My boy would have me sitting at home watching television instead of doing anything at all." She pulled on the ball of yarn harder than necessary. "If it doesn't work this time, I'll let you call in the big guns tomorrow."

They started again, and this time Angela had the feeling that the entire table was collectively holding their breath. Again she reached and tried to separate the strands. She could feel Clara helping as well, her actions uncoordinated and clumsy, but better than most people during the first shift. Pen helped separate another section.

The whole structure wobbled, flashing between purple and green, but Angela couldn't get it to tip over the edge. When Clara learned how to manage her own magic, she'd be able to flip back and forth with little effort, but right now her efforts were ineffective at best. Gritting her teeth Angela added one last bit of power, knowing that she'd pay for it later, but it wasn't enough. The core refused to flip.

There was a disturbance on the other side of the table, the squeal of a metal chair being shoved back quickly, then a short laugh at the same time as someone else gasped. Before Angela could open her eyes to look at what was going on, Clara jumped and the magical tangle flipped to green.

Decades of training let Angela use the last of her energy to weave a stabilizing spell and toss it over Clara, pulling it tight to make sure Clara wouldn't be able to switch back to her mouse form for at least a week. She mentally tied off the ends and released her control, then slumped back in her chair, exhausted, only then looking at what was in front of her.

Clara in human form was a waifish woman in her late twenties with light brown skin and shiny black hair bobbed at chin-length. At the moment she was curled up on the vinyl tabletop, one hand thrown over her face to protect her from... a mountain lion crouched on the other side of the table.

Angela sat up with a start, but Penelope beat her to it. "Jimmy Miller, what on God's green earth do you think you're doing? We do *not* shift in public, *especially* during fiber night."

The mountain lion sat back, chastened. "I figured if she saw a predator she might let instinct take over." He hopped down to the ground, a huge creature of grace, his pads making no sound on the linoleum. "It worked, didn't it?"

Pen snorted. "You've frightened the poor girl to death."

Angela struggled to her feet, her knees protesting all the stairs she'd climbed earlier, and put a hand on Clara's arm. "Are you okay?"

The woman slowly uncurled her body and swung her feet over on to the floor. "I'm... Oh, I'm back in my own body again!" She sank into an empty chair next to Pen and burst into tears. "I'm sorry, I don't know why I'm crying," she said between gulps of air.

Penelope patted her shoulder. "It's all the adrenaline. You'll be better in a few minutes." The old woman looked over at the large cat. "Jimmy, get over here, apologize, and show her how well-behaved you are so she doesn't think you were about to kill her." She picked up her crocheting from her lap and slammed it down on the table.

The mountain lion padded over and settled down behind her chair. "Sorry." He dropped his head down to the floor between his paws. "I really was trying to help."

Angela went over to close the door in case anyone happened to walk down to the end of the hall. A mouse on the table would be easy to explain away, but a mountain lion was a completely different kettle of fish. A little lightheaded from the effort, she sank back down in her chair, briefly switching over to her other sight to look at Jimmy. He was telling the truth — this hadn't been an uncontrolled change, but he didn't have enough magic to change back yet, which meant they might be there for a while.

Ken appeared next to her with a bottle of water. "Are you quite alright, Officer Jones?" he asked quietly. "You look a bit peaked."

Angela gulped the water gratefully. "Maybe it's good I didn't go try to help with the dragon today."

Ken nodded over at Clara who was wiping her eyes with a paper towel someone had handed her. "We both know what you just did took a lot more power than dealing with the average dragon." He shook his head. "I think the only person I've ever seen hold a shape more firmly is you."

Angela realized she'd never asked him what he'd done for a living before he retired and started spending his days making outfits for his Italian greyhound. She pulled her sweatshirt away from her chest. "Ah, but I don't shift." She took a deep breath, trying to decide whether she needed to take the sweatshirt back off. Some days her arms disappointed her by not being toned by the amount of times she pulled on layers and then yanked them off a few minutes later.

Ken made his way back to his seat and picked up the dog coat again. "If you ever did, I'm not sure all the king's horses and all the king's men could drag you back to human again." With a sniff he turned the coat inside out. "I think this will turn out just fine."

~

PENELOPE LEFT SOON AFTERWARD, but by the time Jimmy had rested long enough to switch back to his aging hippie form and Clara had stopped bursting into tears every time anything moved, it was an hour after the fiber group's room reservation was over, and the building custodian was starting to show his irritation. Angela had already flashed her badge at him fifteen minutes before, claiming a minor medical emergency, which bought them some time, but she was glad when Jimmy finally shifted back. It wasn't always easy to find a spot to have regular meetings, especially if it came out there was a shifter in the group. Having ten shifters together could make even the most liberal of communities blink. Early in her career Angela had threatened to get "shifting isn't contagious" tattooed on her forehead. It was still a source of frustration, but now she educated people when she could, and tried to avoid doing anything that would start neighborhood busybodies talking.

"Are we good?" Jimmy had switched out the bifocals he used when working on his knitting for the round wire frames with purple-tinted lenses, but they didn't disguise the worry in his tone. Perhaps he'd finally realized that shifting in a semi-public place in front of his magical probation officer was not the smartest move.

Angela sighed. "Yes, but please don't do that again. It could have backfired badly." She put her latest potholder, an ugly bit of orange that was even lumpier than her usual creations, back in the canvas bag and got up. Jimmy's intervention may have been the thing that got Clara back to her human form, but she couldn't very well thank him for that. At least not this evening. Maybe later.

She dropped Clara off at her apartment, checked to make sure the binding was holding, and promised to call the next day to give her the details of her enrollment in shifter training. Then it was back to work to update records. As tempting as it was to let the paperwork slide until the next day, she knew from long experience that if she didn't keep on top of it, she'd regret it later. As a reward for getting through the day, she picked up a bucket of fried chicken, not even bothering with a pretense of healthy eating.

Angela briefly considered driving downtown to check out the dragon, but disobeying Matt's directive when she was already magically drained seemed like a recipe for disaster. With her luck, the dragon would charge right at her and she wouldn't be able to do anything other than die messily. Besides, Matt and Caleb were probably already having drinks with their new dragon client safely back in his human form.

Candace was on her way out the door when Angela got

to her desk, the swing shift dispatcher already settling in the office with his headphones on. Candace bit into the offered chicken with a sigh. "You're wonderful. Also," she lowered her voice, "the guys are still out there with the dragon, making zero progress, and the comm chatter today has been worth the price of admission. Matt is freaking out because this is all happening the first day he's in charge. He was hoping to be able to put this on his resume and it's blowing up in his face." She shrugged and let her voice go back to normal. "At least the dragon is staying put. I think they're going to give up for the day and try again tomorrow."

Angela raised her eyebrows at that. The longer the dragon stayed in that form, the harder it was going to be to get him to shift. For a mouse that might be a personal tragedy. With a dragon it would be a nightmare for the whole city.

Candace saw her expression and paused before taking another bite. "Matt was trying to get both Patterson and King to fly in overnight with a draining tap, so I think he's stalling for time." The tap would absorb most of the magic from anything it touched, after which it would be simple to just yank the shifter back to human form. They took a lot of specialized training to use, but they worked. Candace shook her head and added in a little singsong voice "...or he could ask the member of his team with the most experience and strongest M-score to help, but no."

Theoretically the M-scores were a confidential part of the employee records, but Angela wasn't surprised that Candace had peeked. "I'm tapped out at the moment anyhow," Angela admitted. "The mouse is at least an M-3." To determine the official classification required examination by a board, but long practice evaluating her clients had made Angela fairly accurate. When she'd been tested during training, Angela had been given a coveted M-2. Matt and Caleb were somewhere in the M-3 to M-4 range, at least when they weren't getting a boost from an artifact.

"Probably good the guys had a dragon to keep them busy while you were doing the real work. And the paperwork they're going to have to submit for every hour there's a dragon..." Candace picked up her purse. "See you tomorrow."

After Candace left, Angela took the bucket of chicken in to the dispatch office so Tom could get a few pieces, then went back to her desk and started entering notes for all her clients.

Over the years she'd learned a few things on how to handle her case load. First, the more stable her clients were, the less time she had to spend making emergency calls. Second, having a support network made everyone more stable, partially because they had someone to talk to, but also because stable magic tended to calm the waters for everyone. And third, having everyone gather in one spot meant less driving around for her. Put all together, it meant things like yoga classes and fiber arts nights were the key to getting through the work. Matt and Caleb made fun of her approach, but it worked. Angela had no idea how they found the time to see all their clients individually and still help the ones that needed it. The captain hadn't cared either way as long as she got her work done.

The notes on each client were simple, just a quick indication that she'd seen them and that they were stable. Angela added additional information to a couple of them about ongoing issues, but she managed to get through everything in an hour. With that done, she compiled her reminders list to make sure she hadn't overlooked anyone. It helped her keep track of her clients and highlighted any that she hadn't seen in the mandated two week cycle, with the length of time they'd gone without contact coloring the item from yellow to red depending on duration and potential for destruction. A few yellow or orange flags were expected as people went on vacation or had to reschedule. She'd had a red flag once that lasted two months until she'd finally tracked the client down in the city morgue where he'd been listed as a John Doe, but green flags were the norm.

This time her reminder list came up in a swath of angry red and orange, making her heart rate spike. Half a minute of frantic clicking informed her the source of the problem. Matt had transferred all of his and Caleb's problem cases to her, and they'd had a lot of them.

Matt had left her a note. "Angie, you do better with the odd ones, so I've moved some cases around to take advantage of your strengths." Angela suspected that meant he was giving her any client that made him or Caleb uncomfortable. "We're all going to have to work a little harder until the open position is filled." He'd also given her the clients the captain had personally supervised.

"Bastard."

"Not talking about me, I hope." Vicky's voice reminded Angela she was in a public place. She looked up and saw the DDA walking toward her, once again wearing the pink sneakers that she used when she didn't need to look professional. She dropped into the chair next to Angela's desk. "What happened?"

"Matt doubled my case load. Claims I'm really good at the 'odd' ones so I should get them all."

Vicky nodded. "Oh, he's pulling the 'punish competence with more work' maneuver. That's what I would do in his place, if I wanted to make sure you were swamped."

Angela sat back in her chair. "Reviews are coming up

soon. If they calculate client ratings now, I'm screwed."
Angela let her head fall back and rubbed her eyes. "I'm just
going to quit. Let *him* deal with the fallout."

Vicky was silent so long Angela finally looked over
at her.

"You walk away from all this and what happens to the
rest of us?" Vicky said, anger showing in her eyes. "We will *be*
that fallout."

Angela sat up, chastened. "Sorry. I wasn't thinking." She
passed her friend the bucket with the last two pieces of
chicken. "Peace?"

Vicky held Angela's gaze a moment longer, then sniffed
and took the chicken. "Fine. But only because I'm hungry."
She took a bite and dabbed at her mouth with a napkin.
"What can we do to help?"

"We?"

She rolled her eyes. "Oh please. There are people all
over the building who would love to help with this. Just tell
us what to do."

Angela threw away the container of mashed potatoes
that she'd managed to eat while she wasn't paying attention.
Comfort food at its finest. "I appreciate it, but you can't.
There are privacy issues." She looked at the list of new
clients. "How am I going to onboard them all? Just meeting
with them and finding out who actually needs help right
now is going to take weeks."

"So don't do it that way." Vicky took one of the wet
napkins and started cleaning her fingers carefully. "Have
them start coming to one of your groups, figure out who
needs the most help there, and start with those."

In some ways that would work, but... "How do I get them
into the right session? I still need to meet with everyone

individually and find out what types of things they like to do."

Vicky stifled a laugh. "Babe, I love you, but you need to get with the times. Send them an email, let them pick their own thing, then all you have to do is track down the ones that don't respond." She rolled her eyes again and pulled out her laptop. "Look, I'll write a draft. Then you can change whatever you need to do and send it out... I'll help you send it out to the new people," she corrected herself. "Go on, just do whatever it is you need to do for a bit while I write this." Her fingers were clacking on the keyboard before she stopped talking.

While Vicky was typing, Angela made a third call to Lily's mother. Since the woman wouldn't pick up the phone and she wasn't returning her calls, Angela left a more explicit message telling her that she was concerned about Lily's health, that Lily's mother needed to set up an appointment with Lily's doctor, and that it was possible the problem was related to magic so Angela needed to be there. Angela finished by telling her that if she didn't respond with at least a text to this third message, she could expect to receive a visit at home at Angela's earliest convenience. If it didn't work, Angela would probably have to get Child Protective Services involved.

A few minutes later, Vicky sent her the draft of the email she thought Angela should send out. It started with an apology for the impersonal approach, explained that the classes were a way to comply with the legal necessities in a more pleasant manner, listed the current schedule of meetings, acknowledged that meetings weren't a requirement but that the one-on-one schedule might be more inconvenient, and suggested that if the recipient didn't at least acknowledge receipt of the message Angela might have to come find them in full uniform and all their friends and coworkers would see. Vicky was a master at the fine art of legal blackmail. "How do you even know my meeting schedule?"

"Because I listen when we go for walks. Now change what you need to change and let's get this sent out."

A few minutes later they were heading out the door, Angela's phone already starting to buzz with replies.

6

B y the time Angela was in front of her computer
again the next morning, ninety-three people had
replied, including two that Caleb had been overdue
on for three months. She raced through her email, adding
names to lists so she would have some idea of who was
expected to show up at each session. If everything went
perfectly, she'd have just enough time after lunch to sneak
downtown and check out the dragon, assuming it was still
there.

"Angie!" Matt's voice rang out.

She looked up, startled since she hadn't seen him come
in. Matt had dressed in the next level of tacticool, with a
black t-shirt and black fatigue pants tucked into boots, the
MPD logo a discrete addition to the "POLICE" lettering
across his chest. Next to Matt walked a suited man in his
fifties with short black hair, tanned skin, and a squarish face
that suggested ancestors from northern China. She *knew*
that face, even if she hadn't seen it in three decades. Angela
glanced down at his feet. Still wearing cowboy boots.
Benson hadn't changed. She wondered if, given enough

vodka, he still got into arguments about whether a person's alternate form was fixed before they first shifted or if the act of shifting itself solidified the form.

Matt introduced them before she could get to her feet. "Ben Li, this is Angie Jones." From the hint of a frown she saw on Benson's face that she felt mirrored on her own, Angela knew he hadn't started shortening his name.

"Hey, Benson."

His lips twitched and his eyes flicked over to Matt. "Just like the cigarettes," he said, his accent still pure Texas panhandle. He turned back to her. "Angela." His arms went out a little, but he stopped, as if he wasn't sure how to greet her.

Angela moved forward and completed the hug. As their bodies made contact she remembered how they'd left things and stepped back. "How have you been?"

Matt waved his hand before Benson could respond. "You two know each other? That's great. Ben is here from HQ to audit our practices. The captain set it up before he died." His eyes flitted to the office he'd taken over. "Since Young and I are probably going to be busy with the dragon all day, I'll leave him with you." He turned. "Ben, I'll have you shadow Angie today, and then after we get this dragon taken care of I'll give you a tour."

Angela blinked and opened her mouth, but Matt had already turned. "Young. Let's go. We need to get to the scene in twenty." He and Caleb were walking quickly as they headed out the door, but Caleb's "Let's change this!" sounded more forced than it had the day before.

Benson watched them go, then turned to her and shrugged.

Angela bit back the words she wanted to say and forced a smile on her face. "Give me a minute to finish things here and then we can go." She went back to her email, but half her mind was on the man across the desk from her. She'd seen his name on various cultural magic research papers over the years; each time she'd thought about reaching out to him and each time she'd let the moment go.

She glanced over at him. Benson had settled into the chair, reading something on his phone, with the same ability to make any place his own that she remembered from college. His face gave her no hint of his feelings. Maybe she could drop him off near the dragon. After all, everyone wanted to see the huge fire-breathing dragon.

Angela finished up, remembered to lock her screen, and grabbed her purse. "Ready?" She headed toward the door, listening for boots treading the floor behind her.

HER CAR HAD the lived-in look of a constantly-used vehicle that had one driver. Angela transferred the pile of paper-work and seven pens to the back seat, then brushed a few crumbs off the upholstery with her palm before disengaging the passenger side lock. She waited until they had pulled out of the parking lot onto the main road headed away from downtown before she spoke. "So..." She stopped talking, not even sure where to start.

Benson shifted in the passenger seat. "Remember that guy you dated the summer before sophomore year? The *artist* who kept giving me lectures on the only true way to watch films."

Angela glanced over before looking back at the road. "I remember you putting on Disney musicals in the living room every time he came over, just to piss him off."

Benson's laugh was an inaudible rush of breath. "I forgot about that. I wonder what ever happened to that guy."

"We got married." Angela nodded when Benson looked over in disbelief. "Not the best decision I ever made. I supported him for five years while he painted, and then he dumped me for an eighteen year-old who " — she took both hands off the wheel to make air quotes — "'really understood' him." She paused, waiting for Benson to bring up the fact that she and Trevor had first broken up at the end of that summer because of a different girl who had also "really understood" him.

"Sorry." Benson sounded sincere.

Angela shrugged. "Turns out that what he meant was that she didn't call him on his shit. It's okay though, last time I saw him he had a job in finance and had two kids, a gigantic house upstate, presumably an even larger mortgage, and I could see the whites of his eyes as he was trying to tell me how happy he was."

"I can only hope that his kids watch *The Little Mermaid* every time Daddy walks through the door."

Angela smiled. "You and Shawn...?"

"Still together. He and my mom argue about the right way to make biscuits every Sunday at brunch."

Even after a span of decades, Angela could immediately taste Shawn's buttermilk biscuits, fresh from the oven. "Tell him I said hello. And if he wants someone to provide a completely impartial assessment of those biscuits..."

There was silence in the car again as they negotiated traffic, but this time it was more relaxed.

Once on the side streets, Angela drove past the connected lot of their target, the memory unit of the assisted living facility, parking her work vehicle on the street around the corner from the entrance instead. Benson waited for her in silence as she put her utility belt with its pepper spray, gun, and tranquilizer pen in the trunk and pulled on a plain red windbreaker over her MPD polo shirt.

"Going undercover?" he finally asked as they started walking back to the memory unit. His boots clicked on the pavement as he strolled beside her.

Angela mentally ran through the information she was about to give him, making sure there was nothing objectionable. She wanted to trust him, but they hadn't seen each other for decades, and Benson worked at headquarters. "Ellen's family had to move her here two years ago after they couldn't find any place that would take her back in Baltimore. Her dementia has worsened, but she's a sweet person. I come by once a week to renew the binding, and it's not a problem."

"Her caregivers don't know?" His tone was stiff. "Accidents can happen. Surely there would be safety—"

Angela cut him off. "We're not talking about a salamander who's going to level the city if she loses control. She's a frog. Just an M-7 frog. She can't hurt anyone, and even if she shifts and someone sits on her, she doesn't have enough magic to cause a problem."

"Right."

Angela wanted to explain more, talk about the prejudice facing older shifters, but they were at the facility entrance and there were other people around. She steered him up to the third floor, greeting people she recognized along the way. Two years of weekly visits meant she knew most of the staff and a fair number of the patients. They signed in to the ward at the desk.

"Ellen isn't having one of her good days," the nurse said as she took the clipboard back. "She was having a hard time sleeping last night and she's been a little combative today, so... Her daughter is going to take her to get checked out by her doctor at noon. UTIs can sometimes cause that. Hopefully we'll be able to get it under control."

Angela smiled her appreciation for the information, and guided Benson down the hallway toward the third door. The facility smelled faintly of disinfectant and steamed spinach, but on the whole it was clean and quiet, with brightly painted walls and live piano music playing in the distance.

Ellen was in her room, sitting on a high-backed chair next to the bed, a scowl on her pale face as she looked toward the window. She was wearing sagging blue sweat pants and a huge yellow t-shirt, clothes obviously made for a much bigger person. Angela hadn't seen her wearing clothing that truly fit her in the last six months.

She sat down on the love seat next to the chair "Hi, Ellen. How are you today?" Some days Ellen knew who she was. Other times the older woman thought Angela was her aunt or a neighbor she'd had when she was a girl. Occasionally she just refused to speak at all. This looked like it might be one of those days. The old woman turned her head and scowled at Benson.

Angela flipped over to her other sight to see how her binding was holding up. The spell she'd placed only a week before had frayed and was on the brink of failing. She'd seen this problem once before with an Alzheimer's patient. It was as if the magic responded to a loss of self and let slip anything trying to hold it in one shape. If her intuition was right, Ellen wouldn't last much longer — weeks or maybe a couple of months at the most. Angela would miss her, but the Ellen she'd known, the one who had tried for months to set her up with a roommate's son, was already gone.

Normally she would have just bumped a bit more power into the binding, but in its current shape she would need to start from scratch, removing the old one and casting the new afterward. She glanced toward the hallway, wishing the rooms had doors on them. Someone with magical sensitivity might be able to tell what she was doing if they walked by, but that couldn't be helped.

"Okay Ellen, this might tickle a bit." When Ellen had first arrived at the facility, occasionally disoriented but usually lucid, she'd told Angela it tingled when the binding went in place. Angela wondered if Ellen still felt it or if the magic at her core was so disordered she no longer had a connection.

Angela released the binding, letting the tattered magic disintegrate and disperse into their surroundings. The minute the binding fell away Ellen shuddered and rocked to her feet, faster than Angela had seen her move in months.

Angela jumped up and blocked her path to the door, feeling her face flush. "Hang on a sec, Ellen. We're almost done here." She started weaving the binding around what remained of the woman's magic.

Ellen struck out with her forearm, catching Angela on her nose and shoving her to the side. As Angela landed in a sprawl on the couch, her eyes watering, she saw the old woman lurch toward the door. Benson moved into her path and she tried to push him aside and... disappeared.

Still blinking away tears from the blow to her nose, Angela missed what had happened until she saw movement on the floor. "Oh, cheese on rice. Be careful where you step." The frog hopped toward the wall, then leaped behind the furniture. Angela levered herself off the couch and looked behind the dresser. Ellen's frog form was just sitting there, bumpy skin glistening, sides moving as she breathed.

Benson moved next to her and they stared, shoulder to shoulder in front of the dresser. Angela didn't look up at him. Heat rolled over her and she could feel sweat forming on her back but she didn't dare take off the windbreaker and expose her MPD polo. Benson might have changed in thirty years, but probably not enough to actually lie about her job performance in his reports. At this rate she'd be lucky to be employed after he turned in the results of whatever audit he was conducting.

Benson leaned over. "I can pull the furniture away from the wall if you can grab her."

Angela risked a glance. He didn't look particularly bothered, just concerned. "Okay. Ready when you are."

A voice cut in from the doorway. "Is everything okay in here?"

Angela turned and saw one of the caregivers, a stout woman wearing a smock with cheerful toy bears waving Puerto Rican flags on it, "We're fine. Just waiting a few minutes to see if Ellen is going to come back from wherever she wandered off to." She followed the woman's gaze to where Benson was crouched, ready to move the dresser. "My pen rolled back behind the dresser. It's like it figured out the worst place to land or something."

The woman smiled. "If I see Ellen, I'll try to send her back this direction, okay?"

"Thank you." Angela turned back and leaned down as if trying to retrieve a pen, and watched the other woman leave from the corner of her eye. "Ready."

Benson slid the dresser away from the wall and Angela leaned in and grabbed the frog before she could hop away. She sat down on the couch again, leaned forward to put the frog on the chair in front of her, then reached with her magic and *yanked* Ellen into her human form, not waiting for her assistance or permission, a violation that made her grit her teeth. The chair springs squeaked as the woman materialized, her shoes clattering to the floor. Angela held out a hand to steady the old woman even as she worked to weave the binding into Ellen's magical core. With a sigh, Angela tightened the binding, tied off the ends, and released it.

For the first time that day Ellen made eye contact, really looked at her, and the sorrow and confusion on the old woman's face made Angela want to cry. Then Ellen went back to looking out the window. Angela reached out and placed a light hand on her shoulder. "Hang in there, Ellen. I'll come back and see you next week."

She got up from the couch and gestured for Benson to precede her to the door.

"Good-bye, Angela." Ellen's thin voice called after her. It was the first time Ellen had used her name in at least a year. She wondered if pulling her back to her human form had allowed Ellen some clarity, and if so, if that was a blessing or a curse. But when she looked back Ellen was still staring out the window, off in her own world.

7

"Things usually go better than that," she said to Benson as they got back in the car.

He responded with a non-committal hum. "Multi-shape care home?"

That would be the correct thing to do according to the guidelines. "The nearest one is over five hundred miles away, and it's private." Ellen's assets had been transferred to a facility in Baltimore that was supposed to take care of her until she died, but they found out about her shifting and kicked her out after a year. Their bill for services already rendered was more than what she had to start with. "Her daughter tried to keep her at home for a while, but she needs a full-time caretaker."

Angela turned on the engine and blasted the air conditioning, feeling comfortable for the first time since they'd entered the building. Damned hormones. "I had a client who moved to Baltimore. He met Ellen's daughter and they started talking..." She trailed off. The Baltimore MPD had shown up at Ellen's house in full uniform every two weeks, frightening the neighbors and scaring off the hired caretakers. Nothing the daughter could say after that would convince them her mother wasn't dangerous. Shifters had few legal protections, and anti-shifter feelings ran deep. Every few years, someone would shift and injure or kill someone, and the media ran the story over and over until even the most tolerant person wondered why they were allowed to remain in society. An entire restaurant chain had gone bankrupt when a report had appeared that linked food prepared by shifter employees to a rise in children shifting. Even though the report had been debunked and proven to have originated on a satire site, people still brought it up. The only people who didn't discriminate were the ones who found a way to profit from it, like the military and the movie industry. "Anyhow, she called me and we worked out this solution. The captain agreed to it, so they moved here."

If Matt really did end up managing their team, she had no idea whether he would allow that agreement to continue or not, but she suspected it didn't matter. Ellen wouldn't last much longer.

Benson wrote something in his notebook, then flipped it closed. "I'm just a little surprised, that you, of all people—"

Angela accelerated a little harder than she needed to in order to pull into traffic. "That was a completely different situation." Guilt and anger crawled out of the pit where she'd buried them three decades ago. "Ellen isn't going to hurt anyone if she shifts."

Benson didn't even pretend they were talking about something else. "You could have made sure Casey didn't. He just needed some time to get used to the idea."

Angela shook her head. "And what if it hadn't worked and he'd hurt someone else? I saw what he did to you." She'd always been able to see the magic, and she'd learned a few simple spells from other people as a teen, but she hadn't yet had any formal training when Casey had shifted. It was a valid enough reason, but she still felt guilty.

The static of the radio was the only sound in the car. Now Angela remembered why she hadn't spoken to Benson in years.

Benson waited until they were turning into the strip mall before he spoke again. "Where to now?"

"Line dancing." She pulled into a space in front of The Watering Hole and cut the engine.

"Line dancing," he repeated.

"I find it helps my clients with stability if I can observe them while they're doing something else, plus there are the social benefits of seeing other shifters, and it's good exercise to boot." She dangled her keychain in the space between them. "But if you have something against the Tush Push, I'll give you my keys and you can go watch Matt and Caleb handle the dragon." He'd take them. He had to take them. Nobody would give up a chance to see a dragon instead of line dancing at a tacky bar in an aging strip mall. And Benson *hated* country music. He couldn't possibly have changed so much that he'd be willing to suffer through over an hour of it.

Instead, he opened his door. "I can't say I've ever Tush Pushed before, but I can't wait to see how it goes."

Gritting her teeth, Angela got out and led him into the bar.

The Watering Hole had seen better days. The stuffed cow out front holding a sandwich sign advertising line dancing classes and the beer of the day had bare spots and an odd stain near the tail that didn't invite a closer look. Inside the bar, the harsh light of day showed worn railings and cracked saddles on the bar stools, but the mirrored wall of drinks behind the bar was well stocked, and the bartender gave them a smile and a tip of his ten gallon hat. "Drummed up some new people, I see." His accent was pure New York City. "What can I get you?"

"Diet Coke, please." Angela turned to Benson and raised her eyebrows. When he started to shake his head she spoke again. "There's a one-drink minimum. Or you can pay the ten dollar cover fee." Or he could go see the damn fire-breathing dragon and let her get on with her job.

"Then I'll have the same."

They carried their drinks across the room where a cluster of about twenty people waited. Angela noted at least five new faces.

"It isn't working," Benson said, his voice pitched low enough that nobody else would be able to hear.

"Excuse me?"

"This is your idea of stability?"

As much as she wanted to argue, the tension in the magic buzzing around them proved his point. Having new people join a session shouldn't have thrown it off that much, but when she switched to her other sight the cause was immediately clear. The majority of the new people were completely unstable, their magics rocking and wobbling within them, held in place by spells with more strength than finesse. Worse, the spells that kept them from shifting were also blocking their recognition of the instability.

Angela frowned. That was the sort of rough and quick spell you could throw on someone about to go off to training camp, knowing that it only needed to last a short while and the subject would be taught to balance themselves later. Except everyone added to her list had been monitored for months, if not years.

Somehow she doubted she'd be getting much dancing done this day.

But before she could start working with the new people, she needed to do something with Benson. Having him know about Ellen was bad enough, but there were other shifters that it would be disastrous for HQ to learn about. Luckily, the solution presented itself in the form of Sue, the woman who had been leading the line dancing class for years. Blond pigtails at odds with her sixty-five years, Sue was dressed in form-fitting jeans and a gingham plaid ruffled shirt.

"Sue, this is Benson Li. He's just visiting for a bit but maybe you can turn him into a convert." Angela backed away while they were shaking hands, and headed off to the first person she didn't recognize.

She quickly fell into a routine, introducing herself, and handing over her business card with her personal contact information in case they needed to reach her after hours. After a quick conversation about how they felt they were doing controlling their magic, she carefully replaced the spells patching them together with one that helped stabilize them a little but left them cognizant of their own unsteadiness. For the clients who shifted into something dangerous she also added a stricter binding so they couldn't shift.

Caleb — because after a few people she was sure nearly all were former clients of Caleb — had done these people no favors. Not one seemed to have any idea that there was a problem. And none of them were happy with how they felt when she was finished. She couldn't blame them — they'd felt fine and now they didn't. But if Caleb, or someone else, hadn't been around to renew the spells, they'd have had no control over their actions.

Angela didn't understand it. None of these clients would have graduated training camp in the state they were in. What Caleb had done had allowed them to get sloppy.

Unbalanced magic leading to an uncontrolled shift could kill bystanders. Shifters were legally forgiven that sort of thing once, the very first time they shifted, but after that they were held responsible.

Before releasing each new client, she paired them up with one of her regulars under the guise of having someone show them the dance steps, hoping that giving them a more stable shifter to talk to would help change how they felt about the process.

As she worked Angela kept an eye on the dancers. Benson cast her a couple of dark glances from his position in the front center, right where Sue could help him the most, but by the time the dancers took a break he had mastered the Cowboy Shuffle, the Redneck Girl, and the Achy Breaky Heart with more grace than some of the regulars.

"You seem to be giving out a lot of business cards," he said, as she took a break to go grab the drink she'd abandoned earlier.

"We shuffled some clients yesterday." That was the most polite way she could explain what Matt had done. She looked around at the group. She still needed to deal with three people and she was getting tired. If Caleb was able to bind this many people on a weekly basis, his magic was a lot stronger than she'd thought. "A lot of these people are new to me."

"Really." Benson pulled out his notebook and handed her a list and his pen. "Which of these are usually yours?"

Angela ticked off the first seven names, two of whom had moved out of town in the last six months, then went through the rest without recognizing them. When she handed back the list he nodded. "Interesting." Then he didn't say anything else, just pocketed the notebook again.

She waited a moment to see if he was going to explain, but Sue clapped her hands to get everyone's attention so they could start dancing again, and Angela went to find the next person she needed to talk to.

BY THE TIME the line dancing class was over, Angela was wiped out. She'd managed to touch base with all of her clients, but the new ones weren't happy and she overheard two women plotting to get reassigned to Caleb as they left. She silently wished them luck.

Lily's mother had finally left a message, giving her just a time and a place for the doctor's appointment. Angela added it to her calendar. More of the new clients had returned the email she'd sent the night before. Also, there was a text from the dispatcher asking her to call when she was free. She called Candace's direct line to find out what was going on.

"You're going to kill me," Candace started. "It's going to be a bullshit call, I'm pretty sure I heard someone giggling in the background, but Matt said I had to send everything to you while that HQ guy is here, so..."

Angela sighed. "Where and what?"

"The food court at the mall. A cockroach."

Of course. Because she didn't have enough to do today. Still, it wasn't Candace's fault. "Okay, I'll swing by. How's the dragon situation?"

Candace snorted. "Patterson and King are out there with them now. So far all they've done is gotten a bunch of expensive equipment torched. The fire marshal is on the other channel swearing about them. I'll record some of it and send you the highlights."

That made no sense at all. Patterson and King would have brought at least one tap with them, so it should have just been a matter of getting close enough to the dragon to deploy it. But maybe the dragon had holed up in a place they couldn't get to. A joke one of her professors had started class with years ago went through her mind. How do you get a salamander to move? Answer: You ask it very, very, very politely.

As much as she knew it was important to get the dragon shifted back, and soon, Candace's news made Angela feel better. "The word of the day is *schadenfreude*. We're leaving The Watering Hole now. Mark me en route to the mall."

Benson looked up when she put her phone down. "New case?"

"I'd be shocked if it's real, but I have to go check it out anyway." Angela hadn't realized how much she would miss the captain when he was still there. He would never have sent her out on such a call.

They were both silent on the ten-minute ride to the mall. When she glanced over at him, Angela had the feeling that Benson was biding his time, waiting for something. She parked in the red zone next to the doors and cut the engine.

Benson followed her into the mall. "What are we looking for?"

Angela glanced over at him. "Honestly? Two or more teenagers near the food court who are waiting for me to start trying to find a cockroach."

A slight break in his step was the only indication that he understood what she meant. "Second floor, third table from the right. You keep them entertained and I'll go grab them." He broke off and headed for the stairs.

Angela made a show of walking through the tables in the first floor of the dining area, looking around at the ground, ignoring the muffled laughter coming from the railing above her. Even if she hadn't known the call was bogus to begin with, she'd have figured it out after listening to them giggle. Then there was a yelp and the laughter abruptly cut off. She glanced up and saw two white boys, probably still in their early teens, seated at a table with Benson standing nearby. She jogged up the stairs, wondering why the kids hadn't just taken off running, but when she got there she realized Benson was holding both of their phones. The kids were smart enough to realize running wasn't going to help.

What they were going to do, however, was try to bluster their way out of it. "I don't know what you're talking about," the older of the two said with a laugh. "We were just sitting here."

Before Benson could say anything else, Angela pointed to the other one. "Do you know anything about it?" She needed to get a denial from both of them before they went any further, or else they would later claim that the call was in good faith but they were mistaken about what they'd seen.

The younger one smirked and shook his head.

Angela nodded, took out her phone, and dialed Candace again. She turned so the kids wouldn't be able to hear her conversation. "Hey, can you ring the number that called this in?"

"I've tried but they aren't picking up. I'll try again."

Angela turned back and watched the kids while she waited. One of the phones in Benson's hand vibrated. "Winner winner chicken dinner!" She took the phone from Benson raising an eyebrow at the teen who started to protest. He settled back in his chair, cheeks turning red. Angela answered the phone. "Is that you?"

Candace's voice came through. "I take it you found the caller?"

"Yep. Can you have mall security meet us in this location?" Mall security usually meant retired cops who had no patience for false calls. As a bonus, they might not yet have heard about her assaulting an officer and then getting him fired.

They were back in the car in less than ten minutes. Angela glanced at the time on her phone. She had a couple of individual meetings later, but it was nearly noon. "You okay with Chinese food for lunch? We're close and I usually stop there once a week."

"For a client?"

"Only in a better world."

8

The lunch rush was in full swing by the time they got to Jade Palace. The long narrow restaurant was in yet another strip mall, the cool dark interior dominated by a large saltwater tank along one wall. The hostess, a round-faced young woman with short black hair, and lightly accented English, greeted them and immediately escorted Angela and Benson to a booth near the door to the kitchen. Between the end of the tank and the door stood a small table with a simple shrine made of a stick of incense and two oranges in front of a varnished wooden box. Under the table, a yellow beach towel rested on a shelf, the color incongruous among the red leather of the booths and the dark pattern of the carpet. The hostess placed two menus on the table, then continued past them into the kitchen and called out loudly before returning to the front of the restaurant.

Benson opened up the menu and scanned through it.

Angela left her menu at the end of the table. She knew it by heart. A sense of futility swept over her, and she spoke up just so she'd be able to concentrate on something other than why she was here. "I figured you would be running a division by now. Or even the whole service."

He looked up and shrugged. "I got side-tracked for a while in the research department. I'm back in operations now. It's a bit of an old boys' network though."

Angela felt her lips quirk up. "You fit right in." As a gay East Asian man, Benson probably stuck out even more than she did. Her gaze wandered over to the reef tank where a variety of glass vases were strewn in the sand, and then she looked back at him. "But what are you doing here?" Their division wasn't big enough to interest someone from operations.

"I came out here to watch your team work." He closed his menu.

Angela thought about her morning. "You must be really impressed so far." She winced as she thought of the frog. "I swear it usually goes a little more smoothly."

Benson shrugged. "Everybody's allowed to have bad days."

Angela looked back at the tank where a small octopus was now climbing over a rock formation in the corner.

Catching up about mutual friends took the entirety of the meal, with some laughter about the absurdity of the paths different lives had taken, and acknowledgement of the ones who hadn't made it that far. By unspoken assent, they avoided the fight that had kept them from talking for thirty years.

They were nearly done with lunch when an older Chinese woman came out from the kitchen, a stained apron protecting her dress. "Hello, Ms. Jones." She took Angela's hand in both of hers. "How are you today?"

"I'm doing well, Mrs. Chen. Lunch was very good. How is your husband?"

The woman smiled, deepening the wrinkles in her face. "I make him rest today." She looked over at Benson. "You have boyfriend now?"

Angela shook her head. "This is my colleague, Benson Li. Benson, this is Mrs. Chen. She and her husband own the restaurant."

Mrs. Chen said something, and Benson shook his head. "Sorry, I don't speak Cantonese." He gestured to his almost empty plate. "The food is delicious."

She waved a hand, dismissing him, and turned back to Angela. "Maybe this week?"

Angela felt her smile freeze. "Maybe. I'll try."

Mrs. Chen nodded. "You always do your best. Thank you." She nodded and hurried back into the kitchen.

Benson craned his neck to watch the kitchen doors swing closed. "I think I just failed some test."

A mirthless laugh bubbled up. "If she started holding failure against people, I'd never get fed here."

Benson raised his eyebrows and waited.

"The Chens have owned this restaurant for almost twenty years," Angela said. "Well, it used to be about a mile and a half north of here, but it's still the same restaurant really. It's always been a family restaurant, with all sorts of cousins and aunts and uncles, you know how that goes. They had a son and a daughter who worked in the restaurant as well. About five... no, I guess it's six years now. Six years ago, her son and daughter were the last ones here, closing up late at night." She took a moment to pour out a cup of tea from the pot in the center of the table. "A group of men broke in to rob them, and things went wrong. The son was shot. Bled to death on the floor. The daughter disappeared. May was seventeen."

Angela took a deep breath. "The cops assumed she'd

been taken. They had her face on posters and television. And the whole family was grieving for the girl's brother and searching for her, so the restaurant didn't get reopened for a week and nobody noticed anything different in the tank for a while."

Benson turned his head to the tank. "She...?" His eyes unfocussed briefly, and then locked in on the octopus. "Oh."

Angela nodded. "By the time anyone thought to bring MPD in, it had been three weeks." She joined him in looking into the tank. "I've never even convinced her to talk to me. Some weeks when I come by, I find it hard to tell there's a human shape in there." She switched to her other sight. Today was one of May's stronger days. Angela could see both shades of magic, even though the octopus was dominant.

"But you keep coming." Benson was looking at her again.

Angela shrugged. "I try to come by at least once every week. I keep thinking that maybe I'll catch her at just the right time." She looked down at the cup of jasmine tea she was cradling in her hands. "Between her strength and the amount of time she had been shifted before I got here, I can't just force her to shift back, but I'm hoping if she ever decides to help, maybe we'll be able to manage it." She looked up at him. "If you have any ideas, I'd love to hear them."

Benson looked from her to the octopus. "There's no reliable record of a first shift being reversed more than ten days after the fact." His eyes unfocussed again and the octopus jumped, pulling away from the front of the tank. "But she's still in there. And I should know better than anyone how little history we have." He looked back at Angela. "Let me think about it for a bit." His phone buzzed on the table and he brought up his texts. "Ah." He seemed to relax into the seat, as if something had been decided.

Angela glanced at her phone but it was still blank. "Did they deal with the dragon?"

"What? Oh, no. Just confirmation of something else." He turned his phone over and folded his hands on the table in front of him. "Do we have time for me to tell you more of why I'm really here?"

Angela nodded. "I have some client home visits to fit in and a doctor's appointment at three, but we have time." She glanced around the busy room. "I don't think they ever seat other customers here so it shouldn't be a problem to stay." She settled back in her seat.

"My division looks for trends and potential outbreaks — anything that looks like something we need to check out." He poured more tea for both of them. "Most of what we come up with turns out to be nothing, anomalies that fall out the minute someone looks into them. But every once in a while we come up with something real. This city is one of those."

Angela frowned at him. "I thought our stats were average. For a city this size anyhow. I mean, before the dragon."

Benson nodded. "Right in the middle, for almost every performance indicator that HQ cares about. First shift per capita, uncontrolled relapse rate, mortality during first shift, all right in the expected range. At the highest level the only difference is that the city skews slightly young for average age of first shift, but it would actually be abnormal if everything was normal, if you know what I mean."

Angela nodded. "So... you're saying the city is normal for its size."

He glanced over at the tank where the octopus had

moved to the front, two tentacles splayed against the glass. "Is she usually this curious?"

"No, that's new." Angela flipped to her other sight, but May looked unchanged. "What did you do earlier?"

Benson splayed his fingers and waggled them. "I... maybe you'd say I vibrated her magic. It was just something one of my instructors did to make me aware of myself. Sadly, it was the only thing they were ever able to teach me. But it's a good party trick." His gaze went vague for a second and the octopus shot across the tank again. "Interesting." He shook his head. "But back to averages. When you aggregate data you lose information. And your department is hiding some big secrets in the averages."

The mention of secrets made Angela think of the things she'd hidden from the captain in the past. She shifted on the bench. Surely there hadn't been enough omissions to raise flags in headquarters.

"Not a few cases here and there," Benson elucidated. From the twitch of his lips she thought he'd caught her flash of guilt. He'd always been able to read her expressions better than anyone else. "Take something like average time between uncontrolled shifts. You'd usually expect it to look something like a bell curve."

Angela nodded to indicate she was following, relieved that he'd moved away from talking about secrets. "Just remember how much time you spent getting me through my stats class before you get too technical." Benson had always been the logical one while she'd been the intuitive one, counting on her magical ability for a career.

He opened his mouth to say something, then closed it. "Good point. Let's just say that instead of a nice curve, there are two bumps, one slightly below average, and a smaller one way above average. Something's not normal." He sipped more tea. "So here I am."

"And when you figure it out?" The best case Angela could come up with was more oversight from HQ, although if that kept Matt from being in charge of the department it might be worth it.

He raised his eyebrows. "If we could replicate whatever is causing that spike on the high end, even in a small fraction of cases, we could save millions of dollars and potentially a few lives."

Angela nodded.

Benson folded his napkin in half, then in half again. "Honestly, I was expecting to find some young agent screwing up a common spell and accidentally making it more effective. But your department doesn't seem to have a lot of turnover."

Angela thought of the spells Caleb had left on his clients that had come to the line dancing session earlier. She would have sworn those shifters were unstable, but maybe Caleb's methods were responsible for the bump Benson was looking for. The idea of a spell like that holding Vicky in her human form was just another depressing thought in a long day of depressing thoughts. Angela finished off the rest of her tea. "We should go."

9

A ngela left enough cash on the table to cover both the meals that the Chens would never charge her for. May had gone back into hiding in the tank before they stood up to go.

The navigation app sent her to an upscale housing tract with neatly mowed lawns and expensive cars in the driveways. Parking at the curb in front of the address, Angela brought up the case file on her computer.

This was another client transferred to her yesterday, but in this case it had been one the captain had been handling personally. Instead of a simple check to make sure the shifter was maintaining stability, this had additional complications. The house was subject to random searches and the shifter was prohibited from owning rabbits. She dug back in the record to find the reason for the prohibition. Occasionally she ran across shifters, usually coyotes or dogs, that enjoyed hunting in their other forms and liked to stack the deck. That could cause the neighbors to complain, but didn't usually lead to criminal charges.

She checked to see what the client shifted into and had

her answer.

"Problem?" Benson had stopped with his fingers on the door handle, waiting for her.

"One of the captain's cases," she said. "Legal. I'll need to do a full house search." Best for this client to understand from the start that she could and would be keeping tabs on him.

Benson nodded. "What are we looking out for?"

His use of 'we' threw her off. It had been so long since she'd had a partner, even unofficially, she'd forgotten what it was like. "He's a rabbit shifter. He's prohibited from having any rabbits on the premises."

Aside from the ethical issues and the general ick factor of having a private harem of animals, there was a practical problem with such interspecies couplings. Some shifters could get animals pregnant, and some of those pairings led to viable offspring. Occasionally those offspring inherited a human form as well, but they would never pass as fully human. The third season of *Shift Enforcers* had involved a doomed relationship between Guy Barron and a mink-shifter hybrid, and had provided a lot of women with Halloween costumes, but it had no touchstone in reality.

Angela got out of the car and checked her tactical belt to make sure everything was in place before going up to knock on the door. An older white man, too old to be her client, but likely his father, answered, opening the door just a crack, leaving the flimsy security chain in place. "Angela Jones, MPD," she introduced herself, raising her credentials so he'd be able to read her identification.

The old man left the chain in place and shuffled away. "Rupert!" he called out. "It's for you."

Angela and Benson waited.

Two minutes went by. Angela sighed. "This isn't going to

be simple, is it?"

Benson leaned forward to look through the gap in the doorway then stood up straight again. "You want me to go around back?"

Angela rubbed her lower lip. "Have you ever tried to catch a rabbit shifter? Nah, if this guy runs he'll come right back. He doesn't have any resources of his own." She leaned on the doorbell and moved forward to shout through the opening. "I'm about thirty seconds away from ruining your door frame. Please open the door, sir."

From around the corner they heard the sound of a recliner snapping upright. "Dammit, Rupert, why didn't you answer the door?" The old man shuffled into view, still yelling. "If you've gone and started this again, so help me, I'll..." He trailed off as he reached the landing, took the chain off, and pulled the door open, all without looking at them. He headed around the corner. "Upstairs. Don't break anything."

Angela led the way, trying not to wince when climbing the stairs reminded her muscles of the hotel the day before. Upstairs the master bedroom and bathroom were open and empty. Angela knocked on the closed door on the other side of the hall. "Rupert, this is Angela Jones with MPD. I'm coming in." She moved to the side of the door before reaching forward and turning the knob. There was nothing in his file to indicate he'd been violent in the past, but if he was violating his parole he might be desperate.

She wasn't quite prepared for the grown man sitting on the bed, shoulders hunched, eyes red. "I read that Captain Rosenthal was dead and I couldn't help myself," he said, sniffling. "In another two days I'll be able to shift again. It's been so long. I couldn't help myself."

The room smelled of grass hay, wet cardboard, and

unwashed sheets. It looked like the room of a high school boy, with sports posters taped to walls and football trophies lining one high shelf. Rupert was in his forties, but the room felt as if his life had halted when he'd first shifted. In the corner stood a cage with five rabbits nibbling on hay, a water bottle dripping onto the shredded paper lining the bottom of the enclosure. Angela flipped to her other sight and looked at both Rupert and the rabbits. As far as she could tell, none of the rabbits was pregnant, and there was still a binding spell on Rupert that would have kept him from acting on his desires. At least she'd been in time to prevent that tragedy. Now she just had to deal with the aftermath.

Benson caught her eye and indicated that he'd be downstairs, giving her room to work, and she nodded.

Angela crouched by the bed. A wave of heat crashed over her and she tried to discretely flap her shirt to cool the sweat forming on her skin. "Rupert, you know why you're not allowed to do this, right?"

He nodded but didn't meet her eyes. Sweat beading at his temple trickled down his face.

Angela wished she'd had more time to read through the file. "Did Captain Rosenthal talk to you about getting therapy?"

He nodded again.

"And did you?"

He shook his head, still not looking up from the floor.

"Okay, what I'm going to do is set up an appointment with a therapist, and if you go to therapy every week for the next two months, I'll hold off on doing anything else about this, alright? But if you don't make it to your appointments you're going to have to go back to jail. And I'm going to have to take these rabbits with me." What she was going to do with five rabbits was another problem.

Standing up again to give her aching legs a rest, she started weaving the strongest binding spell she could. On a good day she'd be able to create something that would last a couple of months, but it had been a taxing morning after a rough couple of days. Still, she'd be able to craft something that would hold until the next week.

His magic dimmed as she tightened the net, giving her pause. She'd never had that happen before. Switching back to normal sight she looked down at him. His head nodded, as if he were falling asleep.

She crouched back down. "Rupert, are you feeling alright?" If she'd caused two men to have heart attacks in the same week...

His eyes briefly fluttered open, then closed again and he slumped to his side on the bed.

"Benson!" She felt for a pulse even as she was fumbling her phone out of her pocket. She could still feel Rupert's heart beating, but his skin was cold and clammy and he didn't respond when she lifted one eyelid to see a dilated pupil. Benson came in, saw Rupert passed out on the bed, and then disappeared back out into the hallway. By the time she'd explained the nature of the emergency to the dispatcher he was back again, holding three empty pill vials.

Given Rupert's father's comments when he'd let them in the house, Angela had been worried he'd send his son off alone, but as the paramedics had maneuvered the stretcher through the living room he'd placed a gnarled hand on his son. "Ah, Rupert," he said, his voice quiet. "Don't give up. We'll get through this as well."

After the scramble to get the rabbits into a carrier and

get out of the house, Angela had driven halfway to the doctor's office before she thought to ask Benson about Lily's condition.

"What does she shift into?" he asked after she'd given him a quick summary of the pregnancy that might not be a pregnancy.

"That's...a difficult question." Speeding through a yellow light, Angela glanced to the left and changed lanes to go around a delivery truck. "It's not something that occurs naturally, and as far as I've been able to tell it's not from any mythology. I'll show you a picture when we get there. Maybe you'll have a better idea of what it is. I've always assumed it was something Lily came up with." Angela smiled, like she usually did when she thought about Lily. "She's a great kid."

Benson typed on his phone, digging his elbow into the arm rest as they took a corner a little too sharply. "What kinds of influences would she have?"

Pulling into the parking lot Angela scanned for a parking space. "Her parents came here from South Korea, but I think they might be ethnically Chinese. They said they didn't recognize the form, but they've been reluctant to discuss it at all." That was putting it mildly. "I've always assumed it was something from her imagination, maybe based on something from television." She pulled into a space, cut the engine, then pulled up a picture she'd taken of Lily the first night she'd shifted. The sparkly bits in the blue reptilian hide reflected the light, but her basic form was clear. Angela handed her phone to Benson. "Have you ever seen anything at all like this?"

He shook his head. "I'm fairly certain that's not out of any mythology I've ever seen, but let me send it to my team. They have more knowledge than I do." At Angela's nod, he mailed the photo to himself, and then returned her phone.

Angela led the way across the parking lot into the building where they found Lily and her mother in the waiting room. When the receptionist stared at the rabbit carrier, Angela pretended not to notice.

Lily's mother nodded at Benson when Angela introduced him, but then went back to reading her magazine. Once in the exam room with the doctor, Lily grabbed Angela's hand and held it tight as Angela explained to the doctor, a calm woman in her thirties, what she'd seen.

"She's pregnant?" Lily's mother burst out. "You didn't tell me that." She put down her magazine and turned to her daughter. "How could you be so irresponsible?"

Lily's eyes watered, but no tears fell. "I'm not."

The doctor cut in before her mother could respond. "Why don't we find out what's really going on first?" She started her exam, and Benson excused himself and took the rabbits out to the exam room to wait.

He showed up again as the ultrasound technician came in half an hour later. The doctor had also scheduled blood-work, but because Angela was able to pinpoint the extra magical signature she was seeing, they'd skipped forward a few steps.

The screen showed a flurry of snow as the technician squirted gel on Lily's child-flat belly and put the probe on it. Angela leaned forward to look. Lily still had her hand in a death grip, but she too looked at the screen. Rounded shapes showed up on the screen as the probe was moved, dark caverns and white lines.

"There." The technician used her free hand to point to a series of white marks on the screen. "Spine and skull." She tilted the probe a little and something fluttered on the monitor. "Nice steady heartbeat." She hit some buttons, freezing the image, and drew some lines on the screen, then let the screen show the live images again. "I'd say you're about nine weeks along."

Lily stared at the screen. "But..."

Her mother's voice was faint. "What are we going to say to your father? We'll have to take care of this today."

Angela felt Lily flinch, and then there was a magical spark and the ultrasound technician drew in a breath.

On the screen the skull had changed from human to something else, a more angular form which had an elongated snout. The screen went back to random static as the technician jerked her hand back. She swallowed, and moved her hand forward again tentatively, using her free hand to take screen shots of the changed fetus. Another flash, and the fetus went back to human.

Angela took the opportunity to slip a light binding spell over the fetus, encouraging it to stay in human form. Lily's other shape had claws and teeth, and she had no idea what that would do to the girl's insides.

The technician shut down her machine and cleaned up, offering Lily a towel to wipe off the gel on her abdomen, then rolled her equipment out of the room, leaving a silence only broken by Lily's occasional sniffling.

The chill in her mother's voice could have frozen water. "Who is the father?"

Lily shook her head. "I didn't..." She glanced around the room. "I swear, I didn't do *anything*. With *anybody*."

"Don't lie, Lily. You don't get pregnant by doing nothing."

Benson coughed. "Parthenogenesis?"

Angela thought he was making a joke to relieve the tension in the room, then realized he was serious. "A clone?"

He shrugged. "How do we know her other form doesn't have asexual reproduction? You might be able to tell with DNA analysis."

Both Lily and the doctor stared at him, eyes wide.

"If..." Angela stopped herself. If it hadn't occurred to anyone else that parthenogenesis might lead to a non-stop series of pregnancies, she would let them get to that point on their own.

"This is ridiculous," her mother said, standing up. "When can we schedule the termination?"

Lily squeezed Angela's hand tighter. "But..."

Angela switched to her other sight and looked at the fetus, bright and strong and slightly unbalanced. "I'm not sure that's such a good idea."

Her mother stood up and grabbed her purse. "This is a family matter. Get dressed, Lily. We'll discuss this at home."

Angela shook her head. "No, I mean I'm not sure an abortion would be safe for Lily." She had the doctor's attention, at least. "There's a reason they haven't just launched a missile at that dragon downtown. The sudden release of all that magical energy would make a crater the size of a few blocks." She nodded toward Lily's midsection. "The fetus doesn't have the energy of a dragon, but it's got some power. I don't know how safe an abortion would be for Lily. "

Benson stirred. "And maybe for the building she's in."

The doctor stood a little straighter. "That... changes things. Is there a safer way?"

Before Angela could answer, Lily spoke up. "What if I want to keep the baby?"

"Absolutely not," Lily's mother said. "Let's go. We're leaving now."

Lily shook her head.

"Lily! Right. Now." Her mother walked over and grabbed her arm.

"No." Lily pulled her arm back and then with a blast of light she transformed into her other form, blue skin glowing in the dim light of the room. Her other form had grown since Angela had last seen it, the ridges of her skull almost hitting the ceiling, and while her skin had been reflective before, the glowing was new. Her new form was beautiful.

Angela heard something break inside Lily's mother's purse when the woman ran into the door on her way out of the room.

The doctor was made of sterner stuff. She took half a step back, then stopped. "Lily?"

Benson looked her up and down, his face a mask of wonder.

Angela squeezed the hand still holding hers, though their relative sizes were now reversed. "You okay there, Lily?"

"I'm okay. I just couldn't figure out how to make my mom let go." She looked as repentant as a nearly eight foot tall glowing blue lizard could look. "I'm sorry for scaring everyone."

Angela switched to her other sight to check on the fetus. If anything, the fetus was stronger than it had been. Clearly shifting didn't bother it. "You ready to switch back or do you need a few minutes?" A thought hit her. "Do you mind if I take a picture first? You've changed a little as you've grown. Maybe someone will be able to tell us what you are now."

"That's fine."

Angela took a few pictures, then one last one as a selfie of the two of them. Lily tried to smile and they both laughed at that, the sound somewhat odd coming from the giant creature she'd shifted into.

"Should I switch?"

Angela nodded, and then suddenly the teenager was back. Her situation seemed to strike her all at once. Pressing one hand against her flat abdomen, she looked at Angela. "But what do I do now?"

10

Lily's question took on a whole new dimension when they went out to the waiting room loaded down with pamphlets, pre-natal vitamin samples, and recommendations for an OB/GYN, only to find that Lily's mother had left. Not only had she left her daughter behind, the receptionist who'd watched her go beckoned Angela over and asked if Lily had friends she could stay with for a bit. Angela assumed there were laws to keep parents from abandoning their children, but she wasn't about to force Lily to go live somewhere she wasn't wanted.

Angela put a hand on the girl's shoulder while she told Lily the news. "We'll figure something out. Why don't we give your parents some time to absorb this?" In retrospect, keeping quiet about why she wanted Lily to be seen by a doctor might have been a mistake. "You can hang out with me for the rest of the afternoon, and then we'll see."

Lily nodded and trudged out to the car with Angela, Benson, and the increasingly smelly carrier of rabbits.

Angela drove more carefully on the way back to the office, very aware of her passengers. When they all got in the building, Matt and Caleb were both there, sitting in the conference room with two other men, huddled over what looked like blueprints. One of the strangers raised his head, and Angela remembered that Patterson and King had flown in. The four of them in the room looked like a casting call for a spin-off of *Shift Enforcers*, all four of them white men with the conventional good looks that Hollywood loved, but even from outside she could feel the tension in the room.

Candace looked up from her station when Angela came in with the animal carrier. "Are those really rabbits?"

Angela nodded. "Can you contact someone in animal services? I had to confiscate them." She shook her head when the dispatcher raised an eyebrow. "Don't ask."

"Okay." Candace took the carrier and put it next to her chair. "If it makes you feel any better, the testosterone brigade out there is raising failing to an art form. The dragon destroyed another part of the building, and they're talking about whether they need to shut down the gas main that runs nearby."

"Can they not get close enough to use a tap?"

Candace winced. "Didn't work. They tried three times."

Angela blinked. She'd always suspected the "experts" only got such consistent results because they had better tools than the officers in the field, but she'd never wanted to test that theory in her own city. Still, Patterson and King had all the resources of HQ behind them. "What are they going to do now?"

"Plan A is still convincing the lawyer to change back on his own, but it sounds like they're mapping a route out of the city, so I think the backup plan is to try to move the dragon somewhere far enough away that it won't kill everyone if they drop a bomb on it." She shrugged. "I told them they were idiots for not bringing you in to help." She saw Angela's surprise and shrugged again. "Patterson asked me to bring them coffee," she said, enunciating carefully.

Angela glanced over at the conference room. "I'm sure that went over well." Patterson might not realize it yet, but he was in danger from more than the dragon. The dispatchers really didn't appreciate being treated as personal assistants, and Candace might forgive with enough groveling, but she'd never forget.

Candace smiled, her eyeteeth showing. "Also, they've posted the captain's position."

"The other reason I stopped by," Angela said, ignoring the comment about the open position and checking behind her to make sure that Lily was out of earshot, "is to see if you could keep an eye on Lily out there for the afternoon in case I get called out. She's not in any danger of shifting unintentionally," she added. "There's just some drama at home."

Candace leaned to the side so she could look out the door. "Sure, she can hang with me for the afternoon. How is it going with the HQ guy?"

"Benson? It's fine," she said, realizing as she said it that it was true. "We used to share an apartment during college." She shook her head when Candace raised her eyebrows. "Not like that. But it's nice to see him again." Still, she reminded herself that she should keep her guard up. She didn't really know Benson anymore.

Leaving Candace to answer an incoming call, she walked by the conference room, tapping on the glass and waving when Matt looked up. As much as she hated having him as a boss, even temporarily, she had a duty to keep him informed that one client had ended up in the hospital and another, a minor, might have been kicked out of her house. Maybe she'd get to see the dragon as they drove it out of town.

Benson set up his laptop on the corner of Angela's desk,

sitting on the other side so they weren't staring at each other's screens. Angela got Lily settled in at the spare desk in the dispatch office where she started working on homework, and then Angela started typing up the notes from all her client interactions for the day. She still had a few clients to fit in before it was time for book club, but nothing that couldn't get pushed to the next day if necessary.

A few minutes later Matt came over, crossing his arms over his chest. "What's this I hear about some bunny perv trying to off himself?"

Angela sighed. Of course he would have heard about it. The salacious details would have been too much for everyone involved in the emergency callout to have kept quiet.

"Last I heard they thought he was going to be okay." Angela scribbled herself a note so she'd remember to set up therapy sessions for Rupert after they let him out of the hospital.

"Probably should have just left him there," Matt said. "It would be the easiest way to take care of that problem."

Benson's breathing stilled, and Angela hurried on to the next topic. "Also, that's Lily over there with Candace." She nodded over to the dispatch office, hoping that the girl's proximity would be enough to curb Matt's comments. "Her parents just found out she's pregnant and we're giving them a little time to cool off." She steeled herself for Matt's next words, giving even odds as to whether it would be misogynistic, racist, or just rude, but he glanced over at Benson and didn't say anything.

Candace chose that moment to come out of the dispatch office. "Who's up for the next case? Two people have called in about a unicorn in a condo complex."

Caleb had walked by just in time to hear her last words.

He smirked. "That lets me and Matt out. Angie, you're the only one not getting any action these days, unless..." He paused and looked at Benson. "Ben, you got a girlfriend or are you going to be the only one the unicorn isn't going to run away from?"

Benson met his eyes. "I'm not a virgin, if that's what you're asking, but I've also never slept with a woman."

Angela leaned back in her chair and watched as Caleb's confusion give way to stiffness as he worked out Benson's meaning.

"Oh." Caleb took half a step away. "We should probably get going," he said to Matt and left before the other man replied.

Matt shrugged. "We need to finish up with this dragon." He walked after Caleb without looking at Benson

Angela stopped herself from asking how many days that excuse was going to last, and looked at Candace. "I guess I'm taking this one." Hopefully it wouldn't take too long and she'd still make it to book club on time.

Candace nodded. "I'll send the info to your phone. You want me to order something for dinner?" She tilted her head in the direction of Lily.

"You're the best." Angela locked her screen and picked up her bag. Benson followed her out the door. As they got into the car she grimaced. "Sorry about..." She let him fill in the blank so he could pick whichever part of the recent interaction had offended him most.

"Don't be. This way I won't have to put up with the entire array of sexist jokes if I have to shadow either of them."

Angela suspected that was overly optimistic, but she kept that thought to herself as she started driving toward the address Candace had sent her. "If you want to take it to HR,

I'll back you up, but from past experience I doubt anything will be done."

"Honestly, the most offensive part is the ignorance about unicorns."

Angela glanced over at him. "If you find ignorance offensive, this office is going to kill you." She caught a slight twitch of his lips before she had to look back at traffic.

11

Less than an hour later, they were heading back to the car. Benson waited until none of the neighbors were around, then coughed. "Horse?"

Hiding her wince, Angela started the car and turned the air conditioning as high as it would go. "I guess you heard that." She concentrated on backing the car out, trying to decide how to frame her words. "You've met my coworkers. If I put Grant in the system as a unicorn, how long do you think it would take before Caleb was making jokes about it in a bar somewhere? Or a picture was used on some MPD brochure? Things like that get around." Shifting the car into drive she pulled out into traffic. "I'll make a call to a friend of mine who works at the training camp so they aren't taken by surprise. Nobody else really needs to know." Grant and his wife had seemed perfectly happy with a marriage that didn't include sex. In fact, she could make an argument for them being the two most sexually compatible people she'd ever met.

"It's going to throw off the data models to have a unicorn entered as a horse."

Angela glanced over at him to make sure he was serious. In college he hadn't even wanted to be listed in the student directory. "Better that than ruining his life. It's not even insurance fraud — horses and unicorns have the same risk classification." Eyes back on the road, she continued, "And you, of all people, should know the dangers of having data like that in an accessible place."

"Because I'm gay?" Before Angela could answer he spoke again. "I'm not saying you're doing the wrong thing. I'm just saying it throws off the models."

Angela sighed. "Maybe it's time to focus a little more on the people and less on the models."

He hummed what might have been an acknowledgement of her words and then lapsed back into silence.

AFTER THE SIDE-EYE from the uniformed guard at the gate down the hill, it wasn't a surprise that all the cars she passed on the street as she drove the winding road up cost more than her annual salary. "We trade off houses every meeting," she told Benson as she parked on the street a few houses away from their destination. "I haven't been up here before." Perfectly groomed lawns were designed to showcase different aspects of the houses, but after a while the same choices of trees and shrubs, all surrounded by emerald green grass, grew monotonous. Nobody was on the pristine sidewalks. It was as if someone had planned the perfect community and forgotten to include any people.

He got out of the car and waited for her on the sidewalk. "You said this was a book club?"

"Nominally." Angela locked her tactical belt in the trunk

of the car. The neighbors peeking from behind curtains would still know she was MPD, but at least this way it looked like she was just a participant in the group. "There's a book and sometimes people have read it and usually we talk about things that are at least related to it, but mostly it's just an excuse to meet and eat cookies and drink wine. Although," she added as she thought about it, "there may be more people who have read the book this week. It's a Regency romance, and those usually get read more than the non-fiction selections." She thought about the last few times the group had discussed books in the genre. "It might get a little heated."

"About what? The hero's eye color?"

Angela felt a predatory grin pull up the corners of her mouth. "Just for that, you're on your own." Ignoring his confusion, she knocked on the door.

Inside the living room ten people, mostly women, had already staked out places, wine glasses and plates in hand. "What a lovely home," Angela told Geraldine, the woman whose house they were using. That was her standard phrase, but in this case it was also true. Hopefully it would still be true after they all left. The cream-colored carpet, white couches, and dainty accent pieces gave the impression that no human had ever entered the space. Angela hoped Geraldine wasn't serving red wine.

After introducing Benson to the group as a colleague, she put a few cookies on a plate, basing her selection of meringues entirely on how likely they were not to leave a stain on the furniture if she dropped one. She sat down on the couch next to the only person she didn't recognize, a young woman with purple and black hair wearing pink scrubs with cartoon rabbits. "Hi, you must be Lourdes. I'm Angela Jones." Since her files listed the woman's other form as a white deer with a subtype of lampong, Angela assumed she at least had relatives from the Philippines.

As they made small talk — Lourdes was a nurse in a physical rehabilitation practice and she owned two cats — Angela switched to her other sight. The other woman's magical core was mostly balanced, which made her likely one of Matt's previous clients, not Caleb's, but the intertwining of the magical strands seemed more complicated than Angela expected, as if someone had tried to create a form with smooth curves when all they could use was right angles. Even as she watched, the form swirled in one direction then immediately pulled back into its former orientation. Angela couldn't imagine the amount of effort it would take to keep the magical core in a shape that it didn't naturally go into. "Why—" Her quiet question was cut off as Geraldine clapped her hands. "Let's talk later," Angela whispered, then turned toward their host.

Secure in her own environment, Geraldine had traded in her usual sweater and slacks for a sleeveless silk blouse and an asymmetric silk skirt. The new outfit seemed a more personal choice, and it also left the scars on her neck visible. Angela had known that violence had led to Geraldine's first shift into her turtle form, but this was the first time she'd seen the physical evidence.

"So, I guess I'm supposed to open the discussion by explaining why I chose this book. I guess the answer is that I wanted something a little lighter than the last one."

Everyone's eyes drifted to Constance, whose most recent choice had been a dry recounting of struggles over water use rights in a California valley spanning fifty years, with a few characters thrown in to qualify it as fiction. Angela had skimmed the last two-thirds in hopes of finding out how one particular character died, but unfortunately he'd made it to the end. If Constance picked the sequel the next time it was her turn to host, Angela planned on skipping the book completely and she thought she wasn't alone in that plan.

"In any case," Geraldine continued, "I've read other things from this author and this book was on my to-be-read pile. So... any initial thoughts?"

After a few seconds of silence, Piper made a face. "The whole alpha male thing irritated me."

Jen, sitting on the couch next to her pulled away. "What? How can you not love a guy that repeatedly ignores everything the woman says?"

Piper rolled her eyes. "He doesn't even like her. He's just in lust with her."

Jen nodded. "He's a total dick twitcher."

Piper snorted, leaving an opening for Courtney's, "He's a what?"

Jen turned her face to Courtney and spoke clearly so the other woman could read her lips if her hearing aids didn't do the job. "A dick twitcher. It's a term we came up with last year for all those guys in romances who see the woman and their dick twitches."

Courtney's eyebrows went up. "Thank you. Yes, that's exactly what he is. Is that even possible?"

All eyes turned to Joe, who had the distinction of being one of the few men *and* a doctor even if he was a podiatrist. He pushed his wire-rimmed glasses up. "I think it's unlikely. There are no muscles in the penis."

Geraldine was holding a hand over her mouth. "I pictured it as a sort of romance dowsing rod, pulling in the direction of true love. Although that seems like it would be terribly inconvenient." Her comment set off a louder round of laughter.

"I thought the author could have spent more time

describing the Cornwall countryside," Joe put in. A wave of good-natured laughter echoed around the room. Some people read for plot, others for character, and Joe read for scenery. From what Angela remembered, there hadn't been much scenery in this novel.

Courtney frowned. "You mean the section where he's stalking her and finds her skinny dipping. There was two sentences about the hills and then an entire chapter where he thinks about her 'full breasts' and 'forbidden cleft.'"

Piper held up a finger. "It sounds like a phrase from the title of one of those pulp novels."

"'Nancy Drew and the Mystery of the Forbidden Cleft'," Jen offered.

While other ribald suggestions were added, Angela took the time to switch to her other sight and check on everyone. Geraldine had finally softened up the brittleness that she'd always had a problem with, or maybe this was what she was always like in her own home. Either way, it was an improvement that Angela hoped would remain. The others all looked stable enough. Out of the corner of her eye she saw Lourdes's magical core again, stable but looking like it was trying to be something it wasn't. It reminded her of something but she couldn't think what it was.

When she tuned back in to the conversation around her, Danielle was speaking. "... but the biggest problem I had was the racism. The main character is described as being obviously good because her skin is creamy and she has blond hair that is so light it's almost white. Our hero, Duke Rapey McRaperson, has golden hair. And the bad guys in the book are the Viscount with the 'dark complexion' and his Chinese manservant who knows 'the ancient Oriental arts.'"

"Oh, but at least it has diversity," Piper said drily, then mimed pointing a gun at her head and pulling the trigger.

"Okay, but despite all the problems I thought the sex scenes were pretty good," Courtney said after the groans had died down. "Kind of vanilla, but good."

Piper shrugged. "I guess. She was such a strong character until they got to bed and then she did the whole passive 'Do what you want to me while I lie here' thing. I'm still holding out hope for the Regency where the girl ties him up and introduces him to pegging."

Courtney leaned forward and touched her ear. "Introduces him to what?"

"Pegging!" Piper repeated loudly.

When Courtney continued to look confused, Piper pulled out her phone and started typing.

Angela took advantage of the group breaking up into multiple smaller conversations to turn to Lourdes. "I really do want to talk to you about some things, but I'm pretty wiped out from my day and you look quite stable. Can we schedule a few minutes at the beginning of the next meeting?" Hopefully by then she would be able to figure out what was going on with the other woman. At Lourdes's uncertain nod, she waved a hand. "Nothing scary. Everyone reacts a little differently to stress, and I think it's helpful for both of us to know how things go for you. But in the meantime," Angela gestured to the person on her other side, "have you met Jen? I think the two of you live fairly near each other."

Angela made another trip over to the side of the room to snag a few more meringues, and looked over the group. The underlying buzz of magic in the room felt pleasant against her skin and she took a moment to relax. The job was often exhausting and her coworkers might yet drive her over the edge, but moments like this, seeing a group of people comfortable in their own skins, made it worthwhile.

Across the room, Geraldine glanced at her watch and took control again. "You're all welcome to stay longer if you want to keep talking, but I know some people have to leave on schedule. Who is hosting next time? Do we know which book we're doing?"

Jen raised her hand. "It's at my place. I'll mail the directions and the title as soon as I leave here. We're doing a cozy mystery this time. It's the fifth in the series but you don't need to have read the first four. I've read it. It's a fun book and it shouldn't give anyone nightmares."

Geraldine nodded. "Thanks everyone for coming here —" She broke off. "Oh, I forgot we weren't just here for the books." She looked over at Angela. "Did you need to say anything before everyone goes?"

Having people forget that the meeting was semi-mandatory warmed Angela's heart. "Please let me know if you're having problems. With the dragon downtown there's a big magic source, so you might want to avoid the area. If you can't, at least be aware that you might be a little more reactive." She looked back at Geraldine. "Thank you for hosting."

A chorus of other people thanking Geraldine turned into a general conversational buzz. By the time she had pulled Benson away from his conversation about Chinese political culture in the eighteenth century with Danielle, Lourdes was already talking to Piper.

"That was... interesting," Benson said as they closed the door behind them.

"Which part?" Eschewing the paved path Angela, walked across the perfect grass to the sidewalk. "The discussion, or the magic."

Benson followed her. "Both, I guess. I didn't know I'd be

discussing the number of dukes in Regency England when I woke up this morning. But I meant the magic of the woman you were sitting next to. I'd never seen a predator forced into the shape of a deer."

Angela nearly smacked her forehead. *That* was what she'd found so odd about Lourdes's magical core. Outwardly, a lampong might be mistaken for a deer, but they were two completely different things. And yet Lourdes's magical core was being bent to look like a deer. "Thank you! I couldn't figure out what she looked like." She flipped her keyring around her finger. "I wonder who taught her to do that." And how Matt hadn't noticed that, she couldn't imagine.

"I take it she's one of your new clients?"

Angela nodded. "I'm usually a lot more prepared, believe it or not, but I've never onboarded this many new clients at one time."

As they were traveling back down the hill, her phone buzzed with a new text, and she glanced at the time. "I know it's getting sort of late, but do you mind if we make a quick stop on the way back to the office? It's on the way."

"Not a problem."

12

St. Anthony's Catholic Church had been built at the temporal crossroads of when churches were meant to look like churches but buildings were supposed to be built quickly and cheaply. As a result, it had soaring arches, with seams showing their concrete pour, and statues weeping rust where the strengthening rebar had been exposed to the elements. On a weekday afternoon, the parking lot was nearly deserted, but a faded sign on the path to the narthex indicated that confessions were being heard for two hours in the evening.

A few elderly women knelt with rosaries in the otherwise empty nave, and the green light was on above the confessional, indicating the priest was free. Angela went into the booth and sat. The sliding door blocking the lattice was already open and she could see the outline of the priest on the other side.

"Father Sebastian? It's Angela Jones."

"Ah, welcome." She heard what sounded suspiciously like a paperback book dropping on the floor. "How are you today?" His head briefly disappeared, then popped back up again.

"I'm fine. How about you?" She switched to her other sight, the thin wood of the confession booth only hindering her vision a bit. "Oh dear." The priest's core had so much extra energy that the entwined strands almost blurred together.

A quiet laugh came through the grate. "I spent the day helping the homeless fill out paperwork for benefits downtown. I hadn't been paying attention to the news, so I didn't realize how close to the dragon our shelter is. I finally had to claim illness and leave because I was afraid I would let out my darkness if I didn't get away. It's a little better now, but..." He trailed off and took a careful breath and slowly released it.

"You should have called me sooner." Angela dug through her purse until she found her obsidian beads. When Sebastian talked about his darkness he was being fairly literal. His shifted form was a large bat-winged gargoyle, black as night. Angela had seen a picture of it in his file, but as far as she knew he had never once shifted since he'd been transferred to this parish. The beads were just barely small enough to pass through the lattice. "Have you ever used a magic sink before?"

"I can't say I have."

Of course not. The priest had avoided spending any extra time learning about his condition, preferring to learn how to keep from shifting and then pretending it didn't exist. The Catholic Church had decided that the ability to shift didn't automatically condemn a person, but the act of shifting itself was a serious sin and magic use was a route to damnation. After Father Sebastian had shifted the first time and he'd gone to the mandatory training, his superiors had changed his name and sent him to a new parish, far away from the old one, where nobody would know who he was. Sebastian spent his life helping others and praying that his other side would never get out again.

"Not a problem, I can guide you through it now. The idea is that we're going to take that extra magical energy from you and sink it into the stones. Does that make sense?" Angela dropped into the reassuring voice she used on people who had just shifted for the first time. Her confidence would help him.

"It does, yes."

"Okay, the first thing I want you to do is hold the first bead on chain and imagine some of that magical heat you feel flowing into the stone. Flowing very slowly and in a very controlled way. Just trickling into the stone. Just like that, yes." She could see the light traveling into the obsidian, just a drop at a time. "Perfect. Keep going just like that."

Angela let him continue for a few minutes until she could see the obsidian beginning to buzz from the charge. "Okay, now I need you to stop for a bit and move to the next stone. Just hold back for a bit Sebastian, you can do it." The stone buzzed a little sharper now and she realized she should have started getting him to stop the flow earlier.

Right as the stone hit a buzzing that indicated it had reached a charge close to its failure point, she heard the priest grunt with effort and let go of the stone.

"Great, you're doing really well. Now pick up the second stone and we'll do the same thing. Slow and steady, just like you did with the first one." The first stone had just barely taken the edge off his store of magic. He would need to fill six or seven of the stones just to get back to his normal state. If anyone other than Benson was out there waiting, they'd think she had a few years' worth of sins to confess.

As Sebastian switched to the fourth stone, Angela could almost feel him relax, and the flow into the bead smoothed out, becoming a steady current.

And then the steady current became a flaming torrent and before Angela could blink the obsidian shattered, the newly-released magic filled the air, and she felt his other form boiling to the front. The shadow of the gargoyle filled the space in front of her, and she *reached* and held him in place.

Holding the magic burned, and for a moment she thought her aid wasn't going to be enough, that he would overcome her and explode into his gargoyle form, destroying the confessional and possibly killing her in the process. And then, with a catch of his breath, the priest regained control.

Angela relaxed her hold on his form, incrementally at first, and then completely as he stayed. "Are you okay?" Part of the lattice between them was destroyed, shredded by flying shards of obsidian. It looked like most of the blast had been directed upward, but he'd been holding the bead in his fingers.

"I think so, yes. I have a little cut on my finger, but that seems to be the extent of it." The hysterical edge to his voice was muted by his practiced whisper.

Angela took a deep breath and pulled her shirt away from her sweating back. "Let's try again, and remember, just a little trickle."

"I don't think I'm likely to forget that again," he said with a nervous giggle. Then he gripped the fifth stone and started filling it, one magical drop at a time.

By the time he had filled the seventh bead he was back to normal.

"There you go. I bet that feels better, doesn't it?"

"You've no idea." Angela heard him slump back. "What do I do with these?" He held up the beads near the lattice, wiping off a drop of blood with a handkerchief.

"I'll take them." She pulled the chain through the separator, feeling the buzz of the filled beads in her hand, and dropped it into her purse again. "There's a way to let out their charge. In a non-explosive manner," she added. Now that they'd safely come through the episode she was relieved, and also upset that he hadn't called her earlier. "We need to take some precautions so this doesn't happen again. First, I'm going to email you some links so you can order your own obsidian. They probably even make a rosary or decorations on a crucifix."

"I'll order something appropriate," he said.

"Second, I need you to promise that you will call me much, much earlier than the state you were in today. You could very easily have killed someone." She wiped the sweat from her brow.

"I promise."

"Good. I've got to get out of here. Think about installing air conditioning in this box, would you? It's boiling in here."

"Go in peace, Angela."

Angela stood up and opened the door to the booth, the breeze caused by that little air movement feeling like a slice of heaven. Outside in the nave, the old women were still kneeling near the altar, rosary beads held by gnarled hands winking in the light. Benson stood up from his seat in a pew, and walked toward the door with her.

"Do you need to sit down for a bit?" he asked in a low voice.

She shook her head, and immediately wished she hadn't. It left her dizzy. Angela took a deep breath and concentrated on walking normally. "Sorry about that. I didn't think this would take as long as it did." She let him hold the door open and passed into the fresh air gratefully. "Didn't think I had that much to confess."

Benson walked next to her on the path, his boots clicking on the concrete in a measured rhythm. Heel, toe, heel, toe. "Can I give you some advice?"

"I can't promise I'll take it, but go ahead."

"If you're going to try to disguise your visits to a Catholic priest, you should remember to use the font by the door to make the sign of the cross."

Angela stopped and closed her eyes. If she'd compromised Father Sebastian's security, she needed to deal with it now. "Do you think anyone noticed?"

"No. Nobody was looking in the right direction. I'm just bringing it up for next time."

Angela opened her eyes and looked up at him. "Thank you." She resumed walking toward the car, feeling decades older than when the day had started. When they finally arrived at the parking lot, she handed him the keys and he took them without comment.

Once in the car, Benson took a moment to adjust the seat and mirrors. "What... Do you mind telling me what happened in there?" When she didn't immediately respond he continued. "I haven't felt that much power spill out in a long time. I thought for sure a shift was going to happen. And then it didn't."

"It's because of that damned dragon." Angela hoped none of the women in the nave had any magical sensitivity. "The church runs a shelter downtown. Sebastian has a few handicaps. He's relatively new to shifting and he doesn't have much training, so he didn't realize how bad the problem really was."

"And he won't get training because of his religion?"

Benson stopped at the light. "You're going to have to direct me. I'm not sure where we are."

"Oh, sorry. Keep going straight." Angela leaned back and let the seat embrace her. "Yes, the religious aspect adds to his reluctance, although I think I'll have a better shot at convincing him to get trained now."

"What does he shift into? It felt big."

"A gargoyle the size of a horse. I've seen a picture. It's pretty impressive." Angela looked out the window. "Those guys need to quit screwing around and get this dragon taken care of."

Benson cleared his throat. "Is there some reason *you* don't deal with the dragon?" He signaled when she pointed to the left turn lane. "It's just... I've done ride-alongs with both Patterson and King, and I've never seen them do some of the things you've done today."

Angela shook her head. "Right now, about all I'd be able to do is be the marshmallow in the dragon's s'more."

Benson clicked in frustration. "Not now, of course, but why not this morning when you were still fresh? You never used to hide from problems before. Is there something about dragons in particular that you don't want to work with, or just extra-large creatures?"

His words took a few seconds to sink in. She turned to look at him. "You think *I'm* the one who made that decision?" She laughed, genuinely amused that he would come to that conclusion. "Do you know what I would give to go check out that dragon?"

"But—" Benson stopped talking and hit the brakes, sliding into a turn that put them into the work parking lot. "Sorry, almost passed it." He parked the car and turned in his seat to face her. "Are you saying that they didn't offer it to you? Why the hell not?"

A wave of heat passed over Angela's neck and shoulders and she opened the door to create some air movement. "Because if Matt goes, it looks like an episode of *Shift Enforcers,* and everyone believes it will turn out just fine. Reality doesn't stand a chance."

She climbed out of the car and headed toward the building, not waiting to see if he would follow.

ngela opened the door to her apartment, and tossed her keys in the bowl next to the gloves that were still waiting there. "Come on in," she said to Lily. "Make yourself at home." She headed into her bedroom, kicked off her shoes, and swapped her shirt and bra for a light sweatshirt. When she went back out to the living room, Lily was still standing, holding her duffel bag and pillow, with her suitcase on the floor beside her.

The planned trip to bring Lily home and have a calm discussion with her parents had taken an unexpected turn when they'd arrived to find Lily's belongings packed up on the front porch and all the lights in the house off. Deciding that neither she nor Lily had the energy to explain the situation, Angela had called the swing shift dispatcher and let him know she was taking Lily home with her for the night. She suspected that the rules would say she had to call CPS and have them find a foster home that would accept a pregnant teenage shifter, but if Matt had a problem with what she'd done, he could tell her in the morning — after she'd had a chance to get some sleep.

"You okay sleeping on the couch?" Angela asked the silent teenager. She looked around the room, for the first time noticing how boring the place was. Everything was just as it was when she'd finished unpacking fifteen years ago. Before their plans had changed, she'd been going to offer the couch to Benson as an alternative to a hotel, but maybe it was better he hadn't seen it.

Lily nodded but didn't move.

"Alright, let me get you some sheets and blankets." As Angela moved to the linen closet, she saw Lily's shoes placed neatly by the door and made a note to keep her own shoes over there as long as Lily stayed. It might make her feel more comfortable. Decades of living on her own had given Angela a wide variety of mismatched sheets, towels, and blankets, but she made a bundle out of the ones that seemed the least wrinkled and placed it on the couch. "Are you hungry?" She went into the kitchen and opened the refrigerator. "I have... I can make you a grilled cheese if you want." The refrigerator was not exactly filled with items suitable for maintaining a healthy pregnancy. "Or there are some frozen dinners."

Lily shook her head. "No, thank you. I already ate dinner."

Angela put one of the frozen dinners in the microwave for herself. Remembering the charged beads in her purse, she dug them out and dropped the chain into the saltwater fish tank, sprinkling some food for the angelfish while she was there.

"What's that?"

Angela looked over her shoulder to see Lily looking at the tank. "That's my angelfish Romeo. Or Romeo the Fourth really." The first three Romeos had suffered from a series of catastrophes, but this one had stuck around for a year.

"No, not the fish, the bracelet. It's making a weird sound. And it..." Lily drifted forward until her nose was right next to the glass. "There's something coming off it."

That confirmed something Angela had long suspected — Lily wasn't just a shifter. She could see, and most likely use, magic. "It's charged obsidian. The moving saltwater will help it gradually release the energy." The microwave dinged and she took out the container, mixing the sauce into the still-frozen rice center until it was all at least lukewarm. According to regulations, Angela was supposed to update Lily's file to show she was a magic user. That would attract a new level of interest. Luckily, at the end of a long day all sorts of things might be forgotten. "If the sound bothers you, I can put it in my room for the night and throw it in the tank when we're ready to leave in the morning."

Lily kept looking at the beads. "No, it's okay. It doesn't bother Romeo? Why did you charge them?"

"Romeo doesn't seem to mind," she answered. She had some doubts about Romeo the Third and his disastrous escape from the tank, but the current Romeo never seemed to notice. "And I didn't charge them." Angela sat down at the kitchen table, shoving the stack of bills to the side. "One of my clients spent too much time close to the dragon downtown, and he needed to get rid of some of the energy."

Lily moved to the table and sat down in the other chair, straightening the stacks of envelopes almost as if she didn't notice what she was doing. "He couldn't just shift?"

Angela took another bite to delay while she was figuring out what to say that wouldn't break any confidences. "He doesn't shift for personal reasons."

That got Lily's full attention. "At all?"

Angela shook her head. "No."

"Is it because his other form is so dangerous?"

"That might be part of it." Angela thought back to the shadow of the gargoyle as he had almost shifted today. From the pictures in the file, she hadn't appreciated the size of the creature, even though she knew his first shifting had been accompanied by multiple deaths. "But he has other reasons as well, so I taught him how to bleed off the magic in a different way."

Lily was silent for a few minutes as Angela ate. Finally she asked, "Could you teach me how to do that?"

Despite it sounding like an innocent request, Angela had the feeling she'd just stepped onto a tightrope crossing a deep canyon. "I guess I *could*," she answered, scraping the last of the rice onto her spoon, "but you wouldn't need it. You have such great control over your shifting you would be able to shift back and forth a few times and have the same result."

Lily went back to straightening the mail piles, aligning the corners until they were a perfect column. "But if I learned how to bleed off the magic, I could stay human all the time, right?"

Angela knew exactly why this was coming up now, but didn't think either one of them was ready to have a serious conversation about it yet. Lily's parents deserved to be drawn and quartered. She stood up and tossed the container into the garbage. "Being human all the time is highly over-rated." She put her spoon in the sink. "But if you really want to learn, I'll teach you. It's a good way to practice control anyhow. Just not tonight."

After Angela had dropped Lily off at school the next morning, Vicky ambushed her in the lobby. "When's Matt going to let you have a crack at the dragon?" she asked by way of greeting. "The mayor's talking about sending in the National Guard."

"The mayor's going to blow up a chunk of the most valuable real estate in the city if he does," Angela responded, stabbing at the already lit up elevator button.

"Let's hope he realizes that." The elevator doors opened and they went inside. "Although, I'm pretty sure his donors will let him know."

The only person in the office when Angela went in was Candace, who waved from the dispatch office and pointed to the pink box of pastries on her desk without pausing in her conversation. Claiming half a bear claw and a broken-off chunk of chocolate donut, Angela sat down at her desk and started typing in updates for the clients she'd seen the day before. She'd almost finished when Candace came out of the office.

"This day is going to be a total shitshow," the dispatcher said. "All the clients who work downtown are starting to have problems, and there's a freaking mermaid in the river. Caleb took that one, and your guy from HQ went with him. Matt's back downtown with Patterson and King, watching the dragon destroy more stuff, and he sent out some bullshit memo last night about support staff looking professional which includes make-up guidelines." She turned to hold a stiff middle finger in the direction of Matt's empty desk. "Please tell me that you are applying for the captain's job. I will fill out the form and update your resume for you if you want."

Angela looked up at her. "Is he planning on having the men wear makeup too?" She shook her head. "Just ignore it and claim you never got the memo and if he brings it up, ask if he ran it by HR. By the time he works through that hopefully he won't be in charge any more. Or at least he'll be worrying about more important things."

The dispatch phone rang, and Candace jogged back into the office. She came back out a couple minutes later with a strange look on her face. "Caleb called and asked me to transfer the mermaid case to you."

Angela hit the button on her phone to make sure it was on. "Did he say why?"

"He said it was because he needed to go help Matt, but there's no way. He didn't call you?"

Angela looked at her phone again. She hadn't missed any calls. "No."

"I can't even imagine what would make Caleb hand off a mermaid call. He ran out of here talking about what her boob size might be." Candace rolled her eyes. "I'll forward the location information to your phone. Hey, did you work everything out with Lily last night? She seems like a nice kid."

Angela gave her a quick run-down of the evening. "I need to drop by the house at some point today and talk to her mother. And I might need to pick her up from school, or at least arrange something. Don't let me forget, okay?"

"I'll mark you unavailable for that half hour." Candace walked back to the office. "Let me know how it goes with the mermaid."

14

The woman who had called MPD about the mermaid turned out to be a waitress in a cafe along the river, about three miles from where the dragon was currently laired. Benson was seated at a table on the deck overlooking the water sipping a latte. This morning he'd discarded the suit jacket though he'd added a lilac dress shirt and pink silk tie above black slacks. The boots were a constant feature.

Angela sat in the empty seat across from him just in time for the waitress to put another latte down in front of her.

"I assumed your tastes haven't changed too much," he said, swirling his cup. "If you don't want it, order something else and I'll take it."

She cocked her head to the side to look at him. "I'll take it, thanks, but why am I sitting here instead of talking to the mermaid?"

He pointed to a dot just visible in the water upriver. "Your mermaid's going to take another five minutes to get back here again. And you probably want to listen to what the waitress has to say." He leaned back in his seat. "How'd it go with Lily's parents last night?"

"They dumped all her belongings on the front step, locked up the house, and left so I couldn't talk to them. Lily stayed at my place last night," she added when he opened his mouth. "Now tell me why Caleb took off from a case where he'd get a free shot at staring at naked breasts."

Benson caught her gaze and held it. "Because before changing shape and swimming around in the river, your mermaid was a young man named Michael who eats breakfast here every morning."

"Merman?" They were pretty rare but not unheard of.

Benson shook his head. "Nope. Definitely a mermaid."

"Huh. That's different." Angela watched the river flowing by, faster currents rippling the surface near the center, calmer water gently lapping the shore. "That definitely explains Caleb though."

"I've never seen anyone make so many excuses so quickly," Benson agreed.

Angela sighed. "Caleb's so uncomfortable with everyone who doesn't fall into his idea of 'normal'" — Angela sketched quotes in the air — "the captain stopped assigning those cases to him." She thought about all the clients she'd gained in the process and how much those different experiences added to the community. "Caleb's an idiot." Matt wasn't nearly as bad, but the pattern had been set.

Staring at the water, Angela thought about what it meant that her new client was a mermaid. She'd had a few whose alternate form was mythical and the sex was hard to pin down, and she'd had clients who didn't fall into binary classifications in either form, but she'd never had one that was clearly switched.

The last time she'd checked in on the ongoing debates,

nearly everybody agreed that shape was determined by some combination of identification, need, and available magic. A woman in danger might become an armadillo because of need. A dragon couldn't shift into being unless someone had the necessary magic. But identification brought in so many cultural, biological, and personal influences that nearly anything was possible.

"Anyone here know if Michael identifies as male?"

Benson shook his head. "The waitress used male pronouns, but I suspect that was just an assumption."

Angela sighed, feeling completely out of her depth. Still, she'd do her best, and at the very least she wouldn't flee and make someone else deal with it. She finished her latte and stood up, waiting as Benson left a few bills on the table. They made their way down to the section of the plaza that met the water, walked out on the short dock, and waited. A few people going by stared at the logo on her shirt, but they kept walking when she looked at them.

Down by the water the air smelled of wet growing things with a faint hint of organic decay. Angela leaned against a wooden post, enjoying the cool breeze ruffling her hair. "You didn't want to go check out the dragon this morning?"

Benson shook his head. "I thought I'd shadow one of your coworkers for the morning, just to make sure I understood the dynamic of the office."

Caleb showing up and abandoning the job before even making contact with the client pretty much encapsulated his usual performance. Angela bit her lip to hide a smile, but Benson caught it anyway.

"Yes, I think I got what I needed in less than fifteen minutes."

"Our office is nothing if not efficient." Angela watched the shifter in the water coming closer, swells breaking on either side of the lithe form. The mermaid had to be traveling at least fifteen miles per hour, powerful tail strokes propelling her — them? Angela wasn't sure what the correct form was — along the top of the water. The iridescent scales on lower half of the mermaid's body gleamed in the sunlight, and the spray thrown up with each flip made rainbows appear above the surface of the water. "I think this is my cue."

Angela pulled her keys out and put the straight silver whistle to her lips and blew, the sound carrying across the water with ease. When the mermaid turned their head, Angela waved and beckoned them over.

She crouched down on the end of the dock to get more on the mermaid's level. Ideally they'd be at the same height, but that was only going to happen if she got in the water. Aside from a desire to avoid jumping in the murky river water fully dressed, there were also safety concerns. This particular mermaid was straight out of European mythology, which suggested death and mayhem. Long straight green hair flowed down over large breasts, water sheeting off delicate features.

If Angela had not had the waitress's information, she would have assumed the mermaid's human form was female. As it was, when they were within talking distance she introduced herself. "Do you mind if I ask which pronouns you prefer?"

The mermaid smiled, revealing a mouth of pointed teeth, then turned in the water, tail slamming into the dock support with a boom that made all the people in the square look over. The dock itself jerked, and Angela grabbed onto the rope railing to steady herself.

Propelling their torso out of the water, the mermaid ran their hands from shoulder to hips. "You need to ask?" Their voice was husky, but underneath it a whistling chord swirled around the words. Switching to her other sight, Angela saw magic flowing on the air. A quick glance around let her relax. Other than herself and Benson, nobody was close enough to feel the pull. She'd have to trust Benson was able to fend off a magical attack.

Angela sighed, as if bored. "Can you at least tell me if you're going by a name other than Michael? I have to fill out some paperwork."

In the blink of an eye, the mermaid went from a proud figure to a creature just floating in the water. "You know?"

Angela relaxed a bit. One of her fears was that the mermaid would swim away, and she didn't relish the thought of chasing after a potentially deadly magical creature in a boat until the mermaid tired out enough to be yanked back to their human form. "You have breakfast at the same cafe every morning." Tired of crouching, Angela sat down on the rough wooden planks, hoping she wasn't going to end up with an ass full of splinters. "Let's talk about how to get you back to your human form."

"I think this is the real me," the mermaid said, magic no longer laced through the words. "This feels right. Or at least more right," they said with a frown.

Usually new shifters were so anxious to get back to their human form that the only problem was getting them there. "Nobody's saying you have to stay in your human form all the time," Angela said carefully, "but you'll want to learn how to go back and forth."

The mermaid swam backward in a wide circle, flukes breaching the surface. "Why?"

"Why?" Angela repeated.

"Yes, why? Why can't I just stay this way? I could do whatever I wanted. No more pretending to be someone I'm not. I could just swim toward the ocean and keep on swimming. Explore the oceans."

Put on the spot Angela couldn't think of a good reason to be human. "Uh..."

"Crossword puzzles," Benson said next to her, his voice pitched to carry over the water. "You do the *New York Times* crossword puzzle every morning, even on Friday."

Angela looked up at him but kept her voice low. "Really? That's the best you've got?"

He shrugged. "Just giving you time to come up with something better."

Angela sighed, then decided to go with the truth. "Do you want to live?" she called out to the mermaid who was starting to drift farther away.

Another flash of teeth. "I feel healthier now than I ever have before."

Angela nodded. "I'm glad. But that's not what I was talking about. What do you know about mermaids?"

The mermaid circled a little closer. "Everything. It's what I am."

"But what is a mermaid's job?"

For the first time, a frown creased the perfect features. "I don't know. Singing? Luring men from boats? Is that a job?"

Angela nodded. "It may not be something that gives you a W-2 in January, but that's what European mermaids do. How many ships do you think you could sink before the shipping companies decided it would be cheaper and easier to put a bullet through your head, instead of trying to catch you and take you to trial? You'll probably make a dent in the ocean when you die, but you aren't going to be able to compete with drones, ear plugs, and a sniper rifle."

Now she had the mermaid's full attention. "But... I would never kill anyone."

Angela shrugged one shoulder. "You won't be able to help it. The longer you stay in that form, the more it will guide your thoughts. You already tried to use magic to lure us into the water, and it's been less than two hours. Maybe you won't do it today, or even tomorrow, but a week or at best a month from now? You'll convince some poor tourist to jump off the dock and drown. That's what a mermaid *does*."

She could see the moment the mermaid accepted the truth, and then the next instant there was nothing in that spot, just a ripple in the water. She held her breath for a second, then sighed. "They have *got* to get that dragon under control soon." Two minutes later the mermaid resurfaced in the same spot, shoulders bowed, not bothering to brush the hair back from their face.

After that, the process of shifting the mermaid back to human went quickly, and Angela made short work of the binding spell that would keep Michael from changing again until they made it to training camp.

By the time Angela got through filling out all the forms associated with a new Shifter of Dangerous Origins, it was after noon.

Angela put the car in gear but didn't accelerate. "Lunch?"

Benson nodded. "Do you mind going back to the same restaurant again? I'd like to take another look at May."

Angela stared at him for a moment, then nodded and pulled into traffic. "Sure, why not? I usually only revisit my greatest failure once a week, but this week has been pretty special in other ways, too."

Once at the restaurant, they were seated immediately in

the end booth, the only open table during the lunch rush. Mrs. Chen came out as soon as the hostess called into the kitchen, making Angela's stomach clench when she saw the hope in the woman's eyes, but the older woman merely said hello, pressed their hands, and then returned to the kitchen.

"You're going to make her think we can help her daughter," Angela said as soon as the kitchen doors had swung closed.

"I have an idea," Benson replied, turning toward the tank where the octopus had crawled over to look at them. "But first lunch, and then maybe a field trip."

The waitress arrived then to take their order, cutting off Angela's questions. When they were alone again, Benson put a finger against the glass of the tank near the octopus. "When you look at May with your magical sight, what do you see?"

Obliging him, Angela switched over and looked. The essential duality of May's nature was immediately visible, green and purple strands entwined, but instead of a vibrant and fluid core, the lines of light were locked into their pattern, the purple strands dominant. "I see a magic twined too long in one state after the first shift." She flipped back to her regular sight in time to see the waitress set down a pot of tea.

Benson poured two cups, the steam wafting the fragrance of jasmine across the table. "Back up a step. Pretend you don't know anything about what caused it. What do you actually *see*?"

Angela picked up a cup, fighting down the rising irritation and frustration that thinking about May produced. Her six-year failure made it like probing a painful tooth, but if Benson could come up with a way to get May into her human shape, she'd take any amount of pain. "I see her locked in a pattern that has solidified."

Benson nodded. "Does it remind you of anything?"

She looked at him in surprise, wondering if there was a collection of stuck shifters littering the landscape. "May is the only shifter I've never been able to get back into her human form."

He nodded, then thought for a moment. "Have you ever looked at someone — not a client, but someone who has never shifted — and thought, 'Under the right circumstances that person might shift'?"

Angela looked back at the tank, the octopus, and the bubbles whirling around the corner, thinking about his words. "A few." Switching back into her other sight, she stared at May again. "Okay, yes, she looks a lot like an octopus that might shift to a person under the right circumstances." Flipping back to her regular vision again she frowned. "But the right circumstances... Oh!"

One of the reasons having a dragon downtown caused such a problem was that the magical energy was being absorbed by people sensitive to it. That led to instability in some, like Father Sebastian, but it also increased the incidence of people shifting for the first time. Michael might never have found their mermaid form if they hadn't worked in a building a few blocks from where the dragon was currently settled.

Benson nodded and the edges of his mouth curled up. "Hence the field trip."

Angela stood up. "I need to talk to Mrs. Chen."

15

Two hours. It took two hours to convince the Chens that they should allow Angela to take their octopus daughter downtown to be near a dragon for some unknown length of time, and then figure out how to do so without killing May in the process. In the end Angela and Benson left the restaurant with the octopus in a large bucket full of saltwater and a portable pump that would be plugged in as soon as they could find a socket. The entire time, Angela was cursing herself because she hadn't thought of this earlier, and also hoping that Matt and Caleb didn't have sudden success in ridding downtown of the dragon scourge.

Candace called while they were in the car, Benson driving so Angela could sit in the backseat with the bucket and work out some logistics. "I have a location for you. There's a cafe that's within the evacuation zone managed by my cousin. It's as close as I can get you where you'll still have electricity. I'll text you the location. He'll meet you there in fifteen minutes if he can get past the cordon. If he can't, I'll have him call you."

"Thanks. Can you get in contact with the hip-hop dance group and let them know I probably won't be there this afternoon, and that they need to call me if they need help sooner than next week?" Angela thought about who was in that group. "Especially Ellie. If she's worried I can meet up with her sometime this weekend, or even whenever I get finished here tonight."

"Got it. And I'll get someone to cover the phones for a bit so I can swing by and pick up Lily after school."

Angela closed her eyes briefly. "Tell her I'm really, really sorry I won't be able to talk to her parents today. Hopefully she's okay with staying at my apartment again tonight." And hopefully CPS would be okay with her not getting in contact with them for a second day. She wanted to sit down with Lily's parents first before making everything official. She hung up the phone, crossing her fingers that this wasn't going to be a huge waste of time.

The car went over a pothole, water sloshing, then slowed at the barrier that had been hastily erected two days earlier. Fast talking by Benson and a flash of her badge got them through the outer barrier, and then she just held up her badge and Benson rolled past the inner cordon. Aside from a few emergency vehicles, the streets were deserted.

"We should evacuate this area more often," Angela said as they proceeded down the street unhindered by traffic. "This is the fastest I've ever made this drive." She looked out the window and tried to ignore the tingling of her skin. She would have known they were near the dragon even without the pall of smoke and smell of burning plastic. "There it is." She pointed, and Benson parked in the red zone right in front of the cafe. When Candace's cousin arrived, they carried the bucket in and hooked up the pump so the water would get aerated. From what Angela had read during her hasty internet search, May would be okay for a while like that. The Chens were back at the restaurant arranging ways to transport fresh water from the tank in a few hours. Angela suspected May would need at least six hours near the dragon before they could tell if anything was going to happen. Father Sebastian had spent the better part of a day nearby, but he'd been a little further out.

Now they just needed to wait.

Using an outlet away from the bucket of saltwater, Angela plugged in her laptop and started working through her email. Three different people had sent her the link to the captain's job posting. She pulled up the online application and looked it over.

The first section contained standard personal, education, and job history information, and the second section contained a series of free-form questions: What do you see as MPD's role in society? What measures do you think should be put in place for a known lethal transformee after the initial shift has been successfully managed? And where do you see opportunities for growth and change in MPD now?

Angela and the captain had certainly had more than a few run-ins over the years, and she'd never thought of him as any sort of friend, but she hadn't realized how much she would miss having him in charge of the group. At least she'd trusted him to look out for the interests of the shifters as well as the general population. From the few brief interactions she'd had with the chief, she didn't think he had the same concerns. Matt was a political animal. If he thought keeping a hard line would get him the job, he'd stop just short of demanding the shifters be rounded up and conscripted. The chief would be just one person on the hiring committee, but city politics were so incestuous he might as well have been the only one. She closed the browser with a sigh.

"Not going to apply?" Benson's voice from the other side of the table startled her.

"How did you know what I was looking at?"

"Lucky guess." He raised his hands then dropped them. "That and Caleb was talking about applying this morning."

Angela suppressed a shudder at the thought of Caleb in charge of the department. "I'm fairly certain no hiring committee would make that big a mistake, although that *would* get him out of the way." She closed the laptop. "But yes, I'll probably apply."

He tilted his head and looked at her. "You don't actually want the job."

Angela shrugged and stood up and walked over to check on the octopus to get some airflow over her suddenly overheated skin. "I don't particularly. I hate worrying about budgets, and I'd probably piss off someone important by accident."

"Or on purpose."

Angela turned her hands up. "That's a given."

"So why apply?"

She turned back to Benson. "Because even on paper I'm more qualified than Matt. If I apply, they'll have to look at bringing in someone from the outside just so they aren't forced to hire me. Maybe we'll get lucky." She sat down at the table and pulled on her windbreaker. "We need someone who is willing to stand up to the chief and the city council." When Benson put his phone to the side and waited, she continued. "You know how it goes." Angela wandered over to the bucket, trying to order her thoughts. The octopus was examining the pump, but didn't seem to be impeding the water flow. "The chief thinks all the resources should be thrown at making sure people never shift. I think there are... nuances. Shifting isn't always a bad thing. I think we've managed to over-regulate things."

Benson blew out a breath. "You really have changed."

Angela stiffened. "Hang on, *that* was a totally different thing." She dug a bill out of her purse, put it near the register, and took a bottle of sparkling water out of the cooler, taking a long drink before she looked at him. It always came back to this. "Casey needed more help than I could give him."

Benson stared at her for a moment. "You didn't even *try*."

Angela thought back to that night in college, when Benson had come back to their apartment with what she first thought was a dog, asking for her help. Casey had shifted into a coyote, and he was afraid if he called MPD now he'd have to redo the entire semester.

Even then, Angela had known the basics of a binding spell, though she'd never helped anyone shift. But blood was dripping down Benson's arm, and every time either of them moved the coyote's teeth flashed.

When she'd picked up her phone to call the local MPD, Casey had jumped out the window and run off. The police found out he'd changed and stopped looking. After a week of fighting about it, Benson and Angela had broken their lease and moved out of their shared apartment.

Angela still wasn't sure how she'd done both the right thing and the wrong thing at the same time, but Benson was right about one thing. She hadn't tried.

The ground shook as smoke poured out of a building a block away.

Angela turned toward the window as a fire truck went speeding past, grasping at the excuse to change the subject. "I don't think we need to worry about the dragon shifting back before we have a chance to see if May responds to this."

They sat in silence, carefully not looking at each other, and watched the flashing lights.

BY THE TIME Candace called in the late afternoon, Angela was riding the line between bored and anxious. May's magical core was showing signs of destabilizing, but the energy absorption was going more slowly than Angela had planned. The Chens had brought a huge plastic tub along with more bagged water from the restaurant tank before the police had escorted them back behind the barricades again, so at least May had more room to move around, but Angela was still only getting brief glimpses of areas in her magic where the human side of her was coming through. And May still hadn't started talking to them.

The dispatcher sounded as unflappable as always. "My shift is almost over, so I'm going to take Lily with me to get some dinner. I can either take her to my place or drop her off at yours afterward. Does she have your key?"

Angela rubbed her tingling arms. "No, but Vicky has a copy. I'll text her now and see if she can bring it down to you."

"Sounds good. Also, Matt just found out from one of the cops maintaining the blockade that you and the HQ guy are there, and he's not happy. So I guess you can expect some sort of phone call soon in case you want to dodge it."

"Wonderful. Have they made any progress with the dragon?"

"Not as far as I can tell. This afternoon they were trying to figure out if they could somehow immobilize and transport him out of the city. I did ask if they wanted to try to get you in on it, but I got shot down. That's probably why Matt's bent out of shape that you're there."

"Okay, thanks. Hopefully we aren't just wasting our time here."

"Fingers crossed. Talk to you soon."

Angela hung up and muted her phone. "I don't think we're going to have much more time before Matt comes by to get us thrown out," she said to Benson, who was typing on his phone again. She tried to bury the irritation she felt toward him. "Can you do whatever you did yesterday that got her attention?"

Benson picked up his chair and put it down next to the tub. "Ready?"

She nodded. "I just want to see what happens first."

"Here goes."

The octopus jerked in the water. Through her second sight, Angela saw the strands of May's magic flex, letting her see more of the human strands than she'd ever seen in the six years she'd been trying. Unfortunately, it wasn't going to be enough to get May to transform on her own.

Switching back to her regular sight, she pulled another chair over next to Benson and sat down. "I *think*," she said, pausing to give the word significance, "if you do that, I might be able to grab hold of her human side and pull it forward." It would require timing, speed, and strength, and she wasn't sure she had it in her, but she'd be damned if she would let their only opportunity to recover May fade. Behind her on the table her phone buzzed.

Benson nodded. "Tell me when."

Tensing, Angela held out her hand. "Three... two...one...go!"

The light strands parted and she *reached*... and missed

entirely, almost falling out of her chair when the expected pushback never happened. Now she was frustrated with herself as well. "Try again?" She counted down. "Go!"

This time she managed to snag a strand, but it was merely peripheral, not a part central enough to yank May's human form to the front.

Benson sniffed. "The energy she's absorbing is making her shape unstable, but it's also making it harder to work with. I didn't think about that."

"I almost grabbed it that time. We can do this." She held out three fingers. "Three...two..."

The front of the cafe exploded, glass and bricks flying in, followed by a cloud of dust as the mid-section of a dragon tail bulged into the building from the street. Bricks knocked Angela from her chair, and she hit the side of the tub, and curled up on the ground. She heard the roar of flames, felt a wave of heat, and then the roof collapsed.

In the darkness and quiet that followed, individual bricks fell, and then something heavy fell off the wall and hit the ground. On the other side of the rubble that had been the front of the building, Angela heard muffled sirens and heavy machinery. "Benson?" Coughing on the other side of the tub greeted her and she held back tears of relief. "Are you okay?" He responded with a strangled affirmation. Angela sat up, dislodging a couple bricks and shards of safety glass. Rubbing her eyes to clear the dust away, she strained to see her surroundings, finally realizing that the problem wasn't as much the settling dust as the lack of light.

Rolling to the side, she dug out her keys and found the mini-light by touch. The room resolved into dingy shades of brown and grey. Most of the structural damage was confined to the front of the cafe, but glass glittered like diamonds thrown all over the floor, and a brick had gone through the pastry display on the back wall. Fearing the worst, Angela looked into the tub which had gone from clear moving water to a brown puddle, but the octopus was still alive, half of the tentacles out of the dirty water and gripping the side of the tub. Two of the tentacles had open wounds, blue blood oozing out, but on the whole May had survived without serious injury.

On the other side of the tub, Benson rocked to his knees, glass and a piece of metal that looked like it had probably been the door handle sliding off him. The dust coating his face and hair made him look like an old man. He looked into the tub and coughed again. "We need to get her into fresh water."

They weren't leaving through the front of the building — that much Angela could tell when she climbed toward it. Not only was the roof sagging, but the rubble underneath was too hot to touch, the brick radiating heat as if it had just been pulled from a blast furnace. Turning away from the front, she picked her way to the back of the shop, rounding the counter and through a doorway. A narrow hallway ran behind the businesses with access to a shared pair of restrooms, with a door to the outside at one end, but it was closed with a deadbolt that required a key to open. She assumed it would be open during a normal day when customers would be present, but unless she could find a key to the door somewhere in the café, they weren't going out that way any time soon.

Angela went back into the cafe, rifled through the cabinets she could get open, then sat down next to Benson and turned the light out to conserve the battery. "We need the key to get out the back." Her phone was lost under the rubble at the front of the shop, but Benson had found his on the ground nearby. After three attempts to make a call failed, he was finally able to text their location to Candace and get confirmation that someone would be there as soon as possible.

Angela turned on the light and looked in the plastic tub, the water unmoving now that there was no electricity powering the pump. The octopus was still half out of the water, but the tentacles didn't seem to be gripping the sides as tightly. She caught Benson's eye as they both leaned over the tub. He nodded.

There was only one way May was going to survive this.

16

Angela switched to her other sight and looked back at May. Their close encounter with the dragon had added even more energy to May's core, the strands practically dancing in Angela's vision. Completing the shift would be easy, but Angela wasn't convinced she was fast enough to grab the human form to pull it forward. Worse, it seemed like May's human form was intentionally hiding within the octopus form.

She'd thought this before, both as a reason May's human form was so hard to see and also to explain why May had never spoken or responded to her, but this was the first time she was sure. Angela thought back to the conversations she'd had with the Chens and the circumstances around May's one and only shift.

"May," she said, speaking directly to the octopus, "you're safe now. But you have to stop hiding and come back to us. Your parents miss you." She shrugged and decided that the truth might be good in case May really was listening somewhere in there. "And we're sort of stuck here and your water isn't going to get any cleaner for a while."

Unfortunately, her words didn't have any effect.

She looked over at Benson. "You ready?"

He croaked his way through the countdown. This time when he nudged May, the change was extreme, the strands flying everywhere, and Angela's grab missed completely. A second attempt fared even worse.

Angela's keychain light flickered and died.

May was going to die because she hadn't thought about keeping them all safe. The Chens had trusted her with their daughter, and all she'd done was get her killed. For six years they'd been feeding Angela, encouraging her, and placing no blame and now she'd taken the only child that remained.

Benson coughed again. "What was her brother's name? The one who was shot in the robbery?"

"His American name was Robert." She'd heard both Robert and May's real names a number of times, but the syllables hadn't stuck.

"I'm going to try something. Be ready."

Angela flipped back to her other sight, the switch requiring more effort now. "Go ahead."

In the darkness across from her, Benson cleared his throat. When he spoke again, his voice was sharp with anxiety. "May! May, Robert's been hurt! He needs you!"

Shock almost switched Angela's vision back.

Benson continued. "May, hurry! Robert's bleeding, May! He needs you right now!"

In the tub, Angela could see the strands of May's magic dim, and then for the first time her human strands peeked out. Taking a firm hold of the most solid clump she could see, Angela *pulled*.

May's magic resisted, trying to hold the formation it had been in for six years. Angela's vision dimmed with the effort, but she kept up the pressure and yanked again.

With a pop that felt almost audible, May's core inverted and the tub deformed as the weight of a woman pressed against the inside. Slow to release May's magical core, Angela struggled with a wave of nausea. Sweat rolled over her.

Benson's voice cut in. "The binding spell, hurry!"

Reminded of her task, Angela quickly wove a binding around May's unstable core. Halfway through, it tried to flip back to her octopus form, leaving Angela gritting her teeth and hanging on. She finished the binding and tied it off, letting herself slump down to the ground until she was lying flat, waiting for the flashes crossing her vision to fade.

The blue light from a cell phone screen lit the room. Benson loomed over her. "You still alive?"

"Yes?" Deciding that she could probably move without vomiting, Angela pulled herself up into a sitting position. A young woman sat in six inches of water, her straight black hair, free of the dust surrounding them, pulled back into a ponytail. A few wisps of hair escaped, as if she were at the end of a long shift in the restaurant. She looked around in confusion, her whole body trembling.

Angela put a light hand on the woman's shoulder. "May?" The smell of fried food briefly overrode the burning insulation smell from the building.

"Where am I? Robert... They shot Robert!"

BETWEEN THEM, Angela and Benson got May out of the water and seated at one of the few unbroken tables. Angela took a few snack bars for them from the display that had scattered around the register. She thought about leaving cash in exchange and then remembered that her money was in her purse which was underneath the still steaming rubble.

A little sugar and some time to get oriented made May look less in shock, but Angela held off talking to her too much about what had happened. If May didn't already know six years had gone by while she was an octopus, learning it while trapped in a half-demolished building with two complete strangers probably wasn't the best option. Benson managed to text an update to Candace before his phone battery died.

Still, May avoided Angela as much as possible while trapped in a small space, which suggested that she remembered all the time Angela had spent trying to convince her to come back over the years. Or else she knew it had been Angela who forced her back to her human shape and she resented it.

Either way, when the back door was opened two hours later, Angela was just happy that Benson was willing to ride with May in the ambulance to the hospital where her parents were waiting. She didn't have the energy to deal with the Chens' gratitude. She'd go by the restaurant in a day or so and check on them all, and get May enrolled in shifter training. After six years in another form, it might be better for her to stay human for a while instead of going to training right away.

Only after she'd opened the door to her apartment did Angela remember Lily would be there. The smell of fried garlic hit her as she walked in, reminding her that the snack bars were no substitute for an actual meal, but it was the sight of Vicky and a gigantic glowing blue lizard creature in the kitchen washing dishes that made her laugh.

Vicky rinsed her sudsy hands off and pointed Angela

toward her room. "Go ahead and get cleaned up. We saved you some."

Angela opened her mouth to ask why Vicky was there, then closed it. It could wait. She left her shoes with the growing pile next to the door and went to her bedroom where she plugged in her new phone so it could start charging.

After taking a shower to get all the plaster dust and glass shards off her, swallowing two aspirin, and putting on the most comfortable clothes she owned, Angela went back out to the kitchen. Lily, back in her human form, handed her a plate of rice topped with stir-fried beef and vegetables along with a glass of water.

Vicky poured her a martini and sat down opposite. "Candace said that you finally managed to get that octopus at the Chinese restaurant turned back. Six years. That has to be some kind of record."

Angela nodded and spoke around a bite of food. "It was Benson's idea. He deserves all the credit."

Vicky narrowed her eyes at her. "Don't do that."

"Do what?"

"Minimize your accomplishments," Vicky replied. "You always do that."

"You do," Lily added from where she was curled up on the seat next to her.

"What? I just said it was Benson's idea because it really was."

"Maybe, but who's the one that's been going to that restaurant every week for six years? And who actually shifted the girl? Last I heard, that guy Benson wasn't a spell caster."

"We did it together." Angela held up her hands at Vicky's stare. "I swear. Cross my heart and hope to die."

"Even so, you deserve a lot of the credit."

Angela took another bite. "The important thing is that May is back with her parents. Who cares who gets the credit?"

Vicky put down her drink. "See, this is why you are not the temporary manager despite being so much more qualified than those other two idiots, and also why there's still a dragon downtown. You need to promote yourself. You're setting a bad example." She glanced over at Lily. "This is an important part of any professional career. You need to learn how to get your accomplishments known."

Angela looked at the girl. "Definitely listen to Vicky when it comes to career advice. And now," she said before Vicky could speak again, "tell me how much I owe you for groceries." She suddenly remembered that her purse was buried under a pile of hot bricks. "And I'll have to owe you for a bit."

By the time she'd told the entire story of how her purse had been lost, it was getting late and Lily was yawning. Angela walked Vicky to the door. "Thanks for coming over and hanging with Lily."

"Not a problem. She and I agreed that the Little Bit needed a home-cooked meal and this was the only way that was ever going to happen over here." She dug her keys out of her briefcase and opened the door. "See you on Monday. Have a good weekend."

Angela closed the door and turned back to Lily, who was cleaning the dishes off the table. She went over to the sink and started washing. "Hey, I just wanted to apologize. With all the other stuff going on, I didn't get a chance to talk to your parents today."

"That's okay." Now that Vicky was no longer there Lily

had gotten quiet again. Or possibly, Angela thought, it was just the subject of the conversation.

"The thing is," Angela continued as she handed Lily a plate to dry, "I sort of feel like I owe you an apology for not sitting down with your parents a long time ago. I thought they'd eventually get used to you being a shifter if I gave them some time, and they never did."

After a few seconds of silence, Lily said, "My great-grandmother was a shifter. A fish. My aunt told us, last year. My father didn't even know. The first time she shifted was after my grandfather was born, and the midwife told the neighbors. They had to move to a different city because it was too dangerous to stay."

Angela nodded and scrubbed at a spot of dried oatmeal. "That used to be a big problem. Things have mostly gotten better, though." Now shifters faced discrimination, but generally not physical danger.

"That's not really why they're so upset." Lily moved her shoulders, as if trying to dislodge some weight. "I was supposed to be a doctor."

"Sorry?"

"I was supposed to go to medical school and be a doctor. But nobody would ever hire a shifter for a doctor."

Angela spent a moment looking at that statement in her mind, sparks of anger giving her energy. "First of all, who says nobody would ever hire a shifter as a doctor?"

"My dad."

"Well, he's wrong. I have multiple clients who are doctors. So don't let that stop you. Do you *want* to be a doctor?"

Lily reached up, then shifted to her other form and placed the plate in the cupboard that she could now comfortably reach, and shifted back. The ease of her transformations took Angela's breath away. "I don't know. I guess it wouldn't be that bad."

Angela turned the water off. Lily was not her child, she reminded herself. "I think you can be anything you want to be, whether that's a doctor or not." Multiple military and governmental organizations were just counting down the days until Lily turned eighteen, but she'd been trying to insulate the girl from that pressure.

"What if I want to do what you do?"

Angela drew her head back and raised her eyebrows. "I'd think you were wasting your talents, but it's certainly something you *could* do if you wanted to." She took the dish towel from the girl and hung it up on the handle to the oven. "Do you mind going in to work with me in the morning? I know it's Saturday and you probably want to sleep in, but I need to get a few things done." Her laptop was buried in the rubble with her old phone and purse, so she needed to borrow a computer at work to enter her notes on her cases and start getting May's forms filled out.

"Okay." Lily went over to the couch and picked up her book, *A Tale of Two Cities*, and opened it to the bookmark. "Good night."

17

Normally on Saturdays the office was an oasis of peace, only a skeleton crew in the building and those people in casual clothing, making it obvious that it wasn't a typical work day. With the dragon still active downtown, though, Angela wasn't surprised to find evidence that Matt had come in. The captain's office door was open and a duffel bag flopped open on the extra chair.

"He's in with the mayor," Candace said from the dispatch room. Instead of her usual MPD polo and khakis, she was wearing a tank top that read "Dispatch Princess: Classy, Sassy, and Smart Assy" and shorts. "Oh hey, Lily, welcome back!"

Lily waved and went in to put her things down on the empty desk.

Angela leaned against the door frame of the dispatch room. "Why are you here today? Don't weekend calls go to the 911 operator?"

"Not when there's a big event happening. They're too busy to take the extra traffic so I'm on overtime." She smiled.

"I've already sent Caleb on a call about a bat in an abandoned church downtown, and a goose at the city park." She held up her hands. "What can I do? Matt says we're supposed to respond to everything. I figure Caleb will be back in another half hour, just in time for a cricket at the convention center." She smiled. "They're having a reptile show there. A bunch of lizards eat crickets. There ought to be quite a few."

Angela shook her head. "Do you know where the captain's laptop went to? I need to borrow one until I get a replacement."

"In the supply closet."

The first thing Angela found when she sat down at her desk with the new computer was an email from Vicky. "This is what I was talking about. If you don't promote yourself, somebody else will steal the credit!" The link below sent her to a news article. *MPD recovers woman after six years underwater.* In the article they quoted Matt, who had been waiting at the hospital with the press when May's ambulance arrived. They'd titled him the Acting Commander of MPD, and he'd managed to get quoted multiple times, all with references to the doggedness of "his" division. There wasn't one mention of Angela in the entire article.

Angela sighed and closed the browser tab. What Vicky didn't understand was that Angela would never think to call the press and take credit like that, but Matt would every time. And Angela didn't want to be like that.

Matt breezed through a few minutes later, Benson following behind him. "Candace, I'm going back downtown to deal with this dragon once and for all," he called into the dispatch office as he went by. "I'll need Young, so have him meet me down there and assign any new cases that come in to Angie." He looked over at Angela's desk. "You owe me for that stunt yesterday. I had to promise a case of beer to the lieutenant so you didn't get arrested for breaching the perimeter." With that he grabbed his duffel bag and headed out the door.

Angela stared after him. "Nice job yesterday, Officer Jones," she said, affecting announcer tones. "It's great that you went above and beyond."

"If it helps any," Benson said from the chair next to the dispatch office, "he just got chewed out by the mayor. He was talking to the press from the hospital at the exact same time the mayor was holding a press conference praising his single-minded devotion to dealing with the dragon. It's never a good move to make the mayor look bad."

Angela leaned back in her chair so she could see around her laptop screen. "You're not going with him this morning? You're going to miss your chance to see the dragon if you're not careful." Her irritation with Matt spilled over onto Benson. He'd been at the hospital when Matt was taking all the credit.

"He didn't like me telling the reporters how to spell your first name. I think you're right. I think he looks so much like Guy Whats-his-name that everyone gets confused. Anyhow," he finished, "I got a great view of the dragon yesterday afternoon, or at least a great view of its tail."

Angela sighed. "How was May when you left?"

"Human. Grieving for her brother. Her parents want to thank you, you know."

"I'll stop by in the next couple of days." With any luck she could time it during the lunch rush. There was only so much praise she could stand after taking six years to get their daughter back to them.

Angela went back to her report, describing how she and Benson had forced May to shift back. Somehow, despite having written up the exact steps she and Benson had taken, she suspected this would end up on Matt's list of accomplishments. Or worse, the report would get buried to keep her name out of it, and Benson's idea of using the extra disruptive energy would be lost. "You should write a paper on your idea of harnessing the dragon's energy. Or at least give talks about it at conferences. It was a really good idea."

Benson moved across the room and sat down in a chair next to her desk. "Why don't we write it up?"

"They're not going to publish something from a field agent with no credentials. But it would be good to get that out there as a technique." She thought about it. "Maybe minus the almost killing the shifter in the process part."

"I'll never be able to look at an aquarium the same way again," Benson said with a sigh. "But how about this — I'll write up the first draft based on your report, you add anything that I might have forgotten and fix anything I got wrong, and we'll list ourselves as co-authors."

"I think you're getting stuck with most of the work, but if you don't mind, then sure." Angela met his eyes. "It will drive Matt crazy if he's still in charge by the time it gets published."

"Tragic."

Angela had finished filling out most of the new shifter forms May would need to sign when Candace called her from the office. "Shit, Angela, you need to hear this!"

Both Angela and Benson crowded into the dispatch office. Candace hit a button and the call went out through a pair of speakers on her desk. "Go ahead and repeat that."

"We're trapped in the access tunnel between the stadium and the main library," a man said, his words nearly drowned out by the sound of a roaring river. With a start, Angela realized the voice belonged to Matt. That meant the roaring sound was likely fire, not water. "The tunnel is —" His words were so garbled she couldn't understand the rest of the sentence. "— a beam that melted and the whole thing collapsed. The dragon's at the other end, near the stadium. We're trapped down here."

Candace hit a button. "Who's there with you?"

"It's me and Young and Patterson and King. We were going to come up behind and drive the dragon forward so the National Guard could net it and transport it out of the city, but we didn't get that far. Angie, I need you to get behind the dragon and get it to move far enough forward that we're not stuck here. Then we can take over again."

Angela stared at the phone. That was a plan just stupid enough to be a plot from *Shift Enforcers*. The best thing she could say about it was that it would provide a nice visual, but there were too many things that could go wrong. Like the dragon could cause a tunnel to cave in and trap all of the idiot MPD officers in one place.

She leaned forward. "How were you planning to make it move?"

"With the stunners. We have them with us, but I can't get a clear line of sight."

Angela knew Matt well enough to know he was holding something back, but he kept talking.

"You'll have to use a gun and aim to wound it. That should get it moving away from you and then we can get to a spot where we can use the stunners and take it from there."

Angela felt her eyebrows go up. "You want me to run up and shoot a dragon in the ass and hope it moves forward and doesn't just destroy me? I'm not doing that."

"Angie, I'll have you fired for insubordination so quickly when I get out of here —"

Angela leaned forward and hit the disconnect button.

"Oops, looks like his call dropped." She got up and headed back out to the main office. "When he calls back tell him I left already and you can't reach me."

Candace stood up so she could see over her monitor. "What are you going to do?"

"I don't know yet, but I'm sure as heck not going to go on some useless suicidal charge just so he doesn't look bad."

When Benson and Lily followed her to her desk, she pulled up a map of the downtown area. If the dragon was in the lower levels of the stadium, there'd be no way to sneak up on it, and there'd be nothing to do even if she could.

She looked up at Benson and Lily. "I think I need to go talk to a dragon."

18

Convincing Lily that she couldn't go along took longer than Angela thought it would. She'd finally had to promise to come back for her if she thought Lily could be helpful there, a promise she made with her fingers crossed behind her back. There was no way she was letting Lily get anywhere near the dragon.

Benson had offered to come along, and she'd taken him up on the offer gladly. While he wasn't a spell caster, he had a different way of looking at things that might help her come up with a plan.

The drive downtown seemed to take forever, and the air conditioning in the car wasn't working quite right after all the smoke and dust from the day before, so Angela was already sweaty by the time she felt the tingling on her skin that said they were close. She made a quick call to Candace to make sure nothing had changed while they were driving.

"Nothing new," the dispatcher said. "But I did hear Matt arguing with someone about why the stunners didn't work."

Angela blew out a breath. "I knew he was hiding something. He was going to let me go after a dragon with a pistol

knowing that they wouldn't have anything to back me up
with."

"Just be careful, okay?"

"I always am. Take care of Lily." Angela hung up the
phone and followed Benson to the barricades.

The commander who finally let them through the
blockade gave them a rough idea of where the dragon was,
but Angela didn't need it. She could feel the magic stabbing
at her skin like magnetic north.

"There's something wrong with this whole picture," she
said to Benson as they hiked across the empty stadium
parking lot. "The lawyer shifted, what," she counted on her
fingers, "over three days ago, and they haven't gotten a word
out of him? Have you ever met a lawyer who didn't want to
talk?"

"A few," he admitted, climbing over a turnstile. "But only
because they weren't getting paid. So what, you think the
dragon isn't speaking for a reason?" He put out a hand to
steady her when she boosted herself over.

"Thanks. I don't know. I just think it's odd. The only
shifter I've had who didn't speak after the first six hours or
so was May, and she was pretty traumatized. Plus, I didn't
see her until weeks later."

"You think the lawyer suffered some sort of trauma first?"
His voice echoed around the concrete walls.

"Nobody said anything about it, and from what I've read
he was the one most likely to traumatize someone else."
When even other lawyers called him difficult to work with,
that meant something. "Maybe he had a stroke or something
right before he shifted."

Benson stopped and looked at the colored lines painted
on the walls, then pointed to the left. "We want to follow the
purple line?"

Angela read through the descriptions. "I think so." They headed to the left. "If it's not trauma, what else could it be?"

"Maybe the dragon side has just completely consumed him." He looked over at her. "I wouldn't expect that to happen so quickly, but I think we've left 'normal' behind."

Angela frowned and stopped, holding up a hand for silence. A low rumbling noise waxed and waned, similar to the sound of waves crashing on the shore. "Is that *breathing*?" she whispered. The tail crashing into the front of the cafe the night before hadn't given her a true appreciation for the size of this beast.

Benson nodded. They found the entrance to the tunnels behind the burger stand, the metal grate opening silently with the key they'd been given.

The dragon's breathing got louder, the sound accompanied by a hot wind on the exhale. Around the next corner was a wide pathway that ran the length of the stadium, built to be one of the exits in case of emergency. That had to be where the dragon was resting.

Benson stopped three feet from the corner. He kept his voice low. "What now?"

Angela shrugged. "I guess we try to talk to him." She quietly walked forward.

The dragon was twenty feet away, head resting on the concrete, golden eyes half lidded. Angela's first reaction was disbelief that anything could be that big, accompanied by an atavistic fear that raised the hair on the back of her neck. The head had to be at least ten feet long from snout to crest, and its shoulders scraped both sides of a passageway meant to accommodate five people walking abreast. The gentle curve of the tunnel hid the back end. Probably a mortal animal couldn't make it to that size without being crushed under its own weight, but magic had no such rules. One claw, long and sharp enough to pass clear through a human torso with ease, was visible on the paw resting next to the neck.

Locking her legs to prevent herself from fleeing, Angela just stood and looked. Even in the dim light of the tunnel, the blue and red scales gleamed. As Angela watched, the dragon finished exhaling, and on the next inhale the nostrils widened slightly to reveal a glow coming from within. Wind whistled past her, stirring her clothing.

Angela switched to her other sight and blinked at the amount of power contained within the duality that was the dragon's magical core. And yet...

Angela had examined a lot of shifters over the course of her career. She'd seen everything from insects to large carnivores to magical creatures out of fables and even Lily, a magical creature from no fable at all. The structures of their magical threads varied as much as their shifted forms did. But the human structure matched the human inside.

This was not the core of a young male lawyer at the top of his game.

Angela tiptoed backward around the corner and leaned against the wall, letting out a long breath. She looked over at Benson who had followed her out and back. "Did you notice anything funny?" She deliberately didn't give him any hint of what she meant, not wanting to taint his thoughts.

He shook his head. "Other than how big and powerful that thing is? I got a little stuck on that part."

Angela shook her head. "Maybe I'm seeing something that doesn't exist." Still, her coworkers were trapped but otherwise okay, and it didn't hurt to do a little more research. She pulled out her phone and walked toward the seats where she had a signal.

Candace answered on the first ring. "How's it going?"

"Still alive. So far, so good." Angela moved so she could watch the tunnels where Benson still stood peeking around the corner. There was no way a regular creature that size could sneak up behind her, but magic changed all rules. "Hey, I never had a chance to read the reports on this thing. Can you look something up for me?"

"Sure, what do you need to know?"

"Everything about this lawyer."

The clack of typing came through. "Let's see... James Carter, thirty-three, twice divorced, no children, no pets, white guy, parents deceased, practices corporate law, top earner in his firm for the past two years, made partner three years ago." She was silent again for a few seconds. "Sounds like everyone he works with is either afraid of him or wants to be him, or both. Am I looking for anything specific?"

Angela sighed. "I don't know. He's not sick or anything is he?" Maybe he had some sort of terminal disease that was warping his core out of alignment.

Candace hummed as she looked. "I don't see anything." A beep interrupted her. "Can I put you on hold for a sec?"

"Go ahead." Angela looked up at the sky, trying to figure out how to reconcile the reality of the lawyer with what she had seen in his core.

A minute later, Candace came back on the line. "What else do you want me to look up?"

"I don't know..." Angela kicked the base of the railing. "Wait, there were fatalities when he first shifted right?"

"A couple, I think. Let me find it again... One of the other partners and an admin assistant."

"I'm guessing it was kind of a mess. Was anyone else missing?"

More silence as Candace went through the reports. A flock of ravens circled the field. "Here we go. Nope, nobody else is missing. The other partner died on the way to the hospital, and they got parts of just one body out of the office. It says here DNA is pending, but since nobody else is missing they're pretty sure it's going to come back as the admin assistant."

The ravens landed on the far side of the field and started picking at something in the grass. Angela's skin itched from the magic so much she wanted to claw it off. "Do we have anything on the admin assistant?"

"Hailey Thompson, forty-five, no family. Or maybe Holly Thompson. It's in here two different ways." She clicked some more. "Pretty sure it's Holly."

Angela shook her head. From Matt's point of view, Holly wasn't important enough to worry about getting her name right. She was just an unfortunate victim of a dragon's first shift. In fact, Matt had probably said as much to the dragon when he was trying to get it to talk to him. Accidents happen with the first shift, it was sad about Holly or Hailey, but hey, she wasn't that important and legally you aren't responsible... She'd heard him give the speech before, trying to reassure new shifters who were panicking that they'd ruined their own lives in the chaotic moments after they'd first shifted.

Candace's voice broke into her reverie. "What are you thinking?"

"I'm thinking Matt and Caleb are idiots. Hell, all four of those guys have been chasing after this thing for days and not one of them thought to look at it." The ravens took to the air as one again. "I think the dragon might be Holly and the crispy bits back in the office are the asshole lawyer."

Candace's intake of breath came through clearly. "Oh shit."

"Yeah, exactly. I'd probably be pretty pissed off if I turned into a dragon and the first person I ran into said, 'Hey, don't worry about that Angela person you killed, she wasn't as important as you anyway.' No wonder they couldn't get the dragon to talk to them." Someone who'd had an easy life with no conflict wouldn't shift into a dragon. A dragon was already a creature of rage. "I'm just amazed she hasn't destroyed the whole city by now."

The phone rang in the background. "Can I put you on hold again?"

"Thanks. I'll call if I need anything else." Angela ended the call and looked at the tunnel where Benson still waited, trying to figure out where to start.

After three days in the form of a dragon, Holly was already going to have a difficult time shifting back. Add to that the anger that had been driving her since the shift, and Angela thought this was going to be near-impossible. She'd have to bleed off some of that rage or she'd never get the woman to listen to her. Even then, she might just need to convince her to move out of the city for a while.

Part of her wanted to call Matt and let him know this was entirely his fault. If he hadn't made so many assumptions in the beginning, this whole episode could have been resolved days ago. Calling him would probably just irritate her more, though, because he'd keep insisting that he was right until they managed to get the dragon back to a human form as proof one way or the other. A wave of heat passed over her, making her walk toward Benson to get air flow across her skin.

A burst of flame at the end of the tunnel lit up the concrete walls.

Benson met her at the edge of the seats. "I know Western dragons are supposed to be easily angered, but this guy seems to be taking it to the extreme. He took one look at me and tried to light me on fire."

"I have a theory about that." Angela told him what she'd learned from Candace. She wondered how long Holly had hidden her rage under polite smiles and deferential nods. Her job probably depended on being able to put up with abusive behavior from everyone around her, and all the while her anger would have been growing. "We're probably lucky things aren't worse."

Benson looked back at the tunnel. "So what now?"

Angela shrugged. "I do my job."

19

Talking to an angry dragon meant dealing with some logistical issues. Normally, Angela preferred to talk to the newly-shifted at eye level and from just a few feet away. That wasn't going to work.

She called around the corner to the dragon. "Hey, Holly?" With any luck, the tight corridor would give her some time to scramble away if the beast came after her.

A blast of flame along the hallway in front of her greeted her words, the heat causing her to take a step back.

She tried again. "Holly Thompson?"

This time there was just the hot breeze of exhaled air smelling faintly of sulfur. Angela decided to take that as an encouraging sign.

"Holly, my name is Angela Jones. I'm an officer with the Magical Probation Department. Can we talk?"

A long pause, then finally a voice came back, huge and gravelly with disuse. "I've seen the officers. They're all men. I'm going to kill them all."

Angela nodded and looked at Benson. His thumbs flew across the screen of his phone as he texted Candace on their progress. At least now they had confirmation they were on the right track.

Edging closer to the corner, Angela raised her voice again. "I'm not going to lie to you, Holly. I end plenty of my days thinking the same thing about those guys." Finding common ground wouldn't be a problem. "But I promise you, I am indeed an officer." She pulled her badge out of her pocket and held it out. "Can you see this?" After a few seconds of silence, she let her arm drop to her side again. "Holly, do you mind if I come around the corner? I find it easier to talk to people when I can see them." She paused, then took a step forward, ready to jump back.

Heat radiated from the blackened concrete wall, proof that the earlier gouts of flame had been aimed in their direction, The dragon's head was still eight foot away, but the eyes were open and focused on her now. Angela stared into rust-colored irises flecked with gold. The rest of the dragon's head was covered with shimmering green scales, intelligence and anger clear in every muscle twitch.

Angela shook off the trance she was falling into. "Let's talk about how to get you back into your human shape, okay?"

The massive head lifted. "Why?"

Angela resisted the urge to sigh. Most people jumped at the chance to get back to their human form, and now she had two who wanted to refuse in one week. "Well," she drew out the sound, trying to come up with a good reason, "it's going to make it hard for them to hold the next home game here unless you move." She felt Benson stare at her. "And really, do you want to spend your days setting things on fire? What if you want to read a book? Or watch a movie?"

"I wouldn't be able to do that from jail anyway."

Angela shook her head. "As far as I know, the only two

people who died were two partners at the firm, and that was all during the first few minutes. You can't be charged for that. Everything else has been property damage. You might be held liable for some of that, but Holly, I've been doing this for a really long time. Believe me when I say the second we get you back in your human form, people will be throwing cash at you. You'll have everything paid off before the end of the year."

"Do you know what he *said* to me?"

Angela grimaced. She'd been hoping to focus this conversation on what came next, not on rehashing what had already happened, but it didn't look like that was going to work out. "Whatever it was, he'll never say it to anyone ever again."

The dragon ignored her. "Twenty-five years, I've worked there. Twenty-five years of late nights, and getting in early, and never taking breaks, and never planning anything for the weekend because I might get called in to work at the last minute. I flaked on so many plans that all my friends don't even bother trying any more. I know more about that job than half the partners, and after all that, after twenty-five years, he said to me I was being demoted because I didn't fit the image they were trying to project. I wasn't young enough." Wisps of flame escaped from the dragon's nostrils, making Angela take a protective step to the side. "I gave up *everything* for that job and they just tossed me away."

Angela nodded. "I hear you—"

"You don't understand. I'm forty-five. I was going to have children. I've always wanted children. And now it's too late. I couldn't have them even if I wasn't a dragon."

"Holly—"

Angela jumped to the side as the dragon opened her

mouth and roared, the sound echoing all around the stadium. Flames billowed behind her.

Benson pulled her a few steps down the tunnel, away from the still-roaring dragon. "You okay?"

Angela nodded, pulling her sweat-soaked shirt away from her body. "I can't tell how much of the anger is hers and how much is just the natural form of the dragon."

"A feedback loop," Benson agreed. "Somehow we need to break it."

The roaring continued unabated. Angela rubbed an ear. "Let's go find some water and let her cool off a bit."

They ended up having to leave the stadium to find water, but one of the guardsmen manning the barricades nearby took pity on them and pulled bottled water from his truck. Angela sat on a bench next to Benson, examining the charred ends of her hair while she tried to figure out what to do next.

"Maybe we could do the same thing we did yesterday with May," he suggested.

"Her own magic isn't going to make her unstable. It's just going to cause trouble for everyone else." Angela rubbed her arms again, trying to ignore the prickling that wouldn't go away. "But I might be able to pull her back into her human form if she wasn't fighting me. I'd feel better if we had some obsidian around to bleed off the extra magic, but we're hundreds of miles away from any natural deposits." She pushed her hair back so she wouldn't keep looking at the damage. "We need a distraction."

They sat in silence for a moment, the bird songs distinctive in an area normally filled with human noise.

Benson cleared his throat. "You really need to come up with a better bucket list for when people ask you why they should shift back." He shook his head. "Because we need the stadium for football games?"

Angela kicked at his ankle. "I got caught off-guard. I didn't hear you come up with anything either."

Benson propped his foot on the other knee, took out a handkerchief, and wiped away the ash she'd just transferred onto his boot. "I'm pretty sure any suggestion from a man is not going to go over well."

"Point." Angela took another drink of water. "There are so many things that drive me crazy, but I would never trade my job for anything. It's just... Look at Lily. And Father Sebastian. Almost all my clients, really. I feel like I'm making a difference. But I still understand where Holly's coming from."

Her phone rang and she pulled it out of her pocket, making a face when she saw who it was. "Speaking of things that drive me crazy...." She accepted the call. "Matt. You're on speaker."

Her attempt to shame him into good manners didn't work any better than it had on the captain a week earlier.

"Dammit, Angie, I gave you one simple thing to do and you can't even get that right!"

"Matt—"

"Get your ass over here and—"

Angela disconnected the call. At Benson's raised eyebrow she shrugged. "I think I'm done putting up with shit today."

Benson nodded. "Maybe tomorrow."

She considered. "Or even Monday. Just not today." Standing up, she looked for a recycling bin. "I wonder if anyone has a fireproof suit we can borrow."

20

N obody had a suit, but they did give her a few extra bottles of water and used one of the trucks to drive the two of them across the parking lot again. On the way, Angela sent Matt a text telling him they were going to try to shift the dragon back to human, then turned her phone off. They thanked the driver, and walked into the stadium and back to the tunnels where the roaring and flames had stopped.

Angela cracked open another bottle of water and took a long drink. "Hey Holly, it's Angela again. Can I come talk to you?" At the silence she peeked around the corner, and when that didn't produce a ball of flame, walked out to where she had been. All the walls were radiating heat now, making her feel like she had entered a sauna while fully clothed. "I really do want to help you get out of this. Is there anything we can do to make you more comfortable?"

The dragon's head stayed on the ground. "I'm not going back. They'll just have to kill me if they want to play games in their damned stadium again."

"Holly, I'm not that worried about the stadium. I don't really care about sports anyway, so a few less games won't affect me. But I *am* worried about you. The more time you spend as a dragon before shifting back, the harder that's going to be." She sucked in a breath that felt like it charred her lungs. A quick perusal of Holly's social media had suggested some avenues to try. "Wouldn't you like to get out of here and go travel the world some day? That's going to be easier if you can get on a plane."

A warm exhale of air met her words, but the dragon didn't comment.

"You won't have to go back to the same job, you know. You have other options." Not to mention the firm was down a few partners and most of a building. "People pay good money to get dragon shifters to work for them. You can do pretty much anything you want." She paused to let that sink in and take another drink of water. "But we need to get you shifted back first."

Another exhale. "What kind of work?"

Angela hid her smile of relief. "You realize you're basically a crane, demolition ball, and tractor rolled up into one, right? Plus you're easy to transport in human form, and you can figure things out on your own. Everyone from the military to construction companies to movie studios will be trying to hire you. You can pretty much write your own ticket." She'd let Holly find out later that she wouldn't be able to fly commercial ever again — airlines being unwilling to risk losing hundreds of passengers through an accidental shift — but there were enough private jets and pilots who would take the job, and she would have the money.

Out of sight of the dragon, Benson waved to her and pointed to his phone. Angela strolled around the corner.

"Patterson's having chest pains," he told her in a low voice. "They need to get him out of there and to the hospital."

Angela nodded and walked back around the corner. "Hey, Holly, would it be all right with you if we moved out to the field? We need to get one of the guys trapped in the tunnel some medical attention, and it is really hot right here." She tried to think of something she could use as inducement. "If you want, I can see if they can turn on the Jumbotron for you. There must be something you'd want to watch."

Another heated exhale. "Fine."

Benson moved out toward the field, and after giving him a head start, Angela followed. Behind her, the sound of thousands of scales scraping along concrete walls told her that Holly was coming as well. Angela headed toward the sunlight. This would be the test. With no side corridors to duck into, Angela would be dead if Holly coughed out any flame behind her.

"Have you thought about what you want to watch?" Angela asked the question over her shoulder and kept walking toward the field.

"I'm thinking." The dragon's gait was measured, individual claw tips clicking down on the floor like a drum roll, followed by a scraping sound as her body was dragged forward. "What do I need to do to shift back?"

Angela didn't try to keep the smile off her face this time. She kept walking. "Mostly I need you to not fight me on it. They'll teach you in training how to control your shifting, but for the first time I'll draw you back to your human form, and then throw a temporary binding on you so you can't accidentally shift back again." She looked backward when the dragon slowed. "It only lasts a week or so, but it will keep you from destroying your apartment while you're packing a suitcase."

Angela reached the opening of the tunnel and walked out under the open sky, rows of seats on either side. She continued toward the center of the stadium, stopping only to try to figure out how to get onto the field. After a moment of study, she gave up on opening the gate and instead climbed over the low fence, hopping down onto the close-cropped grass. The barrier didn't even slow the dragon. She flowed over the top, the movement as graceful as a snake's, first the head, then the front legs, body, back legs, and finally the tail. By the time she was completely on the grass, the dragon covered most of the field.

Angela looked over at Benson and saw him texting. A group of soldiers jogged along the edge of the seats and ducked down the tunnel, on course for the previously trapped MPD officers. At least now they'd be able to get Patterson to a hospital, while she tried to figure out how to shift a dragon who had been stuck in the form for four days.

The huge screen over the end zone flickered to life, first showing a test pattern, and then the manufacturer's logo. After a few seconds more, it cut to a close-up of an oil painting in progress, where trees were being added to a mountain ridge.

The dragon raised her head to look at the display. "Is that... Bob Ross?"

The familiar head of curls filled the screen, answering the question before Angela could. She looked over at Benson, who shrugged. "I think it's supposed to be calming, but if you want to watch something else let me know."

A low rumble vibrated the ground and a few wisps of steam came out of the dragon's nostrils. Angela realized Holly was laughing. She walked along the length of the dragon until she reached the shoulder. At this distance, she could distinguish individual scales, each one a shining dagger. The scales rippled as the dragon stretched both front feet forward, looking for all the world like a giant cat waking from a nap.

Deciding that her position was safe for the next few seconds, Angela switched to her other sight. After the workout she'd had the day before while trying to find May's human side, Holly's magical core seemed ridiculously simple. Both colors shone brightly, neither hiding the other. She'd be able to touch the human side easily. Pulling the dragon to her human form would be simple enough, but if she did that there was a possibility that all the extra magic in the mix would be set free instead of folding down with the dragon form.

With a low-magic porcupine, free magic loosed during the switch wouldn't even be felt. It dispersed into the environment and caused no problems. If she tried the same thing on this dragon, there would be a crater where the stadium had once stood, and the surrounding few blocks of downtown probably wouldn't fare much better.

The trick was going to be to guide Holly into the other shape in such a way that the dragon side took the extra magic with it. Angela took a deep breath and wiped her palms on her trousers. "You ready to get started? I'm going to tug on something and I want you to tell me when you feel it..."

Angela worked with the dragon, the familiar steps of teaching a new shifter calming her even as a part of her worried that the amount of magic Holly needed to be able to store with her dragon form was too much. For a seasoned shifter, it might cause a few moments of extra effort as they worked through the best way to pack it all together. For a new shifter, it meant the shift was exponentially harder, as if a huge spring was keeping the lid on the box holding the alternate form from closing. Lily, she thought with an affectionate smile, would have no trouble with some extra magic. Her next form just might be a little more ridiculous, with bigger spikes on the back or spouting rainbows.

Or even — everything slowed as Angela considered the possibility — with a child created from all that extra magic. She forced herself to file that thought away and concentrate on the task at hand.

Four days ago, when Holly first shifted, this would have been straightforward enough, at least after the initial fires had been quenched. Angela suppressed a wave of irritation over the delay. Magic called to magic. As the biggest magic holder for hundreds of miles, the dragon had attracted stray magic the way a magnet collected iron shavings. A more experienced shifter would have known how to mitigate that attraction, but Holly had been busy being told that her life hadn't been important by the very agents sent to help her.

"You're doing great," Angela said after Holly changed her magic in a way that brought the human side a bit forward before it fell back. "It looks like you've got the basics figured out. Now we just need to do a little bit of fine-tuning so it's more efficient." A bottle of water was pressed into her hand, and she blinked back to regular sight to see Benson next to her. The position of the sun in the sky had changed while she'd been teaching Holly what to look for. Uncapping the bottle, she took a long drink and realized how dizzy she was.

"There's pizza," Benson told her, gesturing to the edge of the field.

Angela nodded. "Hey, Holly, let's take a break for a few minutes." She waited until the dragon huffed acknowledgement, then followed Benson to the edge of the field.

"We need some way to siphon off that extra magic," she said as she collapsed on the ground, pizza in hand. "Any thoughts?"

"Truckload of obsidian?"

"If we could get some I'd be all for it, but I wouldn't even know where to start looking. I've never seen it available in anything other than jewelry accent amounts." Angela imagined trying to teach the dragon to fill the obsidian slowly enough that it didn't explode, and shivered. "Maybe I could get her to swim in the ocean." They weren't impossibly far away from the coast. The salt water would keep more magic from accumulating and would even leach off a little, the same way it could be used to drain charged obsidian. Bleeding off this much magic might take years, or even decades, but at least that would buy them some time to work on training Holly without the problem getting worse.

"Would a ring of salt keep more magic from accumulating?"

Angela looked over at him. "I think it would." She looked at the perfectly manicured grass. "They're going to lose it when we put a ring of rock salt on their field, aren't they?"

"I'll tell them the alternative is building a new stadium and most of the city around it. That ought to clarify things for them."

Angela made the effort to smile. "Let's do it. And if you can find a source of bulk obsidian, see if we can get it."

The sound of boots running on concrete was the only warning she had. Suddenly there were troops in camouflage swarming the field and the sound of pneumatic bursts as nets were deployed and bolted into the ground.

The dragon erupted, spouting flame that lit a group of men on fire, even as another group deployed a net over her head and a blanket to mask her eyes. A jet of flame caught the edge of the blanket, making it smolder.

Angela was running across the field toward them before she even realized she was on her feet. "Stop!" She pulled a man back from one of the stakes holding a net to the ground. "What are you doing? Stop!"

The dragon rolled, the nets giving her just enough play, and three soldiers near her shoulder went down, their voices cut off mid-scream. From her position near the hind leg, Angela could see the metallic strands of the net cutting into the flesh between the scales. The dragon bucked and spit fire, and another soldier went up like a candle wick, the stench of burning flesh filling the air.

Angela spotted Matt on the other side of the field, safely away from the dragon. She ran around the tail to get to him and slammed a hand into his shoulder, knocking him back a step. "Stop this! What is wrong with you?"

He held up a hand to ward her off. "This is our best chance to grab the dragon and transport it somewhere it won't do any harm."

"But I had her talking to me..." Frustration and horror made tears rise.

"Don't be so emotional. We had to take this opportunity. For the good of the city—" His last words were cut off by the collective yell as three of the spikes holding down the netting popped loose, freeing one front leg. Hampered by the blanket still over her eyes, the dragon swept out, impaling the soldier working on the blindfold. She roared and another stream of flame melted a section of stadium seats.

The netting around the dragon's back legs cut deeper as Holly struggled. With another twist of her torso, she freed her other front leg. Two seconds later, the front half of the dragon was completely untethered, and the remaining soldiers near the front were running. Charred husks of over a dozen people remained on the field.

With another roar, Holly tried to turn around, but the lines holding her down didn't come free. Green blood pulsed to the ground from a grid pattern where the strands had buried themselves under her skin.

"You have to release her!" Angela moved forward and pulled at one of the spikes, accomplishing nothing other than bloodying her hand. When she looked back, Matt's face was pale. She stood up. "We need bolt cutters!"

Matt looked at her as if she'd gone crazy. "If we release it now, the dragon will kill us all."

Another burst of flame set a banner on fire and scorched a line up the wall. Angela saw with horror that Holly was thrashing about near the high-voltage conduit going to the Jumbotron. The dragon was beyond reason, flinging her head and shoulders back and forth, biting and clawing at anything in her way. With every move, the netting cut deeper into her flanks, soaking the ground with her blood.

"If we don't release her, she might die and take half the city with her." Angela gave up trying to convince Matt. One of the soldiers wrestling to hold the bolts in place had a knife sheath attached to his leg and she grabbed the knife, moved forward and started sawing at the netting. The knife slipped in her bloody hand, but she got one strand parted.

"Here, use this to hold it." Benson was suddenly next to her, a green t-shirt in one hand and a second stolen knife in the other. They attacked the other strands anchored by the bolt together. If they could just release the section holding her pelvis down, Holly would be able to move forward and free herself completely.

They were on the last strand when an electric shock

knocked them both backward. The Jumbotron, still showing oil-painted lakes and mountains, flickered and went black, and the overhead lights went out.

A sudden silence filled the stadium. Angela looked over and saw the dragon's jaw clamped on the metal conduit, eyes glazed. Even as she watched, the shroud of death passed over the dragon's features.

Panic welled up in her. "Holly?" She put a hand on the bloody scales, closed her eyes, and switched to her other sight.

Inside the dragon's magical core, the threads were loosening, the enormous power bound within starting to flex outward. Angela reached with her own magic to try to hold it back, her efforts like trying to stop a raging river with one finger.

Magic exploded, punching through her as if she were a wisp of paper.

The deluge was matched only by her anger, rage that her plan had been derailed, that she was going to die here, and for no good reason. All the fury she had held inside, every dismissal because she didn't look the part of a magical probation officer, all the petty ways she'd been held back over the years — all of it came together and for a moment she was more powerful than the magic.

Power called to power. The unleashed magic turned and filled her, burning away everything not connected to her anger. She felt her skin split and boil away, and still the magic flowed into her. Dimly she felt herself growing and changing shape, but most of all she was power and fury, a being so pure she didn't need flesh.

The magic flowing from the dragon slowed. She pulled it to her, devouring the final drops, and drew in a breath to scream out her rage.

Only then did she open her eyes. The first thing she saw was the corpse of a magnificent dragon beneath her, small compared to her new shape. She turned her head to gaze upon what she had become, though part of her already knew. Shape was determined by identity, need, and power. Only one creature could hold this much power.

A fiery salamander.

21

The salamander taking control of Angela looked upon her body, watching a wave of flames speed from shoulders to tail tip nearly one hundred yards away. The gold and white skin of her feet darkened to red as it approached her body, then deepened to brown and finally pure black over her back. Under her skin, chaotic magic roiled.

On the formerly pristine turf of the football field, chaos reigned. Black smoke billowed from the remains of a jeep, and people in uniform were screaming all around her. The dragon — *Holly*, the part of her scrambling to throw off the effects of the salamander insisted — lay crumpled in death beneath her, all her power and grace gone.

A cluster of people edged away when Angela turned her head to look at them. *Caleb.* He tried to run and she pounced. Pinning him to the ground in a pool of clotting dragon blood, Angela leaned her head closer, pleased by his shaking. She pulled off a bit of his magic and savored it. Resting her head on her paw, she breathed in the intoxicating scent of his fear mixed with mud and burned flesh.

Then she ripped the last of his magic from him, leaving not even a speck to anchor more, and pushed his screaming body away to find other prey.

Ah, there. *Matt*. He didn't run, but started yelling at her. "Angie! Stop! It's me!"

Angela tore out a chunk of his magic. He doubled over and screamed then, a pleasing counterpoint to the nearby sirens and thrum of the helicopter overhead.

A softer voice spoke near her ear, barely audible over the crackle of flames. "Angela."

She knew that voice. *Benson*, the fading part of her whispered. She growled and peeled another layer of magic from Matt, snagging his vest with one claw when he fell and tried to crawl away.

"Angela, stop," the quiet voice repeated.

Don't hurt Benson. She tossed her head to push him away.

Matt screamed again when she took most of his remaining magic, but his terror didn't satisfy her as much as it had the time before. Flames of frustration erupted from her body.

Benson's voice was weaker, as if he'd taken harm when she'd knocked him away. "Angela, I know you're in there somewhere. Please don't do this."

Under her claws, Matt reeked of urine and terror.

"Angela. Please." Benson had come close to her again and placed a hand on her neck. She watched him, wondering why he would risk burning his fragile human skin. *Don't hurt Benson.* The idea of restraint disoriented her, and she closed her eyes, holding onto her anger tightly. She would *destroy* this city.

Angela opened her eyes and backed away, leaving Matt curled on the ground. The turf charred beneath her feet as she moved to the exit. The encircling wall was no match for her magic, and she climbed over a pile of rubble to reach the parking lot.

"Angela." Somehow Benson had caught up to her and was trotting by her side, one hand held tightly against his ribs. She increased her pace and he sprinted to keep up, his cowboy boots clacking unevenly on the asphalt. "Listen." He held out his phone.

"Angela?"

Angela stopped. *Lily.* Wonderful, smart, amazing Lily. Lily depended on her. Lily would need the city to be there for herself and her baby.

Angela couldn't destroy the city.

Her rage was the one thing holding her together, and she *needed* to destroy everything around her. Instead, she ran to the river, where she dove down through the cool water, pushing past the murky weeds, and swam toward the distant ocean.

22

The cool Pacific waters slid over her skin, stilling the buzzing of magic, and allowing for some little amount of tranquility. Gradually, she came back to herself.

At first, Angela spent her time off the coast during the day and resting on the beach after dark, but by the second evening her appearance began to draw crowds within an hour of her arrival. Between the staring people and the ever-present media drones, she found herself longing to run up the beach and gorge herself on the magic held within the onlookers. Some of those people were just curious, but Angela knew more than a few were hoping to be the first to get through to her, to convince her to sign a contract, or to turn her to whichever cause they supported. Contenting herself with crushing a drone and hurling the remains over the heads of the crowd, she dove back into the soothing waters and escaped.

This body wasn't particularly built for swimming, having a tendency to sink if she didn't keep moving, but it allowed her to see the ocean bottom in a way she never had before. Only her tendency to heat up the surrounding water kept her from exploring more slowly. If she stayed in one place for more than a minute, bubbles of steam began to rise and any life not mobile enough to move away withered and died. Death was a part of life, but that sort of pointless destruction just made her sad.

Well past the breakers, she found a large cluster of rocks that stuck out above the water, covered with barnacles and abandoned bird nests. From the side facing the land she could just make out the shore, but on the opposite side she could curl up and see no evidence of humanity other than the occasional cargo ship passing in the distance.

There she stayed, swimming in the nearby waters when she needed to cool off, climbing on the rocks when she tired. Birds came by to examine her but flew off quickly, the flames coming from her skin warning them away. Fish, too, fled at the sight of her, though a pod of dolphins stuck around long enough to circle the length of her a few times. A colony of sea lions spent almost an entire day trying to bully her off the rock, climbing to higher vantage points and barking at her, but they eventually tired of the sport, leaving her to the relative silence of the water.

After the first few days, Angela felt more like herself, though she knew the form of the salamander was affecting her thoughts. Waves of overwhelming and irrational anger passed through her, and she would have to close her eyes, grip the rocks, and wait for it to pass, listening to the spray sizzle when it hit her overheated skin. Eventually the feeling would subside, and she could think clearly again.

Shifting back to her human body was impossible with the amount of magic she'd acquired from the dying dragon. Unlike every other shifted creature, the size of a salamander was directly proportional to their magic. She'd started out nearly the size of a football field, and after four days of letting the salt water receive what magic she could give it, she wasn't noticeably smaller. She suspected it would be years, if not decades, before she would be close to shifting again.

Grief passed through her at the thought of being alone all those years. She knew she couldn't be anywhere near people, or eventually the salamander side of her would kill them. Even now, when she thought of the dragon being captured and dying, she wanted to swim to the land and lay waste to the cities of men. Salamanders in history books had been described as solitary for decades until they died or disappeared, but she'd never considered the profound loneliness they must have felt.

Two days after she'd retreated to the rock, a boat of sightseers showed up, the stink of diesel caustic in her nose. A dozen people in bright orange life vests crowded to the railing, cell phones and binoculars aimed right at her. Flames ran across her skin and she closed her eyes and hung onto the rock, feeling the skeletons of long dead barnacles pressing into her toes. Snatches of excited laughter and shouting came to her on the breeze, making her cling more tightly.

When the motor roared and the boat moved closer, the salamander would no longer be denied. She opened her eyes, swung her head toward them, and deliberately climbed into the water and swam straight for the boat. Even then they didn't seem to understand their peril, the boat still coming toward her as she crossed the distance. It wasn't until she was within twenty feet that anyone took heed, the boat suddenly changing direction at full throttle, but by then it was too late. The first blow by her tail knocked most of the people into the water, and the others soon jumped in as the boat caught fire. She ignored the people, focusing on the boat until she'd battered it apart, diving down to smash the pieces that had sunk before she'd had a chance to obliterate them.

After the boat had been demolished, a sheen of oil covered the water. She couldn't hold the salamander back any longer. None of the people were shifters but two of them had minor magic and she stripped them of it, a fierce joy filling her as they screamed. Only then could she force herself to return to the rocks, leaving the terrified people bobbing in the waves, tiny pieces of their boat floating on the water nearby.

Angela allowed the rescue boats to enter her waters unmolested, watching from her perch on the stones, the flames coming off her causing a steam plume that would be visible for miles.

When all the people had been retrieved, the rescue boats retreated and she was left to the silence of her anger. No boats dared to come close to her rock again, though when she swam she occasionally ran across patrolling Coast Guard vessels. She left them unchallenged, recognizing they were there for a purpose, and swam on, allowing the salt of the waters to soothe her.

Another week passed. The only contact she had with humanity was a drone carrying an offer from the *Shift Enforcers* producers who wanted permission to photograph her destroying a decoy boat. Angela had knocked the drone out of the air and lobbed it back on the shore. She pushed the decoy boat onto the beach three times before they stopped towing it back into the water.

The moon drew her out into the water, the cool light illuminating the top few feet below the surface so she could see the different fish active at night. A huge container ship

moved by, oblivious to her travel underneath. The salamander within wanted to punch holes in the hull and watch
it sink beneath the waves, but Angela kept going, traveling a
course that gave her the taste of different waters until she
finally headed back to her rock.

Exhausted from the swim, she pulled herself onto the
rock, only then noticing two kayaks on the top where the
waves wouldn't batter them. In an instant, her rage burned
off her weariness. She roared, the sound causing ripples on
the waves as far as she could see. She'd spared the lives of
the people on the boat, but no more. These intruders would
be destroyed.

A blue glow lit up the top of the rock, making Angela
pause. "Lily?" It felt as if she whispered, but a sparkling
reptilian head poked over the side.

"Angela!"

Back when she'd been human, Angela had found Lily's
shifted form pleasing with its glitter and oversized eyes.
Seen through the gaze of a salamander, Lily was just amazing. Her magic blazed in the night, a beacon that Angela
couldn't believe hadn't been visible miles away. Lily's baby
raced in the womb, strong threads of magic running
through it as well.

Angela backed into the water. "Lily, you can't be here.
You have to go." She couldn't trust herself around that much
magic, and she would swim away from shore until she
dropped dead from exhaustion and blew a hole in the ocean
before she hurt the girl.

"Angela, wait!" The blue glow abruptly quenched, Lily
having apparently decided she could climb on the rocks
more easily in her human form. She swung down and
jumped to the flattest part, skidding a little on the wet stone.
"Please don't go."

Angela stayed in the water, head pressed down, nostrils just barely above the waves. She needed to leave, to keep Lily safe, but the need to be around humans, ones she had known before, held her in place. "How did you get here? Who brought you?" She wouldn't allow herself to hurt Lily, but she'd destroy whoever had been stupid enough to let a pregnant teenager kayak on the ocean at night to go visit a salamander.

"That would be me," Benson's voice came from just beyond the ledge at the top of the rock. "Except I didn't exactly bring her. I followed. It was the only way I could keep her from going alone."

"The credit card company called him when I reserved the kayak. They thought I stole his card."

Benson cleared his throat.

"I guess I sort of did," Lily added.

Angela stared at the girl. Somehow the idea of Lily using a stolen credit card shocked her more than any of the other events of the previous month. A ripple of saltwater crested over her back, soothing the buildup of magic on her skin. "Lily, you have to go. It's not safe to be around me." She watched the fetus shift, and couldn't stop herself from reaching out with a tendril of magic to caress the fragile form. It responded by pushing back, and then shifting again.

Lily ignored her and moved forward, then sat on a rock, feet dangling in the water. She was wearing cut-off jeans and a t-shirt that Angela recognized as one of her own. The shirt hung down to the girl's thighs. Over it all, she wore a foam life jacket and a helmet. "You would never hurt me. You didn't even really hurt that guy from your office that's always staring at my boobs when you ate his magic."

It took Angela a few seconds to realize Lily was talking

about Caleb, and then she had to back up into the water so she could completely submerge and allow the water to carry her rage away. She should have killed Caleb when she had a chance. Legally she could have done so without any repercussions since she had just shifted for the first time. Now it was too late. She'd never be able to get near him.

When she came back up, Benson had joined Lily on the rock. The water near her rock had heated to a temperature that would kill anything nearby, so she forced herself to climb out all the way and curl up on dry ground. If the salamander began to take over, she'd just have to head out into the water again.

"Why are you here? And why in the middle of the night?"

Lily pulled her feet out of the water and turned to face her, the girl's face lit by the moonlight and wisps of flames from the salamander skin. "I didn't think I could get past the Coast Guard during the day." She shrugged and then shifted, her larger form almost knocking Benson into the water. "And I wasn't sure I could swim like this."

"But you could have gotten lost and ended up in the middle of the ocean. I can't believe you would do something so crazy."

Lily and Benson looked at each other, then back to her. "Uh, Angela," Lily said, then shifted back to her human form, "your magic is like a bat signal. It's pretty much soaked into the rock. Even when you were out swimming around, we could always see this spot. There's no way I could have gotten lost unless there's another salamander out here."

Benson spoke up. "It's been nearly four hundred years since the last salamander was seen, so I think that's unlikely."

Lily shifted forms again, her skin glittering in the moonlight. "You have to come back with us. We need you."

Rock cracked under Angela's claws and she moved her feet to loosen the muscles. "Even if I could shift... they wouldn't let me anywhere near a city. And I can't shift."

"Why not?" Lily spoke with the innocence of a child who shifted whenever she needed something she couldn't reach.

"Because I'm too full of magic. I can't get rid of it any time soon." She rested her head on the rocks, scratching an itchy spot on her chin. "Maybe in another thirty or forty years." Or fifty if she lost control around another boat of idiots and absorbed even more.

When Lily shifted again, Benson gave her a look and stood up. "What if we could help you with that?"

Angela closed her eyes, trying to stop hope from slipping through a crack in the wall protecting her. "What's the point? At least this way, I don't have to worry about what I'm going to eat or where I'm going to live. If I could go back, what then? A cabin in the woods? How would I live?"

"I know you didn't have a chance to turn in your application for the captain's job, but I don't think they've closed the position yet." Benson hopped forward as saltwater surged up toward him. "Or you could go back to your old job if you didn't want to sit in the office. Or my group would be more than happy to hire you to train MPD officers in less coercive methods of maintaining the shifter population."

Chartreuse and aqua flames rippled over her body, lighting up the rock face. "Don't. I'm a f—" She turned her head to look at Lily. "—freaking salamander. Nobody in their right mind would let me anywhere near a city. I could lose my temper and kill everyone."

"Angela, you saved hundreds, or maybe thousands of people and a huge chunk of the city a couple of weeks ago." Benson picked his way across the rock to come closer to her.

Angela blew out a breath, turning her head so the

heated air blew against the wall of rocks instead of anywhere near either of the humans. A clump of dried seaweed crumbled, smoke drifting up to the sky. "So they'll throw me a parade after they run me out of town."

"Would you at least be willing to try? I have three trucks of obsidian on hold."

Angela closed her eyes. The urge to return to the life she'd carved out before this disaster almost overwhelmed her, but it wouldn't be the same. It couldn't be.

Even if the city didn't ban her, people would avoid her. She'd spent her entire career helping shifters deal with the fallout. She knew better than anyone what would happen. Those who didn't outright abandon her would still whisper about her when they thought she couldn't hear. *I certainly wouldn't trust her with anything important. Sure, she seems stable now, but you never know when she's going to explode.* In some ways it would be the same thing she'd faced throughout her professional career, except this time there would be a good reason for it. The hissing of steam got louder as she thought about it, and she knew she couldn't even blame all of the anger on her salamander side. The reaction to decades of being treated as *"less than"* refused to be buried again. The salamander flared in joy at the thought of going there right now and obliterating the entire MPD building.

Benson shifted on the rock. "I also wanted to come out here to apologize."

Angela cracked an eyelid open. "For keeping me from killing everyone?"

Benson made a little snorting noise at the back of his throat. "No." He paused. "You were right. About Casey."

She let her eye close again, but all her attention stayed on him.

Benson continued, his voice pitched for her ears alone. "I checked in the MPD database, and he's there."

Angela's first reaction was to warn him that unauthorized database queries could get him fired. Then she thought about why Casey would be in the database. "He made it back to human again?" All those years, they'd assumed Casey had been stuck living as a coyote.

"He found someone else to help him that night." Benson's voice was rueful. "I was so busy blaming you, it never occurred to me that there were other people he might have gone to. They got him shifted back, and then his parents helped him move out of the state. Found someone to keep spelling him, got a job, got married, had a kid."

When Benson paused, Angela took over. "Except then he shifted again." It had to be what happened, or Casey wouldn't be in the database.

"And bit his daughter in the face," Benson said. "I saw the pictures. After surgery it wasn't too bad, but she'll have that scar her entire life. His wife found out it wasn't the first time he'd shifted, and divorced him. She ended up with full custody of their daughter. I should never have asked you to help him."

Angela tried to make her body relax. "I could have at least made sure he was in a secure place before I tried to call MPD." She thought back to that night. "We really were young and stupid then."

"Yet somehow lived to tell the tale." Benson tapped his palms on his thighs and his voice went back to normal. "In other news, Vicky told me to tell you that she wants you to meet someone."

Angela opened her eyes. "Really?"

He nodded. "There was something about a triple latte. Hopefully that means something to you."

The salamander couldn't smile, but Angela felt part of her heart warm.

While Angela was still thinking about that, Lily jumped off the rock in her human form and scrambled between the boulders until she was crouched right next to the salamander's head. Angela froze, not even daring to breathe in case the exhaled air burned the girl. She couldn't even back out into the water with Lily blocking the path.

"I need you to come back," Lily pleaded, her voice just barely above a whisper. "I'm going to need someone to help me with the baby, and everyone else is afraid of her already."

Angela looked at her, really *looked* at her, seeing not just the resilient and amazing child, but the scared young woman.

Carefully, very, very, carefully, Angela took a breath. "Where's the obsidian?"

Lily jumped up and clapped. "Yay yay yay!" Shifting back to her other form, she jumped to another rock and did the oddest victory dance Angela had ever seen.

After Angela had escorted the kayaks back to the beach and returned to her now-empty rock, she felt a glowing ember of hope for the first time since she'd left the stadium.

23

That bit of hope lasted until she climbed onto the beach two mornings later to find a pile of obsidian she could wrap her body around twice. Benson got out of his rental car and came down to greet her by himself. He was still wearing a dress shirt and tie, but had his slacks rolled up to reveal bare feet.

"It's not going to be enough," she said as he picked his way across the loose sand and kelp.

"Probably not," he agreed easily. "I've got more on the way. I thought we might have a better idea of how much you'll need after today."

Angela used the tip of one claw to separate out a small boulder the size of a cat, the largest solid piece of obsidian she'd ever seen. "If this goes wrong, it's going to act like a grenade." Swinging her head around to face him, she felt the seductive call of his magic like a drug. "You should go sit in the car." If he moved farther away she would be less likely to gulp his magic if something upset her. "Please."

"Fine. But I'm only doing this so you can stop worrying."

Ignoring the apparent ease with which he'd seen

through her motives, she contemplated the rock under her toe while listening to Benson walk back to the nearly empty parking lot. She'd guided more than a few clients through depositing magical energy into obsidian, but she'd never needed to do so herself. Added to that, the salamander's command of magic was...different. Instead of the ribbons of energy she had spent her career manipulating, the salamander's magic cascaded through her.

Her first attempt to feed the magic into the stone merely swirled it around and back into herself. She tried again and watched the magic move in the other direction. Flames traveled along her spine as she vented her frustration. Pushing the magic around was hard enough. Aiming at the obsidian was like heaving a bowling ball at a basketball hoop from the other side of the court.

The hum of an airplane carried through the air making her cast a baleful gaze at the sky. Even if she ever figured out how to dump energy into the stones, she'd never be able to finish before they were selling tickets to gawk at her. The thump of her tail in the sand made the pile of rocks shift, smaller pieces raining down like gravel. Even the smallest pebble would have been enough to rescue any of her clients in the past, but she knew in her bones the entire pile would not be nearly enough.

Her toe began to tingle.

Angela looked down at the offending digit. Everything looked the same, from the razor-sharp tip of her black claw to the pale scales that covered the skin beyond, but something was different. When she lifted her toe to look at it the tingling stopped, but the obsidian boulder hummed just the slightest bit.

So. The obsidian had pulled in magic without her help. Not much, of course. Barely more than the ambient energy on the beach, but at least it was a start. She put her toe back on the obsidian, ignored the tingling, and stared at it. Nothing seemed to be happening as far as she could tell.

It occurred to Angela that she might owe apologies to some of her clients over the years for assuming the process was easy. When she tried to push more magic into the obsidian, the tingling in her toe stopped. Dropping her head down to the ground Angela stared across the sand to where Benson waited in his rental car. The wail of a slide guitar drifted across the distance, and all at once she felt a longing for her human body.

Perhaps she could make a cave out of the obsidian and let it leach the magic from her. Over the next decade or two.

The music cut off, the car door opened, and Benson got out. He'd crossed half the distance between them when he spoke. "What's wrong?"

She didn't bother to lift her head. "It's not working."

"Why not? Did I get the wrong thing?"

Angela looked over at the pile of rocks. "I don't think so. I've just never needed to do this before. It's harder than I thought it would be."

Benson picked his way over the last few feet slowly, avoiding the sharp stones that had fallen from the pile. He pulled out his phone and tapped at it. "Hang on, I'll see if I can find something."

Irritation washed through her, and flames erupted over her whole body. "You're going to become an instant internet expert? I used to teach people how to do this as part of my job." Even when she was the most powerful magical creature in the world, men with no experience still assumed they were more competent than she was.

"Angela." Benson's voice carried over the sound of sand melting and bubbling beneath her. "There are a lot of alter-

nate techniques for power creatures. It's not part of the standard curriculum because dragons and salamanders are so
rare."

As quickly as her anger had flared up, it snuffed out
again. She'd heard about that, decades ago, back when she'd
been a new agent. Belatedly, she remembered that Benson
was a friend. He'd never tried to explain anything she hadn't
asked him to in the past. She closed her eyes and listened to
the sound of the waves. When she was ready, she opened
her eyes and looked at Benson. A crackling of glass from the
cooling sand accompanied the shift of her head. "What does
it say?"

He was seated cross-legged on the sand, entirely too
close for her comfort. One excessive breath of frustration in
the wrong direction and she would singe his eyebrows. "The
highlights are basically that you're too powerful to push
magic into the stone. You need to let the stone absorb it." He
looked from his phone to her, and she thought she saw his
lips twitch. "There's a whole paragraph that Heldig the
Elder recited to the dragon Gunthor to allow him to charge
the bones of a weakened artifact, but it's basically one long
description of a woman's body. Very 'male gazey', I think
your book group would term it." He scrolled down. "Full of
raspberries languishing on the vine for want of the farmer's
hand, and flowers ripe for plucking."

The laughter of a salamander was a fiery cough.

Benson put his phone on his knee where he could read
the screen. "Let's try it this way. Close your eyes and I'll run
you through this relaxation exercise, and then I'll make
something up."

"Am I a guinea pig or a salamander?" she groused, but
closed her eyes again, feeling the calming ocean breeze over
her skin and the pull of the moon beyond the horizon.

"You are a shallow vessel. Oh wait, a *hollow* vessel," Benson said. "Hang on, I need to increase the font size." He coughed and started again, his voice soothing. "With every breath you inhale peace and exhale tension. Inhale peace. Exhale tension."

Angela matched her breathing to his words.

"Your limbs are relaxing, peace flowing through you, starting from the tip of your nose, down your neck, and through your legs." He paused. "And your tail too."

Angela cracked one lid open. Benson shrugged then waved a hand at her to close her eyes again.

"You can feel the obsidian beneath your foot. Even though it feels like stone, it's really a power sponge with nooks and crannies ready to hold everything, like a good English muffin holds butter."

Resisting the urge to open her eyes again, Angela let her tail stretch out into the surf. "You should probably keep your day job."

"I skipped breakfast," he responded, before smoothing his voice out again. "Just by touching your foot, the obsidian is going to start inflating, pulling power from you like it is sucking helium out of a balloon."

A cough of laughter overtook her. "Is it butter or helium?"

"Power is all things to all people," he intoned. "Fine, if you want the original version, feel the rock opening itself to you, creamy skin leading to a deep dark well of feminine secrets, pulling your essence from your—"

Peeking to make sure Benson hadn't moved, Angela blew a trail of fire off to the side.

"Okay, the rock is a sponge. It's soaking up magical energy through your foot, and when it does the energy flows from elsewhere in your body to replace it."

Angela tried to imagine the obsidian absorbing the energy. Her foot tingled. She relaxed into the feeling, picturing her stored magical energy oozing toward her foot and into the rock.

"Good. I think you've got the hang of it."

Angela opened her eyes and looked down at the boulder beneath her foot. It pulsed with magic. "Can you tell how full it is? My vision is...different." She moved her toes away so they were no longer in contact with the obsidian, and the glow stabilized.

Benson looked at the stone. "I think it's close. You might want to experiment with something that isn't big enough to make a crater on the beach."

Angela pushed the stone off to the side where she couldn't accidentally add more energy to it. Her skin itched. "I'm going to take a break. You go get breakfast. Your stomach is growling loud enough to interrupt my thoughts of butter or helium or whatever it is I'm supposed to be envisioning."

She had just pushed through the waves, salt water closing over her skin in a soothing rush, when a blast from the beach shook the ground and punched through the air. Angela dove under the water, then turned to go parallel to the beach, surfacing again when she'd slithered a hundred yards. A quick glance showed no movement in the air, and none of the expected chaos of an invasion on the sand. In fact, there was no motion at all aside from dust or smoke drifting away from the area she'd just left, where a large divot had replaced the smooth sands of the beach.

A figure lay flat on the sand just a little farther away from the water. Benson. She couldn't see any movement, but if he was still alive, he had no protection against another attack. Even as she realized that, Angela was scrambling out of the water and running across the beach, flames trailing behind her. Clawing her way through the loose sand, Angela curled herself into a multi-layered coil around the human, wrapping herself as close as she could without singeing him. Blood trickled from his ear, but she couldn't see any other injuries and he was breathing.

Angela looked around, her salamander vision letting her see the magic in every living thing within half a mile. Far from the army she was expecting, there was nobody. A few dolphins played in the waves, already recovered from being pushed out of the way during her mad dash back onto the beach, and out further she could see a few larger fish. The land hid nothing bigger than some crabs. Even the access road was clear of traffic, although she could hear the siren of a lone fire truck a few miles away.

Sand slid down the sides of the hole in the ground near them and Angela realized it was the spot where she'd been resting before she'd gone back into the water. Perhaps the heat she'd generated that had created a thin layer of glass had set off something deeper in the sand, maybe some ordinance that had been buried during a war and never cleared. It couldn't have been buried too far down, though — the hole wasn't more than a foot or two deep.

Benson moaned, drawing her attention back to him. His eyes were open, and while she watched he rolled over and sat up, almost touching her side in the process. She loosened the coils around him, giving him more space now that she was fairly sure they weren't under attack.

He lifted a hand to the side of his face to touch the blood there, then looked at his fingers. "What happened?"

"I don't know. I thought someone bombed the beach, but..." Angela looked back at the spot of the blast and realized what was missing. "It was the obsidian. I must have overloaded it." She'd seen obsidian explode a few times during her career. It had always been while power was being put into the stone, not thirty seconds later, but that was the only thing that fit.

Now that she knew nobody had been trying to kill Benson, that in fact she was the one who had done this to him, Angela unwound her body from around him. The fire truck came around a curve then slowed as the driver saw her. The siren cut out.

Angela swung her head back to look at Benson. "I'm sorry." She climbed across the sand and into the waiting water.

"Angela, wait!" Benson's voice trailed off in a fit of coughing.

She ducked her head under the water and kept swimming.

24

In the deep of the night, beneath a waning gibbous moon hidden by clouds, Angela climbed on the empty beach. Aside from the pile of obsidian that had increased in size, there was no evidence that it was even the same place. The hole in the sand had been filled in, wind erasing any sign of the tools used. The access road remained deserted.

Picking a few boulders half the size of the one she'd worked with earlier, she pushed them away from the rest of the pile. No need to waste the larger rocks on tests. When obsidian hit overload, the resulting blast released all the magical energy it had stored. The local environment already had enough stray magic just from her presence.

Resting one foot on the rock, Angela tried to remember how she had fed her magic into the stone the day before. The relaxation exercise Benson had narrated for her was harder to manage without him. She kept seeing his motion-less body lying prone on the sand. After she'd headed into the water, it had taken the firemen almost no time to rush forward and carry him back to the access road. Once there, they'd crowded around him until the ambulance had arrived.

Her skin heated, this time as anger with herself boiled over. She'd taught other shifters to use obsidian safely during her career, but the first time she'd needed to do it herself, she'd almost killed someone.

The smell of melting sand rose and she dragged her thoughts back to the relaxation exercise. Hollow vessel. That was it.

Dawn light had started streaking the horizon by the time she had calmed enough to feel energy flowing into the first stone. She filled all three with varying amounts, stopping the first when she could see it start to pulse, then putting less in the second and even less in the third, so it was barely glowing in her vision. When she moved into the water to cool off and relieve her itching skin, she tried to evaluate if she'd gotten any smaller, finally deciding that if she had, the change was too small to notice. Letting herself sink down under the water to the trash-strewn sand, she thought about the pile of rock and her size.

She was never going to get rid of enough energy to shift back.

A boom, dulled by the weight of the seawater, broke her contemplation. Keeping her feet on the sand, she stretched her head up above the water and looked back at the beach. As she'd expected, a haze of drifting smoke and sand obscured the spot where the first boulder had been. Now she knew that filling it to pulsing strength was too much. It still didn't explain why it only blew up after a delay, but she supposed that didn't really matter as long as she didn't fill the obsidian so full.

Pushing off from the bottom, she headed back through the surf and climbed up on land. No sirens broke the quiet of the night, but she didn't imagine she was unobserved. Even if Benson had not alerted anyone about what they were trying to do, the events of the previous day would have broadcast her location to everyone.

Angela nudged a larger boulder away from the rest, on the opposite of the rock pile. The extra magical energy released by the rock that had exploded permeated the air, and she fought to keep from pulling it into herself.

Movement caught her eye, making her wheel around with a snarl that her privacy had been invaded again, but it was just her second test boulder pulsing with waves of magical energy. She stared. Surely she hadn't added that much energy to the stone. It had been glowing calmly when she had finished with it. And yet there it was, pulsing, the waves beating faster and faster.

Angela ducked her head down behind the pile of inert obsidian right before the second stone exploded, the blast peppering her body with grit that stung but didn't penetrate her skin. More annoying was the increased density of magical energy in the air. Fighting to keep from reabsorbing it all, Angela rushed back toward the surf, hoping the increased distance between herself and the source would calm the cravings. Anger at her miscalculation left her wanting to find the nearest human building and pulverize it, burning the remains to ash that would scatter in the wind, but she had to content herself with crashing her tail into the pile of obsidian, scattering it over the beach.

She hadn't even reached the breakers when the third stone exploded.

~

THE NEXT NIGHT, while resting on her rocky perch in the sea,

Angela wasn't surprised when Lily and Vicky paddled into view. She'd been listening to the two of them talking with each other for the last fifteen minutes. Or rather she'd been listening to Vicky complain about the end of her promising career in the district attorney's office when she was inevitably convicted of contributing to the delinquency of a minor, and Lily's unconcerned laughter.

"Of course you think it's funny," Vicky said, her voice stronger on the last word as she dug into the water. "You didn't just spend fifteen years paying off student loans." She paddled two more strokes. "Are you absolutely sure we're going in the right direction? I can't see a thing."

Angela realized that her skin wasn't flaming at all, possibly for the first time since she'd shifted. She thought of the trash she'd seen on the ocean floor, and fire erupted lazily over her form. Ignoring Vicky's intake of breath, she rolled away from the easiest landing spot to give them room. "Don't you know it's impolite to just show up without calling?"

Lily giggled and shifted, making it onto the rocks with an oddly graceful leap coming from a large blue lizard. "Angela!" She picked up the kayak with ease and set it up on the rock ledge, out of the way. "Benson sent us out here to talk to you."

As Angela watched, Lily's baby shifted to its human form and back again. "Why do I find that hard to believe?" She looked over at Vicky, who had stopped paddling and floated in the water, just staring at the giant salamander in front of her.

Lily sat down with her feet in the water and shifted back to her human form, her life vest making her small figure look bulkier than Angela knew it to be. "Okay, so it was more like he said he was going to come out as soon as he could, but his collar bone is broken and he can't paddle. I offered to tow his kayak, but he got all grumpy and then Vicky talked to him."

At the sound of her name, Vicky started and then paddled over to the rocks. Angela slid her tail under the water and held the kayak against the rock so her friend could get out without falling. Vicky stood on the rocks looking at her, not speaking.

"You were the one who always said I needed to try something new," Angela said, uncomfortable when the silence lengthened.

Vicky sniffed and wiped her eyes, and Angela belatedly realized there were tears on her friend's face. "I thought you were dead." She waved a hand in denial. "We heard there were bodies and you didn't text me and I didn't find out what had happened for hours. But here you are. And you're this...this *beautiful* thing. And I'm supposed to be the good-looking one!" she finished with a half-laugh half-sob.

Angela closed her eyes and just enjoyed the feeling of having her best friend near her again. "You might have to get used to it. Or up your game." She opened her eyes again, not surprised that there were no longer flames illuminating the rocks. "We've run into a snag in the whole plan to change me back."

Lily unzipped the pack she'd taken out of her kayak. Plastic rustled. "Benson said the obsidian exploded." She pulled out a bag of marshmallows and threaded one on a collapsible pointer. She stood up and climbed over the rocks toward Angela's head. "Can you turn the fire back on for a little bit?"

"Lily!" Vicky sounded horrified.

"What? I'm hungry! I'm eating for two. And Angela doesn't mind, do you Angela?"

Angela responded by blowing out a gout of flame that incinerated the marshmallow. "Oops. Get another one and I'll try again."

Lily dropped the charred remains of the first one into the water, then went back to her pack. The plastic rustled some more. "I brought a whole bag." She climbed back across the rocks. "Take two."

This time, Angela judged her strength better and just lightly caramelized the outside. Lily put it between two graham cracker squares with chocolate and shoved the whole thing into her mouth. "Want one? This is the best thing ever," she mumbled around the food, staring at Vicky.

For a second, the other woman stayed where she was, then she reached forward and grabbed the pointer. "Give me that thing."

Lily laughed and handed her the bag of marshmallows. She turned back to Angela. "So one thing blew up. Didn't that guy destroy one of your beads when you were teaching him? You just have to try again."

"I did." Angela relayed what had happened on her second trip to the beach. "Either I'm doing something wrong, or obsidian just can't hold the energy of a salamander." She stopped to blow out a steady stream of fire near the marshmallow Vicky was holding out.

"You can't stay here. Who am I going to vent to when that dinosaur Judge Carmichael comments on my legs when I'm in court?" Vicky pulled the marshmallow back and looked at it, then moved it forward again. "I like mine more burned on the outside."

"I can go burn down the whole courthouse if you want." Angela dropped her head to the rocks as Vicky went to get graham crackers from Lily. "That might be the only thing I can do these days."

Lily brought another marshmallow over for toasting. "Don't talk like that. You have to come back. I can't look after Romeo forever."

Angela felt a weight she hadn't even known she was carrying lift. "He's still alive?" With everything else she'd gone through, the health of a little fish seemed like a ridiculous thing to be happy about, but there it was.

"Yes, but there's a bunch of green stuff on the tank now. How do I stop that?"

"You're probably feeding him too much." The banality of the conversation only increased her longing to be back in her apartment, snug in her pajamas. Back in her human body. "Only feed him what he'll eat in a few minutes. Otherwise all the extra calories go to the algae."

Lily nodded and shoved another s'more in her mouth. "That's it! That's the problem!"

Her salamander face didn't have eyebrows to raise, so Angela made do with opening her eyes especially wide. "I know. That's why I said it."

"No, no, not that. The exploding rocks."

Angela closed her eyes again and felt her skin heat. Failure wasn't a good feeling. "What about them?"

"Benson told me we'll have to set up a ring of salt when my baby is born, in case she has to learn how to keep from absorbing all the magic in the air."

Angela looked at the fetus dancing within Lily's womb and agreed with Benson's assessment. Most babies didn't have a strong enough core to attract ambient magic, which is why there weren't many infant shifters. Lily's baby might be an exception. If it pulled in magic like the dragon had, they would quickly have a problem. "It's a good idea. But what does that have to do with the rocks?"

Lily looked expectantly at Angela, and then at Vicky

when Angela didn't respond. "The rocks are like a baby. Once you add enough magic they keep absorbing it from the air until they pop. So we just need to surround them with salt."

"But the rocks aren't alive..." Angela trailed off. "Huh." She'd been taught that obsidian was inert, but she didn't know anyone who had ever used anything larger than tiny stones. If Lily was right, the attraction of ambient magic had nothing to do with the shifters' biological nature, and everything to do with the total amount of magical energy confined in one space.

Vicky opened another bar of chocolate and ate it straight. "It should be easy enough to test. After we get back I can stop at the mini-mart and buy some salt. If that works I'm sure someone can figure out a more permanent containment spell."

Lily stood up and shifted, her sparkling lizard form putting the kayak back in the water with ease. "We don't even need to do that."

25

For the second morning in a row, Angela found herself on the beach in the pale light before dawn. She'd covertly followed Lily and Vicky to make sure they made it safely back to land, both of them easy to track from their magical signatures even if their voices hadn't carried across the water. Once they'd waded through the surf, Lily shifted, picked up both kayaks, and then headed toward the parking lot. Vicky turned to wave at the water before following the teenager. Angela hadn't thought they'd noticed her.

When she pulled her body onto the beach near the obsidian, she was unsurprised to find Benson sitting in a cheap aluminum-frame beach chair, his face lit by the blue glow of his phone. Even at dawn on the beach, he was still wearing a dress shirt and slacks. The contrast of his clothes with the surroundings lightened her spirits, and offset the rush of anger at seeing his left arm held close to his body in a sling.

Angela rested on the sand away from the obsidian. "Are you going to tell me what's going on?" She'd spent her time in the water thinking. If Benson had let Lily go after her twice, this wasn't just an attempt to help her regain her human form.

They needed her for something.

Benson put his phone down. "Vicky told me you figured out why the rock exploded."

"Lily did. Maybe. She thinks the rock is hitting the Bernhoefer threshold."

He frowned, his features just visible in the watery morning light. "But they're not alive..." He trailed off and cocked his head as he thought about the implications. "If that's true they're going to have to rewrite some textbooks."

Angela thought about the way new agents were trained as she idly sifted her claws through the sand. "They probably need to be rewritten anyway."

"You ready to try it? I can go buy some salt to make a circle." He looked back at the mound of rocks and frowned as if calculating the amount he would need.

"No need. We have an entire ocean of salt right there. I'll just knock them into the water."

Benson started to get up, but when she didn't move he sat back. "Is there something else?"

"I need you to tell me what's going on."

The light from his idle phone shut off, but she could still see him open his mouth as if to answer, then stop. He took a breath. "I don't want to add to your stress."

"Then don't hide things from me."

"We have a problem." He shifted to adjust his sling, making the chair creak. "One of the buildings the dragon—"

"Holly," she cut in, her skin flaring in the darkness. Even when the woman was dead, they were still erasing her.

He glanced at her, face wary, then continued. "One of the buildings *Holly* damaged was torn down a couple of days ago, and by the time they thought to abandon the area, all the construction workers who had even the slightest trace of innate magic had shifted." He sighed. "There are still three guys missing. They're probably small animals hiding in the rubble, but we can't get anyone in for long enough to search for them."

Fighting against a lifetime of training, Angela forced herself to ignore the missing people. In mass shifting events of the past, anyone caught up in the currents was easily changed back to their human form as soon as they got some distance from the cause. "It's not just residual magic from having a dragon lair there?" Holly hadn't stayed in the city as a dragon for long, but Angela's current form was testament to the sheer amount of magic she had drawn in.

Benson shook his head. "It's getting stronger. They had to move the barrier back another ten feet yesterday."

"An artifact?" There were low-level sources of power that were charged enough to act like a weak magical battery, but various cults in history had managed to forge links between objects and the bones of dead power creatures through spells and the raw power of the followers. It never ended well for anyone involved. There were artifacts in heavily warded and guarded locations around the world. When she'd been younger, Angela had considered trying to become one of the researchers who dedicated their lives to attempting to safely disarm them, but had eventually gone the more practical route of MPD.

Benson tried to shrug and winced. "They're accounted for, so this is either a new artifact or something else entirely."

Angela turned her head to watch the waves breaking lightly on the shore, enjoying the feel of the water moving over her tail. If they didn't know what was causing the power surge, that meant they weren't sure exactly where it was either. That suggested it was hidden in the wreckage of the building or they weren't able to get anything, human or mechanical, near enough to find out.

Moving an artifact with that much power wasn't a simple prospect. More likely it had always been there, warded against leakage or discovery, until a dragon had manifested in the city and crashed through the wards. Unless...

"Holly." She said it aloud and turned to look back at Benson.

"What about her?"

"What if she didn't damage the wards? Or at least, what if that was the second part. The first part was Holly coming into contact with the object. That's why she became a dragon in the first place." Identity, need, and magic. Angela wouldn't argue that Holly hadn't had the seed of a dragon within her, grown from a lifetime of rage. But just as Angela would have remained human but for an unfortunate circumstance, maybe Holly would have remained in her human form, secretly seething, if she hadn't touched the wrong thing.

Her thoughts carried her further. If that was the case, it made sense that nobody had been able to shift Holly back to her human form, even in the first few days. She's started out with such a large reservoir that she'd already been unable to go back without losing a huge amount of energy. Three draining taps hadn't even been enough. No wonder that hadn't worked.

Once again, Angela's rage threatened to overwhelm her. Matt and Caleb *had* to have felt the extra energy in the area, or they would have if they'd been paying attention instead of imagining how good dealing with a dragon would look on their resumes. They'd been wrong about every single thing, and it had cost Holly her life, Angela her humanity, and the city its downtown.

And yet.

Even if that was true, that knowledge didn't solve the problem. Holly was still dead, Angela was still a salamander, and the city still had an artifact drowning the area in magic. The salamander within her rejoiced at the destruction, but she forced that feeling away and thought of all of her friends and clients who would be the first ones hurt.

"What do you need me for?"

"I think you may be one of the only people who can deal with whatever it is. We need an experienced magic user who is strong enough to get near this thing, and then contain it. I've watched you work. You have the knowledge and precision, and now you have the power."

"If I can shift back." Her salamander form had magic enough for any task, but she couldn't work spells in that form.

He nodded, acknowledging her point.

"And if I can go there without giving in to the urge to burn everything down." Angela couldn't tell if she meant it as a joke or not.

The edges of Benson's mouth curved up. "I'll take that chance." He stood up and closed the chair, pushing the frame together against his leg with one arm. "I'm going to go wait in the car."

THE SUN HAD RISEN and set again, a group of thunderclouds on the horizon providing a beautiful contrast to the purple and red sky, and Angela had almost used all of the obsidian on the beach. Lily's plan had worked. After filling the stones with power, Angela used her tail to lob them into the ocean, aiming for a spot well beyond the low tide line. She'd miscalculated once and a chunk had exploded in the air, but it hadn't caused any damage other than a blast of sound. Someday she might need to swim down and disperse the boulders so they didn't end up with a magical hotspot underwater, but it seemed safe enough for the short term.

About the time Benson had returned from buying his lunch, she'd realized it was working, at least in one way. She was getting smaller. Even at high tide, the base of her tail was no longer in the waves, and it was taking more effort to hurl the rocks into the water.

With tangible evidence that her attempt was paying off, she redoubled her efforts, pausing every few rocks to try to shift. On that front, she wasn't having any luck. Worse, she had no idea when it would even be possible. Or if it ever would. Maybe she had stayed too long in salamander form to ever get back to normal.

After the last rock disappeared beneath the surface of the water, with only a few thin shards of obsidian left on the sand to cut the feet of the unwary, Benson returned, a bag of hamburger and fries in his hand along with the cheap beach chair. "How's it going?"

She watched him struggle to open the chair with one hand, and tried to remember what it was like to be human. To walk upright instead of cutting cleanly through the waves. To balance awkwardly on one foot in order to use the other to pry open a cheap aluminum-frame beach chair. To be overcome by hunger and need to eat. To worry about fragile skin and broken bones.

To fear.

"Tell me again why I want to shift back."

Benson laughed under his breath and dropped into the chair. "You're asking the wrong person today. My shoulder is killing me."

"No words of wisdom from Heldig the Elder?"

"Not that I've found. But I did get a text from Lily telling me our training manual was a load of garbage and that she was rewriting it. She may be able to give you some words of wisdom, if you can get her to hold still long enough."

A flush of something perilously close to pride washed through Angela. "Lily is..."

Benson nodded. "Exactly." He opened the bag and pulled out a single French fry. "I have a theory about Lily's pregnancy, if you want to hear it." He ate the fry, and when she didn't say anything, continued. "I think Lily was getting exposed to extra magic — Did you know she has dance classes near the office where Holly worked? It's right in the middle of the hot zone." He stopped to take another bite. "Anyhow, my theory is that Lily absorbed enough energy, and instead of involuntarily shifting... her body figured out a different way to handle the extra magic."

"That thought had occurred to me." Angela tried to shrug, the effort rippling down the length of her body. "But it's a theory without any inconvenient facts to get in the way."

Benson pointed at her with a French fry. "You only say that because you haven't seen what happens when there's a sudden surge of magic around her."

"We're going to have a talk about how you know that. Soon." Angela closed her eyes and thought about her human form. She was used to looking at others, helping them bring the human side to the fore, but she couldn't really look at herself. It felt like reaching around in a dark cabinet with her eyes closed, trying to catch a mouse that was running back and forth. *There!* That was the strand she needed to follow. She grabbed hold and pulled.

A wall of rage slammed into her, the core of the salamander distilled to one instant, and she lost her focus, falling back into her salamander self at the same time that she heard the aluminum creak and Benson grunt. She opened her eyes to find him lying on the ground five feet farther away than he had been, smoothed sand showing the path he had rolled across. The nylon straps of the beach chair were partially melted and smoking.

"You would think," he said as he sat up in the sand, pain hidden in the timbre of his voice, "I would learn not to sit that close when you're trying new things."

"Sorry about that." She quelled her urge to escape back into the water, to run away from the pain she'd caused and this insurmountable task all at one time. She was done running.

Closing her eyes again, she found the strand and yanked, keeping her grip as the anger burned through her. If she stayed in salamander form, she could destroy the human cities, crush the buildings, strip out the magic, and burn what remained. Let them deal with their own problems, artifacts created by idiots that were harming other idiots. None of that would affect her.

No, that was wrong. It would affect her, because it would affect her friends. And her clients. And her goddamn fish, Romeo the Fourth, who lived his life without harming anyone.

The smell of burning plastic hit her nostrils, reminding her of the seabed covered in trash. If she stayed in salamander form, she could end this human infestation and cleanse the earth for good.

But then she truly would be alone. Beautiful and powerful and perfect, but alone.

She pulled the thread harder.

With a nauseating lurch, she felt herself tumble and hit the sand, and then she was burning and everything was pain.

26

Being human hurt.

By the time she'd figured out her bare arms hurt because she was lying in sand heated by salamander fire and scrambled a few feet away, her arms felt sunburned. Then she lay in the cooler sand, trying not to throw up.

The air pushed down on her, forcing her against the ground, reminding her of aching hips, sore knees, and a stiff neck. Everything was heavy. Even breathing took effort. For a moment she was tempted to let herself go back to her salamander form — she could feel the energy within, just waiting to be released — but instead she gritted her teeth and forced herself to get up.

The darkness felt more limiting as a human, the blackness unbroken by visible magical currents swirling around her, but Benson was there, the light from his phone providing a beacon for her to orient herself. Benson himself was still on the spot where he'd rolled to before, but now he was smiling.

"How do you feel?"

"Heavy. Confined. Sore." When she said the last word, she remembered the things she'd been doing the day before she shifted. For this body, it hadn't been weeks ago. No wonder she was sore. She was still wearing the battered uniform she'd been wearing to confront the dragon. "I need a shower."

Benson's eyes unfocussed as he looked at her. "Do you feel ready to face going back to the city?"

Angela paused in brushing sand off her clothes. "You tell me." She'd monitored so many new shifters throughout the years, but she had no idea how to judge her own stability.

Benson studied her face, his eyes still unfocussed. "I can't tell you were ever anything but human." He picked up the ruined chair and walked in the sand beside her, heading toward the car. The dim light picked out new creases around his eyes when he smiled again. "I'm really glad you're back."

Following him across the loose sand, forearms burning and muscles aching, Angela decided she was glad to be back, too.

A TWO-HOUR CAR RIDE, followed by getting back to her own apartment, went a long way to making Angela feel normal again. Vicky and Lily had been waiting for her, but after their initial flurry of greetings, they'd backed off and pretended not to notice that she didn't seem to be responding correctly. Angela had escaped to take a shower, enjoying the solitude as much as the water sluicing over her skin.

After the shower, wrapped in a towel, she stared at her face in the mirror. The arrangement of her features was the same. She had the same wrinkles at the corners of her eyes, the same slackening of the skin on her neck, and yet somehow she looked different.

Not something added, but something burned away.

She spent the night lying in bed, staring at the dark ceiling, and having fitful dreams of destroying the city, until she finally got up and dressed for the day. Lily was asleep on the couch, a slight smile on her lips. Angela didn't even need to switch to her other sight to see the magic swirling around the girl.

Grabbing some money from her emergency stash, Angela slipped out of the apartment and down the stairs. The bagel store provided a handy destination and excuse for going out, but mostly she just wanted a chance to remember what it was like to be human again. Despite the early hour, the streets were crowded with people rushing to work. Even with an artifact slowly swallowing the center of the city, bills still needed to be paid.

A man in a suit walked toward her, phone pressed to one ear, paper coffee cup held in front of him as he walked toward a car parked along the street. He had the air of someone doing important things, unable to stop and acknowledge anyone else. There was room for both of them on the sidewalk if they both stood straight and kept their arms in. In the back of her mind, Angela knew that a few weeks ago she would have crammed herself to the side, ceding him most of the sidewalk, but that no longer felt like something she needed to do.

She kept walking.

The man's shoulder bumped into her, a splash of coffee hitting his lapel, and he wheeled, looked down at his suit, then stared at her, as if she had suddenly appeared out of thin air. For the first time she didn't feel the urge to apologize. She met the man's eyes directly. *You could strip his magic away*, the salamander's voice whispered in the back of her head. *Then you could burn him to the ground.* Instead, she merely raised an eyebrow. "You should watch where you're going," she said. She turned and continued on her way while he was still staring at her.

Her forearms still hurt from where she had burned them on the sand, but she opened the door to the bagel shop with a genuine smile on her face.

BENSON WAS SITTING at her kitchen table when she got back, his cowboy boots next to the pile of shoes by the door. Lily was across the room, eyes closed, headphones on, halfway through a sun salutation, with some modifications to allow for her lizard form. A downward dog pose left the question of whether the tail was supposed to curl up over the back or down toward the floor.

"You're up early," Benson commented, his voice mild. He gestured to the living room walls. "Did anyone ever tell you your decor is kind of boring?"

"Help yourself." Angela pushed the bag across the table to him and went into the kitchen to get plates and knives. "I didn't sleep well and I thought maybe getting out of the apartment on foot would help."

"And did it?"

Angela raised an eyebrow at him. He'd have known if it had gone too badly by the swath of destruction she would have carved through the city. "A bit, yes." She sat down and spread cream cheese over a blueberry bagel, and stared at it before taking a bite. It felt odd to need to eat, a habit lost in just a few weeks after decades of practice. "Are you my babysitter then? I'm surprised they didn't bring someone who can cast spells."

Benson took his time answering, first cutting off a small piece of the plain bagel he'd chosen, and then dabbing it with cream cheese. "There are concerns," he finally said.

"Concerns."

He shrugged. "We don't have any experience dealing with salamanders. The most powerful things we've seen in modern times are dragons, and those can be spelled to hold their human shape." He took a small bite. "You're too strong to let a spell hold you back. If you want to shift, nobody is going to be able to stop you. So they decided it might be better to have someone around to..." He paused, knife in the air. "...insulate you from stressors. I volunteered, at least temporarily."

Angela thought back to her encounter on the street, and the voices in her head. "That might not be a bad thing."

"Relax." Benson went back to dabbing cream cheese on another chunk of bread. "You didn't burn down the block. You'll be fine."

27

Benson drove, dropping Lily off at school on the way. Angela watched the girl walk up the sidewalk. "Her parents still aren't talking to her?"

Benson pulled back into traffic. "Her parents moved and didn't leave a forwarding address." He took his good hand off the steering wheel to turn on the air conditioning full blast. "Vicky's been helping deal with the legal side of things. Last I heard, Lily is applying to become an emancipated minor. I have the paperwork ready to file to make her a department consultant as soon as that goes through. She'll be fine."

"Thanks."

"Don't thank me. She's been keeping things together here while you've been gone. The yoga group, book club? She's been dealing with all that." He took a careful breath. "Not always in the same way, of course. You might need to look into a new location for the knitting group."

Angela stared at him.

"There was an incident. Nobody got hurt, but she shifted to chase down a freaked-out jaguar and someone saw her."

He stopped for a red light. "The city has been a little short on spell-casters and MPD agents, so we've had to get a bit creative about some things."

Short on spell-casters because of her. If she was right, Caleb wouldn't be able to work with magic ever again. Not that he should have been an MPD officer in the first place, but at least he'd been able to keep a shifter temporarily human. "Is Matt...?" She hadn't really thought about him, and what she'd done to him when she'd first shifted.

"He'll be fine. He's still here, but he's going to take a transfer as soon as we fill the other open position." Benson glanced at her. "My bosses thought it would be better that way."

Because of her, Matt would have to upend his life, leaving friends and family behind, starting over in a new place. Angela supposed she should have felt guilty about that. She knew she would have a few weeks before. And yet she couldn't bring herself to feel anything other than anger. If Matt had just let her talk to Holly, if he'd hadn't ordered the final assault... Hell, if he had just trusted her the day Holly shifted instead of turning the whole emergency into a way to elevate his own status in the department, Holly would still be alive and she would still be fully human. *You should find him and strip away the rest of his magic*, the salamander urged. *He deserves it.* "That's probably a good idea," Angela replied out loud.

A wisp of magic brushing against her skin distracted her. Without thinking, she pulled it in and felt her form wobble just the slightest bit, not enough to be visible, just enough to make her realize she couldn't do that again. She wove a repelling spell around herself, anchoring it to her salamander side. If the spell started to fail, the salamander would be fed the increased magic and that would add power to the spell again. In theory, it would be strong enough to hold against anything, but nobody in their right mind had willingly approached an unshielded artifact in the last two hundred years. She would just have to cross her fingers and hope her untested and barely remembered spell would work.

"You can feel it already?" Benson glanced over at her as they slowed for the outer barricade.

"You can't?" Angela rubbed her arms. "Maybe I'm more sensitive to it now."

They parked just outside the inner barricades, the downtown area once again empty of people other than soldiers and scientists. The smoke and haze had cleared, but three weeks of accumulated dirt and trash that had blown in aged the scene, making it look like a post-apocalyptic wasteland from a low-budget 80s movie.

Angela switched over to her other sight. Everything glowed. She blinked and turned her head to look at Benson. Even he radiated magic, although not as strongly as the buildings on the other side of the barrier.

"Something wrong?"

She shook her head, and switched back to her regular sight so she could navigate the sidewalk without mistaking its pulsing surface for physical movement. "Just trying to get used to everything." Not just her skin had become more sensitive.

Benson opened the trunk and began handing her supplies. "Before you go in, I'll need you to spell me so I stay in this form, and then add a repellant spell."

"You're staying here," Angela said, opening the backpack to make sure it had everything she needed. Ten pounds of salt, rope, water, matches, safety goggles, bear spray, a camera with a clip. She zipped it back up and shouldered it.

"Yes, but if you run into trouble, I need to be able to come in after you." Benson handed her a hard hat with a camera mount. "Otherwise, the only person we've found who can go into the buildings without shifting or being repelled is Caleb."

Angela felt her nostrils flare. "If I run into trouble and Caleb is the only one who can help me, just let me die in peace."

Benson held his ground. "Then make sure Caleb isn't the only one who can help you."

Without thinking about it Angela grabbed a wisp of magic flowing by and fashioned it into a shield around Benson's core, both protecting him from magical accumulation and keeping him in his current form. "That should work for a bit, but you'll have to get in and get out." She stopped when she noticed him staring at her. "What?"

Benson started. "Nothing." After another breath he stretched, as if trying to get comfortable in stiff clothes. "I've just never felt anyone use power like that. It shouldn't surprise me." He turned back to the trunk, pulled out a new pair of leather work gloves, and handed them to her. "Be safe in there. I'd hate to lose the first salamander in centuries to tetanus."

Angela laughed out loud, surprising them both. She settled the hard hat in place, and they tested the feed to Benson's laptop that was plugged into the charger inside the car. After a few minor adjustments she was ready to go.

"If you happen to find the artifact on this trip and you can do so safely, try to get video of everything around it, and then leave. Even if all we find out is the location, we can start looking into who was using the space and maybe figure out what we're up against. We have a couple of experts on containment spells standing by, ready to argue with each other over the best approach." He sighed. "Maybe you'll be able to just toss something at it and be done, but let's not take any chances."

Angela nodded and bounced on her toes, adjusting the backpack. "Okay, I think I'm ready."

Benson walked her to the barrier. She was about to make a comment about that being unnecessary, but then two young men, bulky in fatigues and protective gear, came over, clearly intent on warning them away.

Benson held up his badge with his good hand. "We're cleared to go in."

The shorter of the two snorted and put his hand on the butt of his holstered gun. "Right." He turned his head to his partner and spoke in a low voice. "Now we're sending in old ladies and cripples."

You could just turn him to ash now and save time, the salamander whispered. She could see exactly how it could be done. Instead, Angela switched to her other sight and looked at them, noting the wobbling of their cores.

"Both of you need to spend some time away from this area." She switched back to her normal sight and looked over at Benson. "Make sure everyone either spends less time near the barricades, or the barrier gets moved back."

Benson raised his eyebrows, but took his phone out without another word. He chose someone on his contacts and held the phone up to his ear. "General, it's MPD Specialist Li. I'm at the south entrance, and my specialist says these guards need to rotate out and we need to decrease ongoing exposure." He paused and listened. "Yes, that specialist." He paused again. "Thank you, sir. I'll be in touch when we know more." He slid his phone into his sling and waited, rocking back on his heels slightly.

"Nice bit of theater," the shorter soldier said, not moving his hand from his gun. "Now get back behind the barrier."

His partner frowned. "We should check..."

He waved his other arm. "No need." A wave of pain went over his face. "Get behind the barrier!"

Moving as quickly as she could, Angela reached forward and clamped his wavering core, stripping off just enough magic to stabilize him, and converting that energy into a binding spell.

With a grimace and a strangled groan, the soldier dropped to his knees, sweat breaking out on his face. His partner reached for his own gun, then stopped as his radio crackled.

"He's safe enough for now," Angela said, keeping her thumbs hooked through the straps of the backpack, "but both of you need to spend some time away from here.

Benson frowned and stayed where he was as they watched the soldiers move away, one supported by the other.

Angela looked from him to the soldiers. "You don't approve?"

"Don't take this the wrong way, but you used to be more... gentle in your magic use."

Criticism from Benson, of all people, stung. "I'm sorry, I decided to save his life instead of getting a signed consent form." His confused look made her realize he didn't understand why she'd acted so quickly. She took a deep breath and let it out slowly. "Sorry. He was about to shift, and his form would have been a great white shark. I wasn't sure we'd be able to get him shifted back before he suffocated."

Benson's shoulders relaxed. "Have you always been able to tell what someone's about to shift into?"

"I don't know. I've never been around when someone

was about to shift for the first time." Angela pushed the now-unattended barrier out of the way enough for her to slip through.

"Be careful."

Angela sketched a salute and turned to face the city.

28

The first thing she noticed as she moved forward was the quiet. This wasn't the white noise quiet of the open ocean, but the silence of hardscape when everything living had left. No birds chirped. No squirrels raced up tree trunks. No rats scuttled between buildings. There was just the sound of dry leaves scraping along the pavement and her own footsteps.

"Can you hear me?" Benson's voice in her ear made her jump.

"Loud and clear. How about you?"

"Got you. The visual is coming through as well. I'm starting the recording."

"I'll try not to say anything incriminating." The high-pitched beep made her wince. "How many people did you say were still missing?" She turned her head from side to side, exaggerating the movement so the camera would pick everything up.

"Three, but they aren't our primary goal today. Caleb went through a few times to see if he could find them. If they're still alive in there, they're hiding pretty well."

"Right." Caleb would have been able to enter the area, but he wouldn't be able to feel the magic that might direct him to the missing people. She fell silent as she passed the library, and saw the rubble that had been one of the two blue glass buildings that gave the downtown its distinctive look. The entire building canted forward, and one half had been demolished, looking as if something had come down and taken a bite, leaving concrete and steel exposed. A crane with a wrecking ball sat motionless on one side, near an abandoned bulldozer. Even as she watched, a piece of paper floated down from an office. She could almost trace the path the dragon had taken from one building to the next from the swath of destruction on just this one street. "Wow."

"Yeah." Benson's voice in her ear was suddenly reassuring.

Angela switched to her other sight and paused to look at the area. The remaining half of the building was saturated with magic, but most of the energy seemed to be coming from the north. She relayed that information to Benson, switched back to her normal sight so she could see obstacles, and kept walking.

Despite her shield, the magic prickled on her skin, reminding her of her time as a salamander. She longed for the cool touch of saltwater. To keep her mind off the irritation, she kept up a conversation with Benson. "I'm still kind of surprised I was able to move back into my apartment right away." She wasn't sure what she'd expected —staying in an empty motel outside of town, maybe — but there had been fewer than three hours from the time she shifted to the time she got back home. "But I guess with this going on everyone was a little preoccupied."

Benson's silence made her revisit the morning. At the time she hadn't noticed it, but she hadn't run into anyone when she left her building. That wasn't completely unheard of, but it was unusual. "Everything wasn't normal, though, was it? Are any of my neighbors there?"

Benson sighed. "Most of them agreed to move out for the week. The woman with all the cats in the corner apartment is still there, though."

"And the guy I ran into near the bagel shop? Is he one of yours?"

There was a slight pause. "That was my boss." Angela stopped again so she could switch her sight and get her bearings, but Benson misinterpreted her silence. "I told them you would be fine, but you know how the bureaucracy is. The higher-ups wanted some sort of guarantee. Not that there's a procedure for certifying a salamander shifter, but they wanted a second opinion."

Angela started walking again. "Pretty gutsy of him to knock into me like that, though. What were they going to do if..." She trailed off. If she died suddenly in salamander form, the resulting magic release would probably level the city, but if the same thing happened in human form, there was a good chance the magic would stay in her bones. "Never mind. I probably don't want to know the answer to that."

"They need you," Benson reminded her.

"Yeah." Angela looked around again, settling on a three-story building of concrete and opaque glass, everything at odd angles in a style that didn't quite blend with its neighbors. "I think the source is in that building there." Unlike most of the other buildings in the area, this one remained untouched by any physical damage, but the walls were nearly throbbing with energy.

"Give me a second." The sound of tapping on a keyboard came over the line. "From what I can tell, there's a restaurant and gym on the first floor, and the upper floors are medical offices, although..." More tapping. "It looks like the upper floors all relocated within the last few months. Building renovations and asbestos abatement, according to one webpage."

Angela looked at the building with her normal sight. "Asbestos? Really? I would have thought the building was too new for that. Huh. Shows you what I know about architecture."

"No, you're right. It's only about fifteen years old. If they used asbestos in the construction, it would be very unusual. I'll have someone start looking into the owners."

Angela walked up the sidewalk, a smooth curved ramp that led to the front doors of the restaurant. "Any idea if Holly spent time here?"

"Hang on, I have her credit card statement here someplace."

Angela tried the front door, but it was locked. She pressed her face against the glass, shielding her eyes from the reflected light with one hand. "It looks like... a restaurant. Some sort of Olive Garden knockoff with flavored oil and lots of carbs." She vaguely recognized the restaurant logo, as if she'd seen an ad for it, or maybe they'd put a to-go menu in her mailbox. To the left of the restaurant, she could see a short hallway with a bank of elevators. Further to the left the gym had its own entrance, also locked. "This looks like one of those places that caters to women, doesn't have any weights more than five pounds, and emphasizes cardio and cleanses."

"Bingo, Holly had a membership. I can't see how often she actually went, but there are pretty regular charges for meals at the place next door. My guess is that she worked out during lunch almost every day."

Angela circled the building, looking for an unsecured door, but everything was locked. Completing the circuit at the front entrance she stopped, remembering the recording. "Am I going to get arrested for breaking and entering if we don't get the landlord's permission?"

Benson started laughing then trailed off. "Oh wait. You're serious?"

"I could turn off the camera at least, I guess."

"Angela..." She heard him swallow, as if trying to figure out how to phrase something. "I'm fairly certain you don't need to worry about it. This is exigent circumstances as far as I'm concerned. And also...who would be stupid enough to arrest you?"

"Good point." Angela looked around for something to use to break through the glass on the door. A pile of small river rocks in one of the planters caught her eye and she picked one up. "I guess now's a good time to start my life of crime." She threw at the glass only to see it hit and drop to the ground. A small starburst chip in the glass was the only evidence that she'd done anything. She waited for Benson to make a joke about her throwing ability, but he stayed silent, which irritated her anyhow. Reaching up to touch the chip in the glass, she fed just a little of her energy into it, hoping that would extend the cracks so she could break through to unlock the door. A few wisps of free energy swirled around hers.

The entire pane liquefied and dropped to the ground in long, gooey streaks.

"Oops."

"Wait a minute, what just happened?"

"I... uh, haven't quite figured out how much power to use on things." Angela reached her gloved hand through the open space, flipped the lock, and pushed the door open, the frame sliding over the pooled glass on the tiles. "Anyhow, I'm inside." She switched to her other sight and grimaced. "The whole place is just radiating, but I think it's coming from upstairs." She walked down the hallway and pushed open the door to the stairwell, leaving it propped open with a fire extinguisher. She climbed the steps, feeling her knees pop with each movement, and wondered whether a spell to restore damaged cartilage had been invented yet. Then she thought of her knees liquefying the way the glass door had, and sucked in her breath.

"Everything okay there?"

"Yeah, just thinking that I should probably wait to experiment on my joints until I have a better grasp of things." She climbed onto the landing of the second story and found the door mercifully open. If she'd had to destroy a metal fire door, the building might not have survived her magic's eagerness.

In the hallway, the magical currents were almost visible to her normal sight. "I'm not sure I'm going to even be able to recognize this thing if I see it," she said as she walked, the sound of her footsteps deadened by the carpet. All of the offices had exterior windows, and there were enough glass panes lining the hallway that she could read the signs as she passed them. "Looks like plastic surgeons and an orthodontist right here." The hallway turned and went along the front of the building. "Sports medicine." The hallway turned again, traveling over the area occupied by the gym below. "And this side seems to be all physical rehabilitation." She stopped in front of the last door. "I think this might be it." Magical currents swirled and sent pins and needles along her skin.

"Can you go back a couple feet? What does that sign say?"

Angela took a step back so she could see the adjacent sign. "The Cradle Group Physical Therapy."

"Thanks. Be careful. Remember, we just need to get some information this time around." Tapping of keys continued even as he spoke. "That's odd."

Angela pulled on the door. Unlocked. She opened it wider and went in. "What's odd?" In front of her was a reception desk covered in dying plants, with doorways to spacious rooms on either side. A blackened banana oozed next to a computer keyboard on the counter, the smell overwhelming with the ventilation off. She headed right and followed the currents to a room with a padded floor and various sports and rehabilitation equipment stacked against the wall. A plastic wastebasket stood upside-down in the middle of the room, as if someone had trapped a wild animal, a dried white residue in a rough circle surrounding it.

"One of your clients works there."

Angela stopped and stood up straight. "One of *my* clients? Really? Which one?"

"Franklin Reams. He's a physical therapist. Shifts into a vervet monkey."

She crouched again and started making a wide circle around the bin, making sure her helmet camera was pointed in the right direction. "I have no idea who that is. Are you sure he was one of mine? Also, are you getting these images?"

"Yes, I can see, and I'll double-check on the records."

Angela finished her circle and switched to her other sight. She could make out lines on the floor, barely visible in the magic streaming from whatever was under the wastebasket. "Holy crap."

Benson answered immediately. "What's wrong? Get out of there if you need to."

"No, it's nothing like that." She knelt on the floor, trying to ignore the feeling of magic flaying her flesh. "I can just barely make out what looks like a simple circle ward on the floor around this thing." She moved a finger forward into the air above the circle and was unsurprised to feel no resistance. "Whatever's under that thing chewed through the ward and vaporized a ring of salt." She took a breath. "What kind of idiot would...?" She trailed off.

"I'm not a spell-caster, so you're going to have to explain what's wrong."

Angela shook herself. "A circle ward is pretty much what it sounds like. It's related to the ring of salt that even non-magic users can make, but it's meant for warding something that has a fairly small sphere of influence. It's one of the first things they teach you. The larger the power source, the larger the ring needs to be. Once you hit a ring about the size of a building, there are better ways to set up a ward."

"So this ring was too small to contain this thing?"

Angela laughed under her breath. "You'd have to renew this ward at least a couple of times a day to have any hope of containing it. But that's not the real problem." She tilted her helmet up toward the ceiling and down to the floor. "A circle ward is really a cylinder ward. So assuming you set this up and came back every morning and evening to renew the ward, you could stand right in front of it and be fine, but it's still not shielding the floor above and the floor below. That's why you would never use a circle ward anywhere but the ground, and even then you would take precautions above and below. Did you ever hear the story about the mutated voles that they found under the Hemsworth dagger?" Running a finger over the top of the wastebasket, she felt the gritty remains of salt. "It looks like maybe someone thought about shielding above, but there's no way you'd be able to

shield down below this way." Angela shrugged off the backpack onto the floor next to her and unzipped it. "My guess?
Holly's normal workout spot is directly below this."

"She wouldn't be able to feel it?"

"Whatever this thing is, it must have been at least
partially constrained at one point, or nobody would have
been able to move it here in the first place. Holly may not
have been able to tell anything was different, but if she spent
enough time directly under it, she would be getting blasted
with magical energy." Angela reached forward and picked
up the wastebasket, setting it off to the side. Underneath,
resting on black velvet, was a silver dagger with a hilt she
suspected was carved from ebony. "Should have guessed."

"What is that, a dagger?"

"Silver athame with an ebony hilt," she confirmed. "*Shift
Enforcers* strikes again."

To be fair, artifacts had been fashioned in the form of
daggers and other weapons for centuries, but medallions
and statues were much more common. In any case, the
producers of *Shift Enforcers* cared a lot more about visual
appeal than historical accuracy. Silver wasn't a terrible
metal to channel magic with, and an athame didn't need to
hold an edge, but stainless steel would have worked just as
well and wouldn't tarnish. There was also nothing particularly special about ebony. But ever since the season one
finale of *Shift Enforcers*, when the leads had tracked down a
cult of scantily clad cat shifters channeling their sex magic
into forming a link between dragon bones and a silver-and-
ebony athame, those materials had become the choice of
every two-bit magic user in the world. The vast majority of
those ceremonies were just an excuse for an orgy, and
finding the untouched bones of a power creature wasn't

easy, but every once in a while someone got everything right.

The salamander within her eyed the athame like a tasty treat, and Angela pushed that thought away. If she pulled all the magic into herself and survived the process, she'd never be able to get rid of it. That shift would be permanent. That would be the very last resort if something went wrong.

Ignoring the burn in her hands, she picked up the athame and looked at the carvings on the hilt. "Are you getting good images of this?" She turned the blade so she could follow the pattern to the other side, and saw a damaged section where the wood looked like it had been attacked by either an icepick or an angry woodpecker.

"Yes."

Angela put the blade back down and wiped her hands off on her pant legs. "I'm not great with rune magic, but I think there was both a limiting spell and a barrier spell on the hilt before it was damaged." Limiting spells controlled the maximum amount of magic that could enter or exit the artifact at any time. The barrier spell would have kept it from transferring magic to anyone that wasn't holding the athame. "Maybe someone who is better with runes can tell me how to fix it, but in the meantime I'm going to try to ward this thing so we can stop the spread."

"I'm all for this plan. Do you need anything from me?"

Angela picked up the bag of salt. "I haven't done a folding ward since I got out of the academy. I'm pretty sure I remember the steps, but if you want to look it up to keep me honest, feel free." Unlike a simple circle ward, a folding ward redirected the magic inward from all sides of a cube, halting the outflow of energy in all three dimensions. It was a little trickier to get right, and the athame still couldn't be moved without breaking the ward, but it would hold for at least a day and give them a chance to work out better options.

She drew the first rounded square with the salt, binding it with air to protect the sky above, feeling the energy flare when she closed the loop.

Benson sounded hesitant. "Is it supposed to glow like that?"

Angela looked at the beginning of the ward doubtfully. "It never did before, but I've never warded an artifact before. And I didn't use to have this kind of power either. It doesn't *feel* wrong to me anyhow." Her academy instructors, doubtless long dead by now, would probably be shaking their heads at her hesitance and making notes on the evaluation sheet. *Lacks confidence in abilities. B-minus.*

She traced the second barrier with a thinner line of salt, and set it with a dribble of water. When she closed that loop, steam swirled between the two lines, water and air interacting. That definitely hadn't happened during her final exam all those years ago, but the decrease in magic tearing at her skin made her sigh in relief. "It's working."

The salamander within her chose that moment to rear up and try to force her to reach through the ward to accept all the magic that the athame held within. Angela stopped her hand before it touched the salt, and backed up half a step. Her salamander's affinity for fire might be a problem.

"Is it finished?" Benson's voice in her ear reminded her she wasn't really alone.

Angela forced herself to breathe normally. "One more layer. I'm just having some issues walling off this much magic. Give me a second." To buy some time, she went out to the reception area and upended one of the plants, bringing a handful of dirt back to the room with her. The inner barrier had been set with air, the second with water. Fire would be one option to set the final barrier, but she was afraid that would draw out the salamander. Earth would work just as well, and she was a lot less likely to burn down the building with potting soil. She traced the third line of the ward, sending the magic to shield the earth. With a pop that she could feel in her bones, the finished ward folded into place, protecting all sides.

Taking a step back, Angela sighed. "That should buy us a little time." Now that the magic was no longer tearing at her skin, it felt like she was floating in water. She clipped her extra camera to the open door, far enough away that it wouldn't touch the ward even if it fell, and turned it on. "Are you getting a good image from this one? I think we should be able to monitor it remotely by looking at the salt." She had no idea how long her ward would last before it started to break down. She hoped for at least a full day, but if not the camera should give them some warning.

"It's linking. Give it a couple of minutes. In the meantime, I looked up the records on your client, Reams. He was transferred to you two days before you..." He trailed off, as if unsure how to phrase her violent transformation.

"Right. Who had him before then? Matt or Caleb?"

"Caleb. He made notes in the file, but nothing specific. We'd have to talk to him to find out if he noticed anything odd."

Angela sighed. Someday she was going to have to face Caleb and apologize for what she'd done, but she'd been hoping to put it off longer. "Has Reams checked in since then?"

"Not that I can see, but like I said, things have been a bit hectic here. We brought in three agents from other cities, and Lily's been doing her thing, but Matt's the only one who really knows the system. I don't think everything has been getting into the records." He paused. "Okay, the other camera is up."

Angela pulled on her backpack again. "I'll keep an eye out for the missing people, but I think we'll have to wait until the background energy drops a little bit first." She adjusted her helmet as she walked down the hallway. "I'm dying for a decent burrito. Or maybe sushi. You'd think I'd be sick of fish after spending so long in the water, but — Ow!" A sharp pain in her neck startled her, and she slapped a hand over the spot, feeling something under her fingers. "I just got stung by a freaking bee." The last few words were hard to get out, as if she had forgotten how to move her mouth. She looked at the bug in her hand, but it wasn't a bee. It was a mini tranquilizer dart, like the ones MPD carried. "That's so weird ." At least, those were the words she tried to say, but what came out was a puzzled sound, and then everything went dark.

ngela came back to consciousness quickly, one moment asleep and the next fully aware of everything. She was lying on her side on rough carpet, facing a wall, hands bound behind her. Handcuffs, she thought, from the way they cut into her wrists, and spelled ones at that, just like the ones on the standard-issue MPD tactical belt. She was back in the room with the artifact; she could feel it even through the folding ward. The sound of salt being poured on the floor was so familiar that she didn't even need to turn her head to figure out what it was. Angela still had questions, but the pieces were starting to fall into place. There was only one person who could have done this.

"Caleb, what are you doing?" She struggled to sit up enough to be able to turn toward him.

"Just getting things ready." The sound of salt pouring ended, though she didn't feel anything happen. Then she remembered that Caleb didn't have any magic anymore, so he couldn't set an active spell. "There. Now you won't be able to contact anyone until we're done here."

Angela's arm was falling asleep, and the cushioned floor

wasn't soft enough for her to lie on indefinitely. Between her discomfort and the salamander barely restrained within, she wasn't feeling as disposed to placate him as she probably ought to have. "Have you always been an idiot, or is this something that developed recently?"

Caleb's boots came into her field of vision, and then she was hauled into a seated position facing him. There were lines in his face she hadn't noticed before, but other than that he looked the same as he had before she'd taken all his magic. "I have to admit, at first I was pretty upset about what happened." He waved his hand in the general direction of the stadium. "Then I realized it was a blessing in disguise. For a little while anyhow. Having the freedom to move around with nobody watching everything I do has been helpful." He shook his head. "Not that you deserved to be the one to get all the magic, but when has life ever been fair?"

Angela pulled her head back as far as she could. "Hey, I'm not the one who damaged the hilt wards on an artifact with enough power to take out the city," she replied, nodding as she saw his eyes dart away. "What were you thinking?"

He looked at her as if she were crazy. "How else was I supposed to get to the power? The limiting spell was getting in the way." His face changed and the look he gave her was one of frustration. "Of course you don't understand. You've always been happy to run around with your stupid sewing clubs and yoga and all that crap. They were never going to fire *you,* because if they did their quotas would be all messed up." He straightened. "But if you'd ever had to justify your position, you would have seen it. There was no way I could get ahead unless I had more power than Matt. This was the only thing I could do. And then *you* messed everything up."

Angela took a deep breath and tried not to focus on what he'd just said, but the irritation within her grew. "So... this is all *my* fault?" Logically she knew she shouldn't argue with him, at least not until after she understood what was going on, but she couldn't help herself.

"Without a power boost, I would have been stuck in that job forever."

Angela thought about her own career and shook her head. "So you found an artifact."

Caleb sniffed. "This guy didn't even know what he had. He picked it up at a thrift shop out in the desert because it looked 'cool.'" His fingers sketched quotes in the air. "When I told him it had magic, he decided to sell it, but he didn't know who to contact. He said I could have ten percent if I set up the deal."

Legally the artifact had to be contained by the appropriate authorities, and as an MPD officer Caleb would have known that. Still, he would have been set up for life if he'd pulled that deal off. "What went wrong?"

"The captain was riding my ass about getting through my client list and keeping my stats up, and I needed more power." He frowned at her. "You always got all the easy cases. That's the only reason your stats were good. I had all these people who couldn't keep their form if you held a gun to their heads."

Angela stayed quiet with an effort.

Caleb waved a hand. "So I used the artifact to boost my energy a little, but I needed more, so I broke the limiting spell." His eyes shifted away from her again. "But the idiot who inscribed the runes on the handle put the wards too close together and the barrier spell got damaged."

Angela took a breath and let it out slowly. Of course the runes were close together. They needed to be in order to keep from tearing the hilt apart. She'd only taken the required introductory runes class, and rune spacing had been in the second chapter. "And then you had to put your own wards on it."

"It was just temporary until I could find someone to fix the barrier rune. The whole thing was a pain in the ass because I had to keep renewing the ward every twelve hours." Caleb started pacing in the narrow corridor between the outside of Angela's folding ward and the ring of salt he'd poured around the edges of the room. "And then the whole dragon thing happened. I couldn't get the rune master in without everyone else finding out. You know how everyone knows everyone else. I couldn't take the chance. And then you took away all my magic and I couldn't even ward it after that and everything broke loose." He threw a hand out to indicate the whole city. "All of this is your fault."

Angela couldn't stand it any more. "Every single part of that was your fault. Every. Single. Thing."

He stopped pacing and looked at her. "What are you talking about?"

She sat up straighter. "You chose not to turn in the artifact. Then you chose to damage the runes even though you had to have known you couldn't remove just one. And then you put a simple circle ward on something on the second floor." At his look of incomprehension she shook her head. "Holly — you remember her, right?" She couldn't keep the sarcasm out of her voice. "Holly worked out downstairs. You put a simple circle ward on this thing, and she was exposed to so much energy she ended up shifting into a dragon." She took another breath and brought her heart rate under control. It wouldn't do to rouse the salamander. "And even after you lost your magic, you *still* could have gone to Matt or someone else, and told them about the artifact before the wards broke down completely." She could tell from the way he shook his head that he wasn't going to accept any blame, but she kept on. "All those people died because you wanted a promotion without doing any work." She gritted her teeth. "So what's the plan here?"

Caleb tilted his head at the athame, just a few feet away. "Now that it's warded again, you're going to give me my magic back, and then I can work with the rune master to fix the barrier spell. I have a buyer lined up. It's all going to work like it was supposed to in the first place."

Angela raised her eyebrows. "Caleb. Your magic is gone. I can't fix that." And she wouldn't even if she could. There was no way she would allow him to access the magic stored in the athame again.

"You have to."

Angela settled back into a more comfortable position.

"If you don't help me, I'll just lock the door and leave you here. By the time the ambient magic dies down enough for anyone to free you, you'll have starved to death."

Bowing her head, Angela took another deep breath. "Don't threaten me, Caleb."

"Or what? You can't shift with those handcuffs on. I could kill you now and sell your bones and you wouldn't be able to stop me."

The salamander tasted the magic on the handcuffs, and strained at the bonds Angela had imposed. Despite Caleb's naive belief, the handcuffs wouldn't stop her from shifting. The only problem was that if she shifted in this room, there was no way she wouldn't disrupt the ward around the athame, and she was pretty sure she wouldn't be able to stop herself from ingesting all that magic. And even if she could restrain the salamander from intentionally battering Caleb to death, she'd probably crush him during her shift. She had resolved to avoid killing anyone if at all possible. Even if he did deserve it.

"Caleb, it's not like you just need a boost of power. There's nothing to anchor it to." She'd ripped his magic out by the roots a few weeks ago. "Think about it. If there was anything left, you wouldn't have been able to get this near the artifact without shifting." Angela turned her head casually, looking for her helmet with its camera. At some point, Benson would come after her, probably unarmed. If Benson didn't know Caleb was here and stumbled across them, things would be even worse.

Caleb started pacing. "No. You're just messing with me."

Angela tried to stand up, but the combination of her hands behind her and her knees threatening to give out after climbing stairs had her stuck on the floor. She sighed. If she'd lost that extra twenty pounds, her knees would probably appreciate it. She remembered the ease with which the salamander moved with longing.

She fed a bit of magic into the handcuffs and yelped when they zapped her.

Caleb laughed. "Told you."

Angela wiggled into a more comfortable position. "Say you manage to get the barrier spell fixed and sell the artifact. Then what? There's enough evidence around to convict you once someone starts looking for it. They're just going to seize all the money when they catch you."

"I'll be long gone by then. New name and more money than I know what to do with."

"And your wife?"

He focused on her again. "She'll come too, of course."

Angela raised her eyebrows. "Have you told her that yet?

Doesn't she have family around here? Is she really going to be okay with never seeing them again?" She'd only met Caleb's wife briefly, but she remembered the woman mentioning plans for a large family reunion. People who planned family reunions were not the sort that willingly went into hiding.

"She'll be fine with it." Caleb's tone was uncertain.

Despite herself, Angela felt a bit of pity toward him. He hadn't thought through any of this. Then she remembered Holly, and all the soldiers the dragon had killed when they had tried to capture her. Even if Caleb hadn't planned for any of it to happen, he must have seen the possibilities.

Angela thought about the construction of the handcuffs. They carried an energy source to power the spells that restrained the wearer. Even the strongest magic users couldn't overcome it. In her pre-salamander days, Angela wouldn't have been able to do anything about it, but now that she knew what kind of power she could absorb and survive, a different option presented itself.

She could drain the energy source in the handcuffs, pulling it all into herself and rendering the dependent spells useless. That, in itself, was somewhat dangerous given what had happened the last time she'd accepted a huge amount of magical energy, but she was fairly certain the amount contained in the handcuffs wouldn't send her into an uncontrolled shift. She'd used some energy powering the folding ward, so she wasn't full up in any case.

But in order to pull in the power from the handcuffs she'd need to drop the spell that was keeping the ambient magic away. The athame was safely warded at the moment, but everything in the environment had been marinating in magical energy for weeks as the previous wards had failed. The minute she dropped her personal wards, she would start soaking up the flurry of magic she could still see swirling around her.

The alternative was to sit and wait for Benson to enter the quarantine area, probably unarmed, and hope that the wards she had put on him were strong enough for him to make it to her position, and that he was somehow able to take Caleb down. Meanwhile, Caleb had a dart gun, infinite tolerance to the surrounding magic, and the power of personal grievance on his side.

Gritting her teeth, Angela dropped her wards. In an instant, the ambient magic assaulted her. The salamander woke, and for a brief moment she feared her other form would demand the shift just to be able to consume all the magic in the air. She clung to her oh-so-human body, with its hot flashes, twenty extra pounds, aching knees, and everything else that came along with it.

After what seemed an impossibly long time but was probably less than two seconds, the pressure eased. She started pulling in the magic from the handcuffs. Caleb was talking again, but she couldn't hear him beneath the buzzing in her ears. Her skin burned and a blizzard of magic crashed against her.

If she shifted now, she'd destroy her folding ward and half the building. Caleb would be crushed. Possibly Benson, too, if he was nearby. She wouldn't be able to stop herself from devouring the magic of the unshielded athame, and then there wouldn't be enough obsidian in the world to dump all the power into. She'd never get her life back again. Clenching her jaw so hard she could feel her molars grinding, she hung on.

The energy from the handcuffs trickled to a stop. She reversed the power flow, feeling the depleted spells being blown away by the blast of energy she sent through them.

Her wrists burned from the heat of the metal, but there was a click and she felt the connecting links part. Before taking another breath, she recast the ward to repel the ambient magic, leaving her arms behind her to hide the fact that she was free. Her body still buzzed from all the magic she contained, but at least her skin no longer prickled from the energy swirling in the air.

Caleb was staring at her, as if he were waiting for a response.

She shrugged. "Sorry, I got bored and started daydreaming. What was the question?"

He shook his head. "You shouldn't have been the one to become a salamander. That should have been me. I deserved it."

Angela looked up at him. "Why?" She considered her choices even as she talked. The room only had one door. Somehow she had to get Caleb out of the room and then get past him so she could leave the building. "You were there. If that was supposed to be your destiny, why didn't you absorb all the energy released when you idiots killed the dragon?" She shook her head. "Your other form is definitely not a salamander."

Caleb pointed a finger at her, as if he'd caught her in a trap. "Aha! Got you! If I really didn't have any magic left I wouldn't have an alternate form." He took his stun gun from his tactical belt. "Do you remember how much it hurts to get hit with one of these things? I might not be able to kill you, but if you don't fix this I'll make you wish you were dead." He pressed the button and current arced between the prongs.

As part of their training to carry the stun gun, they'd all had to get shocked by one. That had been bad enough, but for three weeks after the training course, Matt and Caleb had stalked each other every time they were in the building, their laughter echoing around the hallway every time one was able to connect. Unfortunately, they didn't just confine their attacks to willing participants, but seemed to think anyone else who couldn't fire them was fair game. Those who complained was accused of being not tough enough. The captain had called a halt to it when he'd come back from vacation to find the dispatchers threatening to sue the department.

Angela tried to ignore the stun gun and her instinctive flinch. "If you had any magic at all, you would have shifted by now." She scooted over to keep him in sight as he came around the athame toward her.

Caleb finished covering the distance between them, and held the stun gun against her bare neck. "Not if I'm a power creature. You did something to me to keep me from building up the power I would need to shift. Now are you going to help, or not?"

Angela met his eyes, his face just inches away, and chose her words carefully. "Do you freely accept this magic I give you?"

Consent, freely given, was a powerful magic of its own.

Caleb nodded. "Yes. That's what I've been saying." He put the stun gun back in his belt and grabbed his keys. "I'll take the handcuffs off so you can do this, but don't be stupid. I still have the darts and the stun gun."

Before he could get behind her and notice that she'd already destroyed the handcuffs, Angela punched into him with her magic, driving energy into the two strands that made up his core so she could separate them, and then grabbed the purple strand and *yanked*, all the while feeding magic to the strands to keep them from collapsing back together.

Identity, need, and power. All the elements that went into determining shape were there, but they weren't coming from Caleb. Even as she let the strands form into their new configuration, Angela recognized the shape was coming from her, based on her magic, her need, and her feelings about Caleb.

Caleb's form shimmered and collapsed into a mottled gray-green slug, and the magic she fed into him slipped away, unable to find purchase. The strands of his core shriveled together again. Now that he had taken his alternate form, he wouldn't be able to shift back to human again without help from a magic user.

He screamed with rage, his voice unchanged in his new form. "I'll kill you!"

"Hush." Angela moved her arms in front of her and stared at her hands, blistered flesh encircling her wrists under the blackened metal. "Ow." Now that she could see the damage, her vision darkened from the pain.

The change in Caleb's screaming, along with a bubbling hiss, finally penetrated her haze. When she looked down at him, she realized that he had landed on the ring of salt he'd drawn to contain her in the room. No slug was safe from that much salt, even one that had started in another form.

Angela reached over and flicked him off the ring, then scrambled to rinse him off. The water she'd used for the first layer of the folding ward was almost gone, but she drenched him with it, making sure it came nowhere near the outer barrier. His screams stopped, and the bubbling slowed. "Caleb?"

The slug didn't respond.

With her inner vision, Angela watched the coils of his core starting to unravel. She threw energy at the limp strands, trying to get them separated enough to grab his human side so she could pull him back to a healthy body. She'd worry about how to disarm him again afterward.

The strands of energy that made up Caleb dissolved and wafted away on the magical breeze just as Benson charged into the room.

30

Six months later, Angela and Vicky loitered at the edge of the crowd, waiting for the groundbreaking ceremony to start. With the artifact safely warded and removed, downtown had quickly become habitable again, although the building housing the physical therapist's office had been broken up and removed to a salt pit three states away.

Vicky glanced up from her phone. "Did I tell you we found a place?" The triple latte relationship, Katie, had progressed. Angela was waiting for Vicky to start ring shopping, but so far they had merely decided to move in together.

"Where?"

"Arden Apartments." She smiled when Angela looked at her in surprise. "We'll be just around the corner in case Lily needs a babysitter."

"I thought you..." Angela let her words trail off. The area around her apartment had changed, with most of the non-shifters moving out and shifters moving in to fill the vacancies. The magical currents were more soothing there, but not everyone was fine with the thought of wild animals walking down the street, even if they were just carrying groceries. Vicky's girlfriend, a non-shifter, hadn't seemed interested in moving into the area, so Angela hadn't realized they'd even been looking there.

Vicky shrugged. "We talked. I pointed out the advantages of living near you. And the Arden has a really nice pool."

"Hey, maybe we can start a water aerobics class during the summer," Angela said, thinking about how good it would be to have a cooler alternative to yoga during the stifling heat of the warmer months.

Lily trotted over, the bulk of her pregnancy only slowing her slightly. "Can't they just start without the mayor? I'm getting hungry again."

Angela reached into her bag, and handed the teen a granola bar without pausing. "He's stuck in traffic, but he should be here soon."

"It's not like he did anything to take credit for." Lily stopped talking to eat.

"He signed off on it," Angela pointed out. The ground where the building had stood was being turned into Holly Thompson Memorial Park, with a jogging path, flower gardens, and a small oak grove. Lately the mayor had been touting the advantages of having a green space in the downtown area. Just a few people knew he'd only agreed to the plan when they'd excavated down ten feet under the spot where the artifact had stayed and the soil had been so contaminated with magic that the foreman had shifted to a zebra and nearly been run down in traffic. None of the many experts the mayor had consulted would give a firm estimate on when that section would be safe again, so the plans for a high-rise were scotched. The oak tree being planted in the refilled hole might be affected by the magic, but at least it wouldn't be able to get up and cause problems elsewhere.

A shiny black car stopped at the curb, and the mayor got out and hurried over to the spot where Benson waited with a few members of the city council, shaking hands with people along the way. After a quick consultation with an aide, he took the microphone.

"I apologize for the wait, ladies and gentlemen." He glanced at the notes in his hand. "While I never met Holly Thompson in person, when I first heard of the plan to create a park here, I immediately thought of her and how much she would have loved this idea."

As the mayor continued on, Benson caught Angela's eye and gave her a slight head shake. They'd made bets on how long it would take the mayor to start talking for Holly in his speech, but neither had expected it to happen in the first sentence. Still, he *had* agreed to the park in the end, and he'd agreed to Angela's first choice in names, so she decided not to begrudge him this moment in the limelight. Benson had suggested that she be the one on the podium for the ceremony instead of him, but she'd quickly turned him down. She had a pretty good rein on her temper, but forced socialization with all the movers and shakers in the city would have been trying for all parties involved. Besides, the publicity over Caleb's contribution to the crisis and his manner of death had only just died down, and she was looking forward to a little more anonymity.

The mayor's speech continued. He'd even listened to her suggestion that the ceremony focus on the person Holly had been before she'd shifted. Not that anyone in the nation didn't know Holly Thompson was the woman who had shifted into a dragon and decimated the downtown, but it was nice to have one day just about the woman.

With a theatrical flourish, the mayor took the oversized gilded scissors and walked to the thick red ribbon that had been strung across the jogging path. He stopped with the blades against the fabric and turned to face the crowd, giving them ample opportunity to take pictures for the morning paper. Then he cut the ribbon to a smattering of applause, at which point the crowd began a slow motion stampede toward the refreshments table.

At the edges of Angela's vision, wisps of magic drifted by, but just background levels that could be found anywhere, a comfortable hum against her skin. She tipped her head back and looked at the clear blue sky. After the ceremony, she had a training session with the new recruits, and then some individual monitoring sessions. Benson had told the dispatchers to block her schedule in the afternoon so she'd have a chance to work on her part of the new training manual.

They hadn't had any luck tracking down the source of the artifact that had nearly destroyed the city, and there was a barely concealed panic in the upper levels of MPD HQ that there might be more out there. It turned out that Captain Rosenthal had passed along one of the memos Angela had written warning about the changes downtown, so now everyone wanted to know Angela's thoughts on all kinds of things, which felt odd. But Guy Barron's contract for the next season of *Shift Enforcers* required him to work with a dragon shifter, and she suspected her own influence wouldn't survive that spectacle.

In the evening, she had a "paint and pinot" group meeting at the library, and she had cleared the perfect spot on her wall to display what was certain to be a horribly executed painting of a zinnia.

Someday soon she was going to have to take a trip back

to the beach to do something with the charged obsidian. Reports had come in of fish acting oddly. The Coast Guard had sent a polite notice to MPD expressing their concerns.

For now though, Angela was content to enjoy the day. Shifting her weight off her bad knee, she pulled her keys out of her pocket, patted her tactical belt to see that she had all her equipment, from anti-shifting handcuffs to protective gloves, and went off to embrace what her city had to offer.

ACKNOWLEDGMENTS

I know I joke a lot about being unable to follow directions, but that only works if you have people around you willing to tell you how to get back on the path when you're lost in the weeds.

Many thanks to my writing groups, both to Yolo Writers' Cramp for always being there with encouraging words, and to WordForge for metaphorically kicking the tires and pointing out that the steering wheel doesn't belong in the trunk. I've received so much inspiration, knowledge, and advice from both groups that I'll never be able to pay it all back. I'll especially never be able to pay Paul back for all the horrible dad jokes he tells, but since he came up with the title, I guess we'll have to call it even.

My editor, K.B. Spangler, helped me transform this book into its proper form. To extend the car metaphor, she suggested the car would go faster if I made the wheels round instead of oval. She also saved me from leaving clownfish in a tank with an octopus, so readers are going to have to find something else that's completely unrealistic in this fantasy novel.

Melony Paradise of Paradise Cover Design managed to get me to answer a lot of questions (a feat in itself!) and then created the amazing artwork you see on the cover.

And finally, thank you to Eric and Karen for doing a last proofreading pass. If you can't liven up your family get-togethers with finger-pointing about who left typos in the book, why even celebrate holidays? You deserve all the brownie and bagel points.

ABOUT THE AUTHOR

T. M. Baumgartner is a speculative fiction writer who has difficulty following directions. This has produced occasional culinary triumphs, but once necessitated lopping off six inches of pressboard when assembling a cabinet. At various times she has been a veterinarian, Unix system administrator, software developer, and after-hours book-shelver in a medical library.

Theresa currently lives in Northern California in a house with too many animals. She knits hats for garden gnomes and runs with scissors only when absolutely necessary.

Shift Happens is her first published novel.

For more books and updates:
https://tmbaumgartner.com

The marketing department here at Speculative Turtle Press is great at tail wagging, but a little challenged by tasks that require thumbs. If you enjoyed this book and would like to help other readers find it, please consider leaving a review at your favorite site.

Made in the USA
Las Vegas, NV
21 December 2020

13994879R00156